Resistance

Port Russell Romance, Volume 1

Isabella -

Keay Francis

Welcome to Port Russell -
happy reading!
Keay Francis

Published by Keay Francis, 2023.

Cover design by Bailey Designs Books

Editing by Melanie Cossey

Published by Keay Francis

1st Paperback edition: March 2023

eBook ISBN: 978-1-7387781-0-2

Paperback ISBN: 978-1-7387781-2-6

Table of Contents

For my parents, Carole and David, for instilling my love of reading and writing, and for my Gram, Norma (Keay) Poll, whose unconditional love continues to help me find my confidence.

I so wish you were here to see this.

Port Russell
Romance
1

Welcome to Port Russell, B.C.!

Resist all you want; love *will* find a way.

Port Russell, a hidden gem nestled amongst the old growth on the west coast of Vancouver Island, is the best place in the world, according to recently returned teacher Courtney Merrick. Back home to recover after her disastrous first relationship implodes, Courtney vows to focus on her career and looking after her wild grandparents, leaving love to those who still believe in it.

Her resolve wobbles when she runs into Josh Cameron, her high school bestie and secret first love, when she's called down to the RCMP detachment to bail out her grandparents following their arrest at the Gnome Lake logging protest. When Josh and Courtney team up to figure out who is behind the escalating threat to their idyllic town, can Courtney continue to resist falling in love?

Resistance is a contemporary Canadian small- town, friends to lovers, medium heat, fade to black romance, set against the backdrop of old growth logging protests.

CHAPTER 1

Courtney sighed, blowing the bangs out of her eyes as she pulled her Subaru into the small lot outside the squat brick RCMP station, the late May sunshine a strange juxtaposition to her errand. Didn't the police have better things to do than arrest septuagenarians?

She threw open her car door, lifted the strap of her crossbody bag over her tangled brunette ponytail, and jumped out. Courtney marched across the small dandelion-spotted lawn to the front door of the detachment she'd always thought looked like something one of her Grade 3 students had built out of Lego bricks—square, with a window on either side of the door. She couldn't believe she was here. What on earth had Gram and Gramps done to get themselves arrested? And who the heck had arrested them?

With Gramps finally retiring from running the logging company, Courtney thought maybe her grandparents would travel or explore new hobbies, like bird watching or oil painting. She hadn't expected them to take up a life of crime.

An electronic buzz announced her presence in the small vestibule as she opened the door. A chest-high counter topped with plexiglass barred the way to the offices in the back of the building. A thirsty plant sat on the dark-green Arborite counter next to a rack of recruitment brochures. Courtney snorted—there probably wasn't a person of recruiting age, herself excluded, for at least forty kilometres. Once most people could drive, they left Port Russell and never came back. She seemed to be the exception to the rule, returning at the start of the school year after six years away.

"Hello?" Courtney called after glancing around for a bell and coming up short. The fluorescent light above her flickered off, then on again, humming loudly. Framed photos of the current detachment officers hung on the wall behind the counter, drawing her eye to a familiar face. Josh Cameron? He was back here? In Port Russell?

"Hey, Courtney," a melodic female voice said.

"Ah!" Courtney startled, raising a hand to hover over a heart racing like a greyhound, her mind having wandered to a decade past upon seeing Josh's photo.

"Hi, Constable Huong. I'm here to pick up my grandparents?"

Emmy Huong, a stocky woman a decade older than Courtney, with raven-coloured hair and warm brown eyes, smiled from the other side of the counter. "I figured. Come on through. Charles and Norma are waiting in the back."

The door next to the counter buzzed, and Courtney pushed it open. As she walked by the photos, she scrutinized the man decked out in his duty uniform with a short-sleeved grey shirt covered by a black vest emblazoned with "police." The skinny arms and slim shoulders Courtney remembered from high school were now replaced by the bulk of toned muscles. It was indeed Josh, her former best friend, and first crush. His kind grey-blue eyes, sun-kissed skin, and clipped dark-brown hair were the only recognizable things about him. The trim beard was a surprising addition. He was barely shaving the last time she saw him, at sixteen. What was he doing back in town? Courtney groaned inwardly.

"Before we go in, I forgot to ask, why were my grandparents arrested?"

"Oh," Constable Huong said, looking over her shoulder. "My bad. I should have said on the phone. We cleared the protest at Gnome Lake."

"Did you arrest them?"

"No, the new guy drew the short stick. Though, maybe you know him? He said he went to high school here. Josh Cameron?"

Courtney's stomach did a slow roll. "Yeah. I went to school with him." The image of Josh on the beach smiling as he leaned in to kiss her just days before he moved away without telling her popped into her head. Then it was replaced in short order by the memory of the anguish she felt when her ex, Nathan, admitted he was cheating on her.

Ugh. Men. She reminded herself she was here for a more important reason. "Are my grandparents okay? I mean, do I have to post bail or something?"

"No, that's an American thing. I offered to drive them home, but they insisted on calling you to come and pick them up."

An alarm sounded deep within. This felt like a setup, but Courtney tamped it down. "They're free to go? I'm sorry. I don't know much about the process."

"That's a good thing," Constable Huong said, swiping a key card over the pad next to the door leading into the administrative part of the detachment. She pushed the door open and gestured for Courtney to go before her. "We've released them on their own recognizance with an order to appear at a later date."

"In court?" Courtney squeaked.

Constable Huong looked over, black brows knitted in concern. "It's just a mischief charge. Given it's their first offense, I'm sure the judge will be lenient."

Her grandmother's distinctive peal of laughter drifted past Constable Huong, and Courtney scowled. Gram was chatting with the dispatcher at the break table set up along the back wall in the kitchen area of the detachment. Meanwhile, Gramps was studying a chessboard on the desk in the first cubicle of four arranged in the large rectangular room.

"Courtney!" her grandmother exclaimed. "Hurray! We're sprung!"

Gramps twisted in his chair to look at her. "Just in time to see me trounce Emmy here." He removed the constable's queen. "Checkmate."

Courtney's face burned. Trust her grandparents to turn getting arrested into a party. Gram retrieved her backpack while Gramps shook Emmy's hand in a show of good sportsmanship.

"Thank you, Emmy dear, for making getting arrested such a lovely experience," Gram said as she slipped her arm through Courtney's. "Please let Josh know, no hard feelings. It was a pleasant surprise to see him back in town."

"I'll pass on the message," Constable Huong said.

Gramps stepped behind Gram, placing a broad hand on his wife's birdlike shoulder. "Hopefully, CFI will listen to reason and leave the old growth alone, and you won't be put in that position again."

"Let's hope that's the case, Charlie. At any rate, you two stay out of trouble," Emmy said.

Gram winked at Courtney. "We'll try." She giggled.

Courtney pulled on Gram's arm, her own face on fire. What was up with her grandparents?

They came out the way Courtney came in, passing the portrait of Josh.

"Such a nice young man," Gram said, nodding toward the photo as the door chimed their exit, "and not bad looking either, don't you think, Courtney?"

Courtney ignored her grandmother's pointed comment. She wanted nothing to do with men for a good long while, even if it was Josh. She fumbled in her bag for her keys, praying no one she knew would drive by and catch her standing in front of the detachment with her jailbird grandparents.

"Ms. Merrick!" A little voice drifted in the early June air before a horn honked. Courtney willed the weed-cracked asphalt lot to open and swallow her.

"Oh, it's Annie's granddaughter. I didn't know you taught any of the Joseph kids," Gram said, unconcerned, as she waved furiously.

Courtney gave a halfhearted wave, and a little hand waved back before the battered minivan turned left and disappeared. Almost a year since she'd returned, and Courtney was still adjusting to being back in Port Russell, where everyone knew everyone—and their business.

With keys located, Courtney pushed the button and unlocked the car. She leaned over the backseat to clear it off, shoving the bin of marking—math booklets and art projects—that comprised the sum of her weekend plans and knocking it over. The glitter from the artwork fluttered onto the upholstery and floor mats, and Courtney sighed. Add vacuuming her car to the excitement of the weekend. She bent to pick up the scattered assignments to make room for her grandmother.

"Don't see why you lock it," Gramps said, settling into the passenger seat. "No one's going to steal it from in front of the police station."

"City habit," Courtney said, brushing the glitter off the back seat. "Sorry about the mess, Gram."

Gram, Norma to her friends, sat in the back of the Subaru. "Oh, Courtney, I hope this isn't what you planned to do this weekend."

Courtney rolled her eyes before yanking her door open to slide behind the steering wheel. She struggled to fasten her belt because she'd forgotten to take her purse off. Frustration threatened to set off an eruption, so Courtney paused to take a deep breath, in through her nose, out through her mouth, before she said something she regretted, just as she taught her students to do.

With her equilibrium restored, Courtney pulled her purse strap over her head and moved it to the floor behind the passenger seat. She caught her grandmother's bright hazel eyes in the rearview. "You know it's report card time, Gram. I have no choice—I'm on a deadline."

Norma clucked her disapproval, "You shouldn't work so hard all the time, Court. You deserve to have some fun."

Courtney smiled, despite herself. "There'll be plenty of time for fun in July."

Fun with whom? her nasty inner voice whispered. She'd spent the year focusing on work rather than relationships and consequently had zero plans for the summer. Courtney shook her head, refusing to listen. Time to change the subject. "What happened, you two? How do you go from saying you were going to putter in the garden this morning to calling your granddaughter to bail you out of jail within a few hours?"

"It's a long story," her grandfather said.

A police cruiser pulled into the lot, and Courtney realized with horror that Josh was driving it. He parked a few stalls over from her Subaru, waving when he saw it was her.

Shit, Courtney thought, stomach fluttering madly. He's going to come over to chat if I don't get out of here. There was no way she was going to talk to him, not with Gram and Gramps in the backseat listening to the whole conversation. She started the car, waved, and backed out of her parking spot, the weighty gaze of the now hunky policeman making her hyperaware of her driving.

"It was a lovely surprise to run into Josh Cameron, wasn't it, Charlie?"

Gramps grunted. "Could have done without him arresting me."

"Who'd have thought such a scrawny little thing could turn out so brawny!" Gram giggled.

"Gram!" Courtney's cheeks heated. "Seriously, though, what were you two thinking?"

"Someone needs to stand up for what's right." Gramps pulled his backpack onto his lap with a work-worn hand as Courtney turned onto the highway out of town.

"But why you? You could get hurt."

"Pshaw, Court—we're not that frail. As to why us, why not us? We have the time, and we helped create the problem in the first place."

Courtney glanced over at Gramps in the passenger seat. He sighed and bowed his head a bit.

"What do you mean you created the problem?" Courtney asked.

For months, rumours had swirled around town about the company that had bought her grandfather's logging company, about who was behind it, and what they had planned. Depending on who you talked to, it ranged from a few road closures to the full-scale destruction of half the town. All too late for her grandfather to do anything about it—the sale was final. Irreversible.

Silence had descended on the car, and Courtney's stomach clenched. She turned off the highway onto the access road that led to Gram and Gramp's acreage. Whatever this company had planned, it was bad. Her stomach never lied.

Courtney pulled through the timber arch her grandfather and Dad had built over the entrance to her grandparents' acreage. The sign affixed to it read *Merrick Manor*, a gift from Courtney when she'd done woodworking in high school.

She parked next to her grandfather's workshop, setting the parking brake before he could remind her to do it. Should she ask or wait for her grandparents' explanation?

"CFI launched their new project today," Gram said, the click of her seatbelt reverberating in the silent car. "They're going to log Gnome Lake."

"No!" Courtney said, laying a hand on her grandfather's arm.

It was worse than she'd ever imagined.

CHAPTER 2

CFI had seemed like a dream come true when they'd expressed interest in buying her grandfather's company, Port Russell Logging, more than a year ago. At the time, he'd still worked fifty, even sixty-hour weeks, despite being ten years past average retirement age, and Courtney worried he'd simply drop dead on the job—never enjoying the fruits of his years of labour. She'd been overwhelmed by her breakup with Nathan at that point and didn't know the details of the deal, only that Gram was thrilled she was finally going to get to enjoy retirement with her husband of nearly fifty years. Gramps had been relieved to sell to a company with Vancouver Island connections, and they'd assured him they would run the company like he had for the last forty years—as a steward for the land and an employer of Port Russell's hardworking people.

The whole family—Mom, Dad, and herself—had travelled back to Port Russell for Gramps's retirement party last June, celebrating with champagne the sale and his well-earned rest. That was the night Gram had told her about the job opening at Port Russell Elementary. Had it been a year already?

"Why log Gnome Lake?" Courtney asked. "I thought that area was off-limits?"

Gramps placed a hand over hers, squeezing. "I could really use a whisky. Can we move this inside?"

Courtney helped Gram put together snacks and tea—Gram rarely drank alcohol—before settling down at the well-worn dining room table. The tang of spirits, with hints of peat and salt water, filled the room as Gramps poured a finger of amber liquid into a cut-glass tumbler. Once

Gramps had taken a sip of whisky, sighing after swallowing the single malt, Courtney pounced.

"Okay, spill. What is going on?" she asked.

Gramps looked tired—more tired than she'd seen him look since he'd retired. Gram kept glancing over at her husband, concern clear on her lined face. When she noticed Courtney looking, she busied herself with stirring sugar into her tea, the spoon tinkling as it hit the sides of the mug.

Gramps took a deep breath, and Courtney's stomach flipped. This was serious.

"Stan called me on Monday to let me know CFI weren't what they'd claimed to be when I sold them my company."

"Stan Jones? I thought he retired just after you?"

Stan and his wife Marilyn were like a second set of grandparents to her—fixtures in her life and in Port Russell. Marilyn was Gram's best friend, and Stan had been the foreman of Port Russell Logging and Gramps's right-hand man.

"One of Stan's many nephews works for CFI and tipped him off. Turns out the CEO of CFI, Justin Cameron, was working as a proxy. His father, Wayne Cameron, has partnered with an offshore company, and the real owner of my company is an Eris Resources."

"Wait, what? Justin Cameron? Why didn't you tell me you sold to him?"

Gram flashed Courtney a confused look. "We thought you knew. CFI is Cameron Forest Initiative. Justin has been the CEO for about five years, ever since he finished business school. The name change was his idea—an updated image."

Courtney flushed. Completely wrapped up in her miserable life, she hadn't put two and two together. "Of course. But how could he log Gnome Lake? He knows what it means to the Pacheedaaht and the rest of Port Russell."

Gnome Lake was a sacred spot for the Pacheedaaht and the beating heart of Port Russell. Courtney couldn't think of a single person who didn't cherish it. It was a magical place. The Cameron family had called Port Russell home and would be well aware of its importance to the community. Wayne Cameron had run his much smaller company alongside Gramps for about a decade before they had moved out of Port Russell.

Justin Cameron. A memory of his perpetual sneer and arrogance popped into Courtney's head. Blech. The once-local boy, and Josh's brother, had straight up lied to her grandfather? Courtney knew he was a dirtbag—lord knew he'd made her life as hard as possible when they'd been in high school—but how dare he!

"I imagine it was for the money," Gramps said dryly. "I'm such a fool."

Gram clucked. "Charles Merrick, you are no such thing. Eris Resources clearly knew you were no fool, or they wouldn't have gone to such lengths to conceal themselves behind CFI. Masterstroke, really, to find a company with a local connection. They did their homework." Gram laced her fingers through her husband's, bringing them up to kiss the back of his hand.

"Thanks, sunshine." Gramps smiled. "Stan also found out they were headed for Gnome Lake. Once we told the band, they mobilized the elders and set up the protest. That area is sacred. It's why I never harvested any of the timber around it, despite its board feet value."

"Won't provincial laws prevent them from logging there? I thought old growth was protected in BC?" Courtney poured herself a small whisky and took a sip.

"Unfortunately, it's totally within their right to harvest up to a quarter. Thing that really worries me is that logging is only part of Eris Resource's business. They operate a bunch of resorts. What if they have plans to develop once the logging is done? If that's the case, then I've opened the door to the destruction of Port Russell as we know it." Gramps's hand tightened around his tumbler, the amber liquid sloshing against the sides.

"Weren't there conditions in the purchase agreement?" Courtney recalled her grandfather's many meetings with his lawyer prior to the sale.

"Yes, for CFI. But, apparently, the company structure with Eris Resources means they aren't bound by those conditions in the same way. I could challenge CFI, but it would create massive legal bills. They've got deep pockets and the support of Eris Resources."

"Oh, Gramps!" Courtney got up and hugged her grandfather from behind. Her heart sank when she thought of Gramps's commitment to sustainable forestry practices ruined by corporate greed and that dirtbag Justin Cameron. Not to mention the Indigenous involvement in the management of their local resources and safeguarding Gnome Lake from being logged, even when it wasn't legally protected.

"We felt we had to be involved in the protest," Gram continued, pouring herself another cup of tea, "and we'll likely go there tomorrow."

Courtney's gut blazed. "Is there any other way you could help? If they're arresting people already, it could get much worse."

Gramps waved away her concern. "I got them into this mess. It's the least I can do."

Courtney recognized the steel in her grandfather's voice. Family and community—they were religion in the Merrick house. She shared a look with her grandmother, who smiled and shrugged. After decades of marriage, Gram knew how to pick her battles.

"What do you feel like for dinner, dear?" Gram asked, rising to head to the kitchen.

"Gram, no, let me..."

"Courtney, I'm fine. You worked all day. Why don't you go for your run?"

A run sounded like heaven.

She had a lot to process. First, she finds out Josh is back in town. Her stomach swooped at that thought, and she sighed. Best not to go down that road. And Justin was back, ruining her life. Gah! Had she gotten into a time machine? She thought better on her feet, running through the forest.

"Compromise? I go for my run, but you order pizza. My treat."

Gram laughed. "Deal. Be back by 6:00."

CHAPTER 3

The astringent scent of cedar needles beneath her pounding feet untied the knots in Courtney's neck and shoulders. This path in the manor's forest, essentially her backyard, was the only place she truly found peace these days. As she cruised down the soft, single track through towering cedar and fir, her brain, which usually replayed every mistake and misstep she'd made the last few years, was quiet.

This was the forest of her childhood. Everything about it reminded her of the rosy days of freedom and joy she'd experienced within the shelter of these green giants. Her childhood had been spectacular, as confirmed by her few years as a teacher in a busier center. She was grateful every day to have grown up in Port Russell, though she cringed when she thought about how she used to disparage the place as a teenager to anyone who would listen. The shame following her disastrous relationship with Nathan and the uncertainty over what to do with the shambles of her life had driven her back here, to her childhood home. But she had to admit that contributing to a magical childhood for her students, and spending time with her grandparents, kept her here. If they insisted on attending the protests, it was good that she was here to keep an eye on them. Once school finished, it might even be a good idea for all of them to go together, so she could make sure they didn't get hurt. Lord knew she'd never be able to talk them out of going unless something changed drastically.

Courtney rounded a bend and settled into a comfortable pace, the tension in her shoulders dissipating and her breathing easy. Halfway along the path, an enormous cedar with unusual horizontal branches dominated the forest. Perched upon one of the weird wide boughs sat the cozy treehouse where she'd spent a good portion of her idyllic childhood. She smiled as she remembered the countless summer sleepovers with her best friend, laughing as they lay tucked beneath the sturdy cedar shakes of the treehouse.

Josh Cameron.

Skinny and loyal, he was her constant companion and partner in crime. Her best friend. A memory of Josh's dancing ocean-coloured eyes, shaggy bangs, and scabby knees popped into her head. He'd spent so much time at her house that her parents had set a place at the table for him every night, and her grandparents invited him to every family event they'd hosted. She'd only realized he was her first love after he up and moved away without even saying goodbye. Port Russell had felt much smaller without him. Now he was back in town. A ripped police officer.

Courtney laughed out loud, cheeks flushing when she pictured him at the detachment earlier. What did her response to his reappearance mean? Why was she so nervous to talk to him? Was she still angry with him? He'd certainly changed on the outside—was he even the same sweet guy she'd known and trusted? Did it matter? She was hardly in the right headspace to do anything about it. She shouldn't be thinking about any guy, let alone Josh.

Scowling, Courtney rolled her shoulders, knots returning with the memories. She slowed as she passed the treehouse and eased her way onto the single track leading out of the trees and down to the pebbly beach. A light breeze, salt laced, lifted the hair off her sweaty neck, and Courtney sighed at the familiar sight. The deep cobalt blue of Little Bear Bay stretched out before her, glittering in the early evening sun. She jogged to the steep path and began to descend it to the private strip of beach below. A copper-coloured blur in the scrub next to the path drew her eye from the water, and Courtney let out a strangled cry as she slid on the conifer cones littering the track. She landed on her ass with a thud. A rusty muzzle instantly obscured her view of the water as a Nova Scotia duck toller, hind end wagging joyously, licked her face and bare arms.

"Russell! Off!" a male voice called from the beach below.

After one last lick, the overly friendly Russell bounded off toward the sound. Smiling, despite the layer of dog drool coating her, Courtney looked up to see Russell run up to his person.

A shirtless—and holy mother of trees, ripped in ways she would have never imagined—Josh Cameron stood on the beach looking decidedly less formal and formidable than he had at the detachment earlier that afternoon. Just past him, perched on the pebbly shore, was a bright-red fibreglass kayak.

It definitely hadn't been purchased at Canadian Tire. Courtney blushed when she found her gaze lingering on Josh's sculpted abs and glistening pecs as he walked up the path toward her.

"Sorry, he loves people. He's young and sometimes forgets his training," Josh said, scowling at his errant dog while extending a hand to help Courtney off the ground.

She was immediately reminded of all the times he'd extended a hand from the top of the treehouse ladder to lift her up, and her stomach clenched sharply. Ignoring his outstretched hand, Courtney pushed herself up to standing, wiping needles and dirt off her running shorts.

Josh withdrew his hand, hurt plain on his face.

Russell was now leaning against her leg, looking up at her with an expectant grin on his face. His soft, floppy ears begged to be stroked.

Embarrassed and flustered, Courtney giggled. "I see that." She leaned over and scratched the soft fur, running the dog's velvet ears between her fingers. Russell closed his eyes in bliss, and Courtney smiled in earnest.

"He normally plays a little harder to catch," Josh said, brow furrowed, the wind riffling his short brown hair.

They paused; the only sounds were the whisper of the waves as they lapped the smooth pebbles on the shore and the sharp cry of a high-circling osprey. Then, they both spoke at the same time. "When did you come back to town?"

Josh chuckled, gesturing toward Courtney. "Ladies first."

Irritation zapped up her spine. The statement reminded her of Nathan, condescending chauvinist that he'd been, but Courtney answered. "I moved here at the start of the school year. I took a position teaching Grade 3 at Port Russell Elementary. You?"

"Just arrived last week. Transferred temporarily from up island. Port Hardy."

How long would he be here? Courtney pushed off another wave of irritation. Naturally, the first guy she'd been attracted to in ages was only going to be around temporarily.

They fell silent again. Russell took umbrage at some seagulls picking at exposed sea life and took off barking.

A million questions darted through Courtney's mind, principally, why Josh hadn't bothered to say goodbye, quickly followed by why he'd never bothered to contact her over the years, but she bit her tongue. This Josh Cameron was a stranger—a hot stranger, yes—but the boy she knew was gone. She had to remember that. Courtney cleared her throat and looked down at her watch, still recording her run.

"I've got to go. Gram expects me for dinner at six."

"Oh. Cool," Josh said.

Courtney swore she saw him wince.

"Um, hey. Would it be okay if I took a walk in your forest? For old times' sake? That's actually why we paddled here today." Josh gestured to the red boat pulled up on the shore. The waves buffeted it, threatening to take it out into the bay.

"Your kayak is going to leave without you," Courtney pointed out, buying some time to respond to his question. It was her grandfather's property. He was right to ask permission. But he couldn't have known he'd run into her. Did the upstanding RCMP officer intend to trespass when he came here today? And what did he mean by old times' sake? Courtney shook the thoughts from her head. It didn't matter anyway.

Josh pulled the boat way past the water line, lashing it to the silvered remains of a cedar driftwood for good measure, stowing one human and one canine PFD in the cockpit. Russell returned to lean against Courtney, triumphant in having chased the intruding seagulls away. He looked up every once in a while to see if she still thought he was cute.

"Yes, Russell, you're adorable," she said, leaning over to stroke his ears again. When she stood up, she got an eyeful of Josh's rock-hard abs. Wowza. His workout regimen must be intense. She straightened quickly. Had he noticed her checking him out? She admired the ink on his upper arm—a half-sleeve tattoo of a coastal scene with a red kayak paddling out to sea in a bay that looked a lot like the one she was currently looking at. Weird.

"Nice artwork," she said, gesturing with her chin.

"Thanks. So would it be okay if Russell and I had a ramble?"

"Were you just going to trespass?"

Josh's ears turned red. "I knew I'd likely run into you."

Heat rose from deep in her belly, travelling toward her head. Her eyes grew into saucers.

Josh put out a placating hand. "When I stopped into the post office after work, I mentioned to Marilyn Jones that I was thinking of going for a paddle. She suggested I might find you here."

Courtney ground her teeth. The Port Russell pipeline. Gram must have called Marilyn as she was getting ready for her run. Courtney blushed when she put two and two together. Gram!

"I see," she said, glancing at her watch again. "Sure. Ramble away. Don't take anything."

Courtney winced. Idiot.

Josh nodded, pursing his lips to stifle a smile. "Sure thing. Hey, is the treehouse still there?"

Courtney's feet itched to get going. Away from Josh and his abs. And the memories.

"Yeah. Just past the top of this path. Can't miss it."

Josh looked up the path, a dreamy look on his face. "Some of the happiest times in my life were spent in that treehouse."

Surprised, Courtney managed a nod. She felt the same way.

"Okay. Nice to meet you, Russell. See you around, Josh."

She turned and started running up the hill at full speed—she was going to feel this tomorrow. She hoped the weight of Josh's wave-blue eyes rested on her upper back and not her running-short-clad rear end.

CHAPTER 4

On the run back to Merrick Manor, Courtney tried to banish the vision of Josh, standing on her beach, bare-chested and chiseled, and attempted to replace it with the scrawny, scraped kid perpetually in need of a haircut she'd once known. And loved. Damn.

How different would her life have been if he hadn't up and moved away from Port Russell? Would they have eventually hooked up? Maybe gone to prom together? Moved in together when they left home? If Josh hadn't left her heartbroken, she wouldn't have given Nathan the time of day when he'd showed up. She'd still be the whole, happy person she used to be. Courtney shook the thought from her head. Playing what-if was a recipe for disaster and disappointment.

A little voice whispered in the back of her head: He's back now. Why not go for it?

"No!" she said out loud, causing a squirrel to chatter a warning from a branch above. "Yeah, yeah. I'm going." Courtney said to the critter, picking up her pace.

Russell was a cutie, Courtney admitted, breaking through the waist-high ferns that edged the manor's boundary. She hit the driveway and glanced at her watch: 5:30—enough time for a quick shower. She'd do the after-dinner cleanup for Gram to make up for her absence.

At five minutes to six, Courtney walked from her place in the guest bungalow—she refused to call it a "granny suite"—to the mudroom door with her wet hair loosely braided and wearing clean leggings and her favourite Port Russell High School gym shirt, holes and all. As she entered the house, Marilyn's wheezy laugh drifted down the hall from the kitchen. Immediately, Courtney prepared an excuse to get out of the inevitable card game that would start after dinner and carry on into the wee hours. Her grandparents were party animals, especially compared to her. Saying she had homework probably wouldn't cut it. Lost in thought, she startled when she saw a tall, broad-shouldered man holding a large bowl of salad in the kitchen.

"Look who I found wandering along the road on my way in," Marilyn crowed, sharing a conspiratorial look with Courtney's grandmother.

Wily old busy body, Courtney thought. Had she and Gram masterminded this whole evening? Courtney stiffened her shoulders.

"Josh, we meet again."

Russell looked up from the stainless-steel dog bowl of water that likely her grandfather had put down for him and wagged his tail joyfully. Gramps was in heaven having a dog in the house again—he'd be no help at all. Stan waved shyly from his usual spot at the table.

"Is that my shirt?" Josh blurted out.

Courtney looked down at the faded T-shirt. Crap, what had she done? She'd forgotten her favourite cozy shirt was the one Josh left behind in the treehouse. Courtney felt very warm suddenly.

"I've asked Josh, and Russell, to stay for dinner, love. Can you get another place setting out?" Gram said. Phew! Gram had impeccable timing, as always.

Relieved to have something to do, Courtney sidled past Josh and busied herself retrieving a plate, cutlery, and a glass. She spied the feast of salmon, salad, and roast potatoes Gram had prepared laid out on several platters rather than the pizza boxes she'd been expecting.

"What happened to ordering pizza?" Courtney asked, her eyes meeting her grandmother's. Gram just smiled and batted her question away.

"Mrs. Merrick, I really just popped in to say hi."

"Nonsense, dear. I insist." Gram smiled, patting Josh on the arm. "Just put this on the table and grab your usual seat."

Josh smiled, acquiescing, and settled in his place on the far side of the table.

Gramps looked around the dining room. "Just like old times, hey, Norma?"

Courtney, seated across from Marilyn and close enough to Josh to feel his warmth radiating along her left side, concentrated on putting her napkin on her lap, praying Josh didn't notice she was sweating.

"Place, Russell," Josh commanded, pointing at a spot beside him. Russell was going to be a very happy boy, Courtney thought; Gramps would be tossing him treats all through dinner.

"You made good time from the beach. You still run competitively?" Josh asked, passing Courtney a bowl of new potatoes with dill.

"Uh, no. I gave that up years ago." Courtney avoided looking at her grandfather. He'd been particularly disappointed when she'd given up her spot on the University of Victoria's track team because Nathan had said it took too much time away from their relationship. Gramps had never forgiven him for it. Courtney should have taken that as a sign.

"That's too bad," Josh said, accepting a platter of salmon fillets from Gramps. "You were so good. It always bugged me that I couldn't beat you."

Courtney kept her eyes focused on the platter as she took the salmon from Josh, willing the hot tears of shame pricking her eyes to stay put.

"This looks amazing, Mrs. Merrick. Beats the sandwich I was going to make myself. Thank you."

Gram clucked. "Sandwiches—how'd you get so big eating those? Stan brought the fish, more than we could eat. Glad you could stay."

Gram caught Courtney's eye and grinned like the Cheshire cat. Courtney fought the urge to roll her eyes. This wasn't the first time Marilyn and Gram had conspired to set her up. Courtney suspected a lot of Marilyn and Gram's conversations revolved around how sad and lonely Courtney must be. They teased her mercilessly for her lack of social life. This dinner was a new low.

"Tell us about your life outside of Port Russell, Josh. What did you get up to?" Marilyn asked, flashing a twinkling smile in Courtney's direction.

Kill me now, Courtney thought, turning her attention to spearing a bone-free forkful of salmon.

"Um, huh," Josh said, delaying as he shifted in his chair, clearly uncomfortable in the hot seat. "Well, right after we left here, Dad enrolled us at Mulligan Lake Prep. He felt it would be best for us, and it freed him to focus solely on building his business."

Courtney noted the bitterness in Josh's voice and glanced at him furtively, brow furrowed.

"What business was that?" Marilyn asked, captivated by Josh's tale as if it were a best-selling romance novel.

"Um, Cameron Forest Initiative?" Josh answered, watching the reaction of everyone at the table.

An awkward silence fell over the room. Anger bubbled in Courtney's stomach, and she lowered her fork, searching the faces around the table to gauge how everyone else was taking this news. How could he so casually mention being associated with the company threatening to log the heart of Port Russell?

Stan was scowling, his furry black brows knitted together. Gram had set down her fork and was wiping her mouth with her napkin, likely to cover her reaction. Marilyn had leaned forward toward Josh, and Courtney could see the wheels turning as Marilyn connected the dots. Curiously, Gramps was still eating, his face calm but shuttered.

"Oh!" Marilyn exclaimed, breaking the silence. "Silly me, I'd forgotten."

Courtney glanced at Gramps again, who was now busy slipping a sliver of salmon to Russell. Stan, ever silent, nodded, then returned to his meal.

"How did you enjoy Mulligan Lake?" Gram asked, sensing the tension.

"I hated it at the time, to be honest. I've learned to appreciate it a bit more as I've grown older. I did find kayaking there, so..."

Glancing over, Courtney noticed Josh's neck had turned red.

"Ooh, I remember now. You competed in race kayaking, didn't you?" Marilyn asked, pausing to take a sip of her ice water, the cubes clinking against the side of the glass.

Wily old fox. How long has she stored that little bit of information? How was it that I never knew that? Because I'd never bothered to look for him, her nasty inner voice whispered. Regret bubbled up from her lower abdomen. Courtney put her fork down to sip her water.

"K-1, yeah. Not a lot of money on the world cup kayak circuit, and I missed qualifying for the national team, so when I ran across a recruiter for the RCMP at one of our meets, I decided I'd try it out. I graduated from depot three years ago. My first posting was in Prince George."

"Why leave there? I hear it's a nice town," Marilyn said, and Gram nodded.

Josh laughed out loud, short and sharp, before schooling his face. "Sorry, that was unprofessional. I didn't really enjoy Prince George. Let's just say it's too far away from the ocean. I always hoped I'd find a posting on Vancouver Island, maybe even Port Russell."

Courtney felt Josh's eyes on her as he said this. Why was he looking at her as he said that?

"Isn't it a conflict of interest to be policing the town where your family's company is in conflict with most of the town?" Courtney asked, uncomfortable under the weight of Josh's eyes.

"Courtney!" Gram admonished as everyone at the table paused their eating to focus on Josh's answer.

"I'm posted here temporarily to lend a hand for the dist—um, demonstration at Gnome Lake. My actual position is up island in Port Hardy. And for the record, it's not my family business anymore. I'm not on speaking terms with my father."

"I'm sorry to hear that," Gram said, her hazel eyes softening as she looked at Josh. "So, you're all they sent to handle the protest? I hope it won't be too much work for you." Gram paused to sip her water. "Today was just the start—things are going to get much rowdier."

"Norma, the boy is just doing his job," Gramps said. "New rule: no shop talk at the table."

"My apologies, Josh. I'm just very passionate about this town and our forest. We've looked after it so long, and old habits die hard. I do hope you'll come for dinner often while you're in town."

Josh blushed. "Thanks, Mrs. Merrick. I hope I'll have the time."

"So, Josh, do you have a girlfriend?" Marilyn asked, causing Courtney to choke on her bite of potato.

"You okay?" Josh asked, his fork clanging on his plate as he readied himself to deliver aid, relief flooding his face as the spotlight moved off him.

Courtney, eyes streaming, nodded before taking a gulp of water. "I'm okay. Just went down the wrong hole." She felt Josh's gaze upon her for a few heartbeats before he returned to his dinner.

"Do you want some more salmon, Josh?" Gramps asked.

"No thanks. I'm stuffed. It was excellent."

"Dessert's not fancy, just ice cream and strawberries," Gram said, getting ready to push herself away from the table.

"Honestly, I couldn't eat another bite, and Russell and I still need to paddle back to Cedar Cove. We're staying at the Cedar Sands cottages while we're here. How about I clean up while you have your dessert?"

"No need for that, thank you, dear. You're a guest."

Courtney glanced at her grandmother in confusion. She never gave up that easily. What was she up to?

"Keep him company on his walk to the beach, Courtney? Us oldies can clean up and then have our dessert round the card table later."Gram fixed Courtney with a pointed stare.

Shoot, no way out of this. She'd been outfoxed. If she made a fuss, it would just end up making her look bad. If Gram and Gramps could stand to have the enemy in their house, she could at least be cordial. But, just because Josh wasn't on speaking terms with his father didn't mean he wasn't involved with CFI. He was a Cameron, after all. Maybe she should refuse. Gram was now frowning at her. Uh oh.

Sighing, Courtney resigned herself to her fate and stood. She was only agreeing to walk him to the beach, not to marry him, after all.

"Sure, Gram. Ready to go, Josh?"

CHAPTER 5

Courtney looked longingly at her cabin as she and Josh walked across the short swath of lawn toward the beach trailhead. What she wouldn't give to be safe inside right now instead of escorting the enemy back to his kayak. She felt jittery in his presence and had to resist the urge to reach for his hand. Her heart wanted one thing, and her head told her in no uncertain terms to leave it be. She would walk him part of the way to placate her grandmother and nothing more.

Russell bounded ahead, barking at a crow perched in a tree at the edge of the forest. At least she'd still have this bit of forest to ramble in. Once Gnome Lake was logged, what would happen to all the wildlife up there?

Josh followed her gaze. "You staying in the cottage? Remember all the stupid plans we made revolving around that little place?" Josh said, chuckling.

Hell. No, Courtney thought, grinding her teeth to keep the word vomit brewing deep within from spewing all over Gramps's well-trimmed lawn. If Josh thought this was an invitation to walk down memory lane, he was sadly mistaken. Her hands formed fists at her sides, and Courtney marched to the trailhead.

Josh started rambling as if talking could dispel the awkward gloom surrounding them.

Good. Let him feel confused for a change.

"Sorry about dinner. I got turned around in the forest—I guess my memory isn't as good as I thought. Anyway, I found myself out on the road as Marilyn and Stan were driving by. I couldn't say no. You know how she is."

Oh, Courtney knew. She felt a pang of empathy; Gram and Marilyn had trapped him right alongside her in their match-making scheme.

"Marilyn is a force of nature," Courtney conceded, regretting it immediately when Josh smiled. She turned and focused on walking.

They entered the forest, the cedars and firs towering sentinels above them. Russell brushed along Courtney's leg, lifting his nose in an explicit invitation for pets. Russell, I like, she thought, ruffling the dog's silky fur and ears.

The crow swooped overhead, an arm's length above their heads, and Russell bounded off after it.

"Whoa!" Josh exclaimed. "Holy crap. That isn't the same crow, is it?"

They'd befriended a crow back when they'd spent every moment not at school or sleeping in the treehouse, their "forest fortress." Concerned for the wildlife on a blistering hot day, Courtney set up a shallow dish of water and shared a handful of trail mix from her bag with the crow. From then on, Edgar the crow had been their official mascot and unofficial security guard.

"No," Courtney said. "Edgar stopped coming the summer after you left." She felt the prick of tears—oh, God; she wasn't crying! Were the tears for the crow or Josh, she wondered.

Neither, she decided. She'd outgrown that version of herself a long time ago. She'd had to. And she wasn't going to go back now.

"Oh, too bad," Josh said. "I dug that bird."

Not enough to come back to visit, Courtney thought. They came to a fork in the path.

"Just stay straight on the path to the left. You'll pass the tree fort, and then about five minutes later, you'll start going downhill to the beach." She pivoted and took a step in the direction they'd just come from.

"Wait! Aren't you going to come see the fortress with me? For old times' sake?"

Irritation, as hot and frothy as an overboiling pot, bubbled to the surface, and Courtney whirled back to face Josh.

"Oh! So *now* you want to visit? Sorry, but you missed your window by, oh, I don't know, ten years or so, Josh. No, I don't want to reminisce with you. The magic sort of drained out of this place when you left and never contacted me again. Do you know how much I worried about you?" Do you know what sort of jerk I got myself involved with because you left me? she didn't say out loud. Courtney clapped a hand over her mouth, horrified she'd let her angry froth splash out all over Josh and herself. The forest was supposed to bring her peace.

Josh took a step back and blinked but immediately took a deep breath and squared his shoulders. “I’m sorry, Court. It was totally shitty of me to leave without saying goodbye. And even shittier to never contact you again.”

Russell sat at Josh’s feet, whining softly.

“I had no idea my dad was going to move us, and I got lost in my anger for a while. When I emerged, I was embarrassed I’d let so much time pass. I convinced myself you’d moved on and were better off without me.”

Her cheeks were burning, and her knees began to tremble as the anger seeped out of her body. Then, in the low light beneath the canopy, for a moment, Courtney saw the skinny kid she’d known and felt her heart open a crack.

“You didn’t know you were moving?”

Josh’s face transformed into an angry mask for a second. “You know my dad. He never felt it necessary to communicate with me.”

Courtney caught the implication beneath his words, and her irritation fell away, replaced by righteous indignation on Josh’s behalf. “He told Justin, but not you? Asshole.”

Josh broke into a wide smile. “There’s the Court I know. Do you mean my dad or Justin when you say ‘asshole?’”

Courtney smiled shyly. “Both. But mostly Justin, of course.”

Just a grade above them, Josh’s brother Justin had spent most of his spare time back in the day finding ways to make his brother’s life as miserable as possible. Courtney had become a favourite target once she started hanging out with Josh.

Justin was the reason they’d spent so much time at the fortress in the first place—it was a place to escape the torment. It was probably the only good thing Justin had ever done for his brother, Courtney mused. And now, naturally, Justin was behind scummy CFI and their plan to destroy Gnome Lake. Courtney rubbed at her chest, anger flaring like heartburn.

“Come with me, just for a minute?” Josh asked, smiling until the dimple in his cheek stood out.

A flash of electricity shot up from her leggings straight to her brain. God, that dimple was even hotter than it used to be. Courtney stood, frozen to the spot. This was a bad idea.

"Please?" Josh pleaded. "I'm worried I'll get turned around and miss it. Show me?"

"Fine, but I'm not staying. I don't want to give Marilyn and Gram anything to talk about."

Josh mock-shuddered. "Deal."

Russell stood and wagged his tail, settling in between Josh and Courtney as they continued down the path, looking up at each of them every few minutes.

They walked in awkward silence to the clearing with the bent cedar tree. Some long-past storm caused the curve, and the elbow-shaped bough had provided the perfect foundation for the tree fort. Courtney had helped her father and grandfather build the first room the summer she was eleven. She remembered every detail of the day in Grade 7 when she'd invited Josh to hang out with her to cheer him up. As an only child, she'd watched in horror as Justin, egged on by his posse of meathead friends, took Josh's lunch bag and then licked everything in it.

Before that day, Josh had been just another kid in her class, quiet and unassuming. Once they arrived at the fort the day of the lunch incident, Josh came alive, and from that day until the day he left, they were inseparable. He got her, and she saw him. They were teased mercilessly for hanging out. Josh took the brunt of that abuse for having a "girl" for a best friend, as if that made him defective. Courtney huffed. They'd always sworn to others and, more loudly to each other, that they were "just friends." Courtney lied through her teeth from the summer of Grade 8 until long after the day Josh left. Once she realized she'd been in love with Josh, never being able to tell him, it had eaten away at her until she'd met Nathan in her first year of university.

Courtney took a deep, cleansing breath, the sharp tang of cedar and the dampness of the spongy moss beneath her feet filling her up. She glanced at Josh—it was so weird to be standing here with him again. She stopped at the base of the ladder, feeling the heat of Josh through her battered T-shirt as he stood close behind her.

"So, here it is," Courtney said, turning to face Josh and getting a face full of his muscular pecs and shoulders. Courtney backed up, bumping into the ladder.

"Oh, sorry," Josh said, sheepishly taking a step back. "Didn't mean to crowd you."

Skin humming, Courtney side-stepped past Josh back onto the path, muscles straining to keep her hands next to her body.

"It looks exactly the same," Josh said, letting out a small laugh, running a hand over the ladder's rungs. "If you only knew how often I thought about this place.

As if someone flipped a switch, the electricity in the air stopped. Courtney scowled, certain her "angry wrinkle," as her students liked to call it, was furrowing the space between her arched eyebrows.

"Yeah. Well, Gramps believes in good maintenance for all his creations." Courtney glanced at her watch. "I've got to get back. Just take that path to the right of that patch of salal to get back to the beach."

Josh raised his eyebrows at her shift in tone. "Uh, thanks. Hey, do you want to have dinner with me tomorrow night?"

He did not just ask her out. Seriously? He was more perceptive when he was thirteen, Courtney fumed. "Actually, Josh, no. I don't really think that's appropriate."

Josh recoiled, blinking as if he'd been slapped. "Appropriate? It's just dinner between friends, Court."

Friends? Your family tricked my grandfather out of the company he spent his whole life building, and they're going to log the most precious corner of the forest, she wanted to shout. Instead, she made excuses.

"That's not what I mean." Courtney's heart thudded in her chest. She fished around for cover. "I've also got a ton of work to get through this weekend. End of year report card time."

"I get how hard it is during report card time. Another time?"

How did he know about report card time? Courtney's belly burned, but she lifted her chin, her family's insistence on good manners taking over.

"Um, maybe." Courtney mentally kicked herself. When would she learn to just say no and move on?

Russell bounded out of the ferns behind the fort and planted a big wet kiss on Courtney's bare leg.

"Russell! Keep it to yourself, bud! Come."

Russell shimmied over to Josh and leaned against his toned leg, looking up adoringly at his master as Courtney wiped the dog drool off her leg and turned to leave.

"Thanks for tonight," Josh said. "I had a great time."

Looking back over her shoulder, Courtney waved stiffly, making a grateful escape back to her cottage. Hopefully, it would be the last time she saw Josh while he was stationed in Port Russell.

CHAPTER 6

Sleep was elusive for Courtney that night. Each time she closed her eyes, Josh, perfectly sculpted and tattooed, standing on her beach, would pop into her head. His lightly tanned skin shone as if he'd just worked out, accentuating the tattoo on his upper arm, his smooth, well-formed chest, and bulging biceps. Courtney imagined what they would feel like beneath her searching fingers—soft, but hard, she decided after ruminating in the dark. She'd kicked the comforter off, suddenly sweltering from lust or anger; she couldn't decide. Come on body, get the memo! There would be no dating until she sorted the mess Nathan had left. It was well past 1:00 a.m. when she finally fell asleep.

Of course, Nathan showed up in her dreams. He was the one walking with her in the forest, instead of Josh.

"Ugh, why are you wearing that disgusting T-shirt? You look like a slob," dream Nathan said, sneering.

She looked down at her worn T-shirt and patted her hastily piled bun. "Sorry, sweetie. I went for a run."

"Why bother? You quit the track team, remember? I was going to take you out, but you're such a mess. I'll go out with my mates instead."

Courtney awoke, tears in her eyes and her chest tight as if it had shrunk in the wash. The familiar urge to shrink herself to fit the small role Nathan dictated overwhelmed her. Josh would never have said those things to her back when they were kids or even yesterday. He accepted her for who she was and treated her as an equal. Why was she so against pursuing a relationship with someone who treated her with respect?

After a slow start to Saturday morning, featuring an extra long shower where she tried and failed to stop thinking of Josh, again, then a monster cup of coffee, Courtney attacked the pile of marking and report card preparation she'd brought home for the weekend. Finally, the work allowed her to get her mind off the shirtless Josh channel and back where it belonged, on her students and her responsibilities. She hadn't come back to Port Russell to find a man. She'd accepted a job at her former elementary school to get away from one, or at least the legacy he'd created. To put herself back together after wasting six years trying to be someone she wasn't.

Monday came all too soon, a dreary June day, or "Juneuary," as locals called it. As Courtney pulled into the parking lot of Port Russell Elementary, she noted low clouds obscuring the mountains surrounding the town and bordering forest. The relentless drizzle splattered the bin of glitter-caked art projects as she dashed from her car into school. She stifled an undignified squeak when a large raindrop fell from the beam above the door, landing on her neck and then running beneath her shirt.

She made it to her classroom, and her nearest neighbour, the Grade 4 teacher, Danielle O'Halloran, popped her head around the door. Danielle had been her former Grade 4 teacher, and now white hair was beginning to overtake the vibrant red. Courtney carefully peeled the damp artwork out of the bin and placed it onto the wire drying rack so it wouldn't congeal before she could hand it back to her students.

"Morning, Courtney. Fifteen days and counting!" Danielle sang.

She knew, to the minute, the duration until every school break and her retirement. It was 615 school days, the last Courtney had heard.

"Is it okay if we use your classroom for the presentation today? I've still got all those project tri-boards taking up space in mine."

"Presentation?" Courtney turned, her mind a blank.

"The RCMP presentation on what to do if you get lost in the forest?" Danielle prompted. "For Social Studies?"

Courtney blinked. Crap. She'd booked that before spring break and completely forgotten. "Right. Yes. Just slipped my mind. Sorry! Report card brain."

"You know, if you need a hand with anything, all you have to do is ask."

"Nah, just lots of work. I've got it covered, Mrs. O'Halloran."

Despite Danielle asking Courtney for most of September and October to call her by her first name, Courtney couldn't bring herself to do it. It was so weird to work with people who'd once been her teachers.

"Okay, see you after the lunch recess," Danielle said with a wave.

Courtney glanced at the clock. Fifteen minutes until the bell. She scanned her plans—good thing there was a surprise guest speaker coming. She really hadn't planned near enough for her Grade 3 students. This would make the day go by much faster.

The morning went smoothly, a small miracle, and her class sailed through their daily language exercises and a math lesson on telling analog time. They even managed to rearrange the desks without any major incidents. Courtney gobbled her lunch, and as the bell rang to release the kids for their outside break, Courtney was grateful she'd stashed an umbrella at work as she was on recess duty, and the day was still relentlessly wet.

Naturally, as she made her rounds in her designated part of the sopping schoolyard, an overzealous soccer player bailed right into a giant mud puddle. Courtney had to escort her—loudly protesting her removal from the game—to the office to call home for dry clothes.

"Sadie, I know Mrs. O'Halloran has asked you guys to have dry clothes at school for just this reason," Courtney said, opening the door to the office while looking back at the soggy Sadie. "Why don't you have any here?"

"Used them last week," Sadie said. "Watch"—Courtney stepped into the office, right into a tall, navy blue-clad chest—"out, Ms. Merrick," Sadie finished.

Rubbing her nose and blushing, Courtney took a step back, nearly tripping on her collapsed umbrella, creating a puddle of rainwater on the office floor.

"I'm sorry!" Courtney said, looking up into Josh's smiling blue eyes, the colour of dark denim under the fluorescent lights. "What are you doing here?" she blurted, making the connection too slowly. Her face could probably be seen from space at this moment.

"I'm here to do the presentation for Mrs. O'Halloran and Ms. Merrick," Josh said, pursing his lips to keep from grinning.

"Really?" Sadie exclaimed. "Cool!"

Courtney hustled back into teacher mode. "You'll need dry clothes if you're going to sit through the presentation." Courtney signalled to the school secretary. "Sadie needs to call home for dry clothes, Mrs. Brown."

"Again? What are we going to do with you, Miss Sadie? Come on over." Mrs. Brown said.

Squelching a little, Sadie walked over to use the phone.

"I guess I can just follow you to class?" Josh asked, bending over to pick up a tote off the floor.

"Ah, sorry. I'm on recess duty," Courtney said, stomach fluttering. "I've got to get back out there." As she turned to leave, the bell rang. Was there no escaping this man? Courtney took a deep breath. "I guess I'm free now. Follow me."

Courtney was hyperaware of Josh walking beside her the whole way to her classroom.

"Wow, it looks just the same," Josh marveled. "Oh my gosh! It's us!" Josh paused in front of the framed picture of the whole school photo taken the year they were in Grade 7.

"I've really got to go. I've got to let my kids in and settle them for the presentation. I'm in Mr. Mitchell's old room. Just head down when you're ready." Courtney started back toward her class, glancing at the time.

"Seriously? That is so trippy," Josh said, catching up with her in just a few strides. "I can set my stuff up while you let the kids in."

Courtney pushed down a wave of irritation. She hated being late, and being so close to Josh, looking like he could be Mr. May in the Hot Cop Calendar, was not helping. She felt the sensation of fingers on warm skin and blushed, remembering her lurid dreams of the weekend. She didn't want to reminisce with him now.

As she entered her classroom, Courtney pointed to the rainbow-shaped table she'd cleared off in anticipation of the presentation by shoving stacks of books and bins of half-finished student work anywhere with the space to take them. She really needed to tidy her classroom. Shaking that thought loose, Courtney rolled her shoulders and concentrated on keeping any sign of irritation out of her voice.

"Just set up there. I'll let the kids in." She glanced at the clock above the whiteboard and prayed her students hadn't taken advantage of her tardiness to run wild.

They were, thankfully, all lined up under the overhang, keeping out of the rain. Bless them. Courtney smiled—they really were a nice bunch of kids.

"I'm late. I'm so sorry! I had to escort our guest down from the office. Remember, class, we must come in quickly and quietly and get ready to listen.

Wet stuff off and head to your desks, please. Once Mrs. O'Halloran's class comes, our presentation will begin.

Courtney stifled a laugh when she overheard the students' comments as they filed in.

"Ooh, awesome!"

"He's so tall!"

"Look at his cool pants."

Josh was dressed in his grey short-sleeved uniform shirt, duty vest, and navy blue pants with their distinctive yellow stripe running down the leg. His RCMP patch covered his kayak tattoo, and Courtney had to admit he did look pretty cool. Capable and trustworthy. Thankfully, he had left his duty belt, with his weapon and handcuffs, off. If he'd worn it, he would have had to answer a million questions about the implements. As it was, it looked like Josh was prepared for today's presentation. He'd set up an array of pamphlets, colouring books, and, curiously, a selection of stuffed animals on the front table. He turned to face the kids, waving back at Ellie and Katherine, who hid shy giggles behind their hands.

"Hey! Where's Constable Huong?" Niko, her challenging student, demanded as he slid into his desk.

Courtney scowled.

"I know Constable Huong normally comes, but I used to go to this school, so I asked if I could do the presentation today. I hope that's okay."

Seriously? It would have been easier to ask for a tour. Why go to the trouble of preparing the presentation? Courtney had to put a hand over her mouth to cover a smile when she saw the kids' eyes grow as large as saucers. She didn't want Josh to get the wrong idea, after all.

"You used to go here?" Brayden asked. "Cool!"

Just then, there was a light knock on the doorframe as Mrs. O'Halloran announced her class had arrived. With a pointed finger, she directed her line of students to sit on the floor between the rainbow table and Courtney's students.

"He was smaller than you, Brayden, if you can believe it," Mrs. O'Halloran said, winking at Josh. "Good to see you, Constable Cameron."

Josh grinned at her. "Lovely as always, Mrs. O. So nice to see you again. Is this everyone?"

Courtney glanced around and noted Sadie, in dry clothes, slip into the room and sit with her class on the carpet. She waved at Josh.

"Yes, that's everyone. Okay, Cougars, it's my honour to introduce Constable Josh Cameron. He's a former Cougar himself and is here to do a presentation on how to stay safe in the forest, especially if you get lost. Remember to listen respectfully, and if you have any questions, you can ask them at the end," Courtney said, addressing the combined class. But then she thought to herself, If there's a forest left for them to get lost in.

Trying not to glower, Courtney nodded at Josh staring intently at her with a look she couldn't quite place. Her heart fluttered for a few beats before settling down.

Courtney fell in beside Danielle at the back of the class as Josh began his presentation. All the students were riveted in place.

"Hubba, hubba," Danielle said under her breath, nudging Courtney with her elbow." He looks amazing in that uniform. Look at those muscles! I wonder if he's single?"

"I don't know," Courtney said. Not that it mattered, anyway. Courtney's face could fry an egg, and she shot a warning look at her colleague. Like her grandmother and Marilyn, Danielle was always trying to fix her up. Did these women not have better things to do?

Josh was having a great time and keeping the kids' attention. Courtney had to give him credit. Having guest speakers in the class could be a bit of a gamble. Not all of them were as engaging as Josh. The memory popped up of the time her ex, Nathan, came into her class. What a nightmare that had been. Nate had been stiff and boring. Her students had started to act up—not that she blamed them—and later, Nate had told her she should work on her classroom management skills.

Josh grabbed the bear stuffie—actually a puppet—and Courtney gasped when he launched into a dopey voice, sending the kids into gales of laughter. The electricity she felt the other day returned, zooming up her spine. Danielle was right; he really did fill out his uniform nicely. Even with a bear puppet on his hand, he looked sexy. Courtney allowed her mind to wander, remembering what was under his pressed uniform shirt until she sensed someone looking at her. Katherine, one of the giggling girls, had turned around and was watching her rather than the presentation. Blushing, thankful Katherine couldn't read her mind, Courtney spun her finger in the air to remind her student to pay attention to the front of the room rather than her daydreaming teacher.

Josh wrapped up his presentation by handing out a colouring book to each student and then cheerfully answered questions for a whole fifteen minutes. After glancing at the clock, Courtney joined him at the front of the room, trying to ignore the pointed looks from matchmaking Danielle.

"I'm afraid it's time for us to say goodbye to Constable Cameron. Mrs. O'Halloran's class needs to get back to tidy up for the end of the day, and my class has to move our desks back and pack up. What do we say, Cougars?"

In unison, the kids sing-songed, "Thank-you-Constable-Cameron!"

Danielle came over and gave Josh a hug.

"Thanks, Josh, that was great. Very informative and entertaining. So good to have you back in town. My class, let's line up and head back to our room." Danielle winked at Courtney before disappearing out into the hall.

Courtney was swept up in the usual end-of-day chaos and was surprised to find Josh still standing in her classroom once she'd ushered her last student out the door to their waiting parents.

"Oh! Sorry, I forgot you were here for a moment," she said, immediately cringing. Way to be grateful to a presenter, Court.

Josh chuckled. "It is full-on at the end of the day. I've never seen it from this vantage point before. You must be exhausted."

How would he know something like that? Courtney scooted past Josh to her desk, taking a look at her to-do list. "I am, but the day isn't over for me, I'm afraid." She looked up pointedly from her plan book, willing Josh to take the hint.

"Right, yeah. Busy time of year." He glanced at his watch. "I should probably get back anyway."

Danielle popped her head around the classroom door. "Oh good, you're still here, Josh. Jen's shower is starting in the library, Courtney."

Courtney ground her teeth. Mother of trees! She'd forgotten about the stupid baby shower. She'd hoped to avoid it but, at worst, planned to make an appearance and then quietly slip away. The last thing she needed was a reminder that regular people her age were beginning to have babies.

"Shower?" Josh asked, lifting his tote of presentation materials off the rainbow table.

"Yeah, Jen Miller—she's Mrs. Cross now—had a baby boy a month ago. We're having a shower for the new family."

"Ian and Jen are married?" Josh asked. "Wild! I had no idea. I haven't seen either of them since the tenth grade days at Salish Secondary."

"You were always so cute, playing man tracker back in the day," Danielle said, causing Josh to blush. "They'll be so surprised to see you."

"As long as it isn't putting anyone out," Josh said to Danielle, looking directly at Courtney.

One of the nice things about living in the small town was socializing. One of the bad things about living in a small town was socializing. Especially when it reminded you of everything you lacked. Courtney pasted on a smile, thinking of her grandmother. She'd promised to open up and be friendly. To try. She reminded herself that Josh, though a Cameron, really wasn't the enemy. If Gram could only see her now.

"It'll be great," Courtney said. "Let's go."

CHAPTER 7

Courtney popped into the dimly lit staff bathroom, running fingers through her tangled shoulder-length brunette waves and inspecting her tired, hazel eyes, so like her Gram's, in the hazy mirror. Why hadn't she at least put on some mascara this morning? She wished she had more than chapstick in her school bag. She needed professional intervention to look presentable at this time of year. As Courtney pinched some colour into her cheeks, she repeated an affirmation. *You are loved just as you are.* She was simply going to the same function as Josh. Being friendly. As long as she set clear boundaries, she'd be okay. He didn't need to know she'd been fantasizing about him with his shirt off non-stop for the last two days. She had no intention of pursuing anything more than mingling.

Courtney wound her way through the now-empty hallways to the centrally located library. This room, full of cozy reading nooks and a bank of windows overlooking the towering forest behind the school, was her favourite place in the entire school. It had been her refuge as a shy kid—she secretly hoped she'd become the librarian one day when Sheila Nash, the current librarian, retired.

Today, someone had decorated the space with blue and white paper lanterns and a table covered with a mountain of food. The scent of coffee and the hum of chatter punctuated with laughter filled the room. Courtney had learned that Port Russell Elementary loved any excuse to get together over cupcakes and dip. She prayed no one had organized any games—the only thing they loved more than snacks. Courtney watched Jen and Ian's faces light up when Josh walked into the room after putting his supplies into his car.

"Oh my gosh! I didn't know you were back in town!" Jen gushed, passing her chubby son, clad in a cream-coloured sleeper, into Danielle's eager arms to give Josh a big hug.

Ian stuck out his hand and pumped enthusiastically. "RCMP! Nice! It's a good thing you've bulked out, man."

They chatted, catching each other up on what they'd been doing for the last ten years. Courtney marvelled at her childhood friends. How could they be adults? It was strange seeing them standing in the same library they used to come to for storytime. They were teachers, police officers—parents! Courtney's stomach clenched at the thought, but she sensed eyes on her and shook the swirling thoughts from her head.

"Congratulations, you two!" she said, hoping the smile on her face looked sincere. She peeked at the snoozing bundle in Danielle's arms. "He's a cutie. Well done."

Jen leaned toward Danielle and stroked her son's cheek."So far, Logan has been a perfect gentleman."

Not for long with a name like that, Courtney thought, recalling the few trouble-making Logans she'd met throughout her career.

"Want to hold him?" Danielle asked Courtney, offering the sleeping boy to her.

"No, thanks," Courtney said, noting Danielle's surprise. "I haven't washed my hands yet. Maybe in a bit."

Courtney drifted over to the food table. She'd linger here for a while and then slip out. Hopefully, Logan would live up to his name at some point and provide the cover she'd need. She sensed Josh sidle up to her, her right side tingling as his arm brushed hers.

"Not a baby person?" he asked quietly, loading a small blue plate with a rainbow of veggies.

"I like babies just fine." Courtney bristled, reaching past him for a chocolate cupcake. Veggies were not going to cut it today. "I'm covered in Grade 3 germs at the moment. What about you?"

Josh grimaced. "I love babies. They don't seem to love me back. He seems to be sleeping peacefully at the moment. If I hold him, he'll wake for sure. Can you believe they named him Logan? If they only knew how many I've met in my line of work."

Courtney caught Josh's eye and smiled, despite herself. "Logans are trouble. What were they thinking?"

"Right?" Josh chuckled.

"I hope I'm wrong, but they may live to regret that choice." Courtney looked down at her cupcake. This felt nice, being friendly. "Want to sit for a bit?" Courtney tamped down the swirl of nerves in her stomach as she waited for his answer. Sitting still counted as mingling, right? She wasn't sending the wrong message?

Josh looked at his watch. "For a bit, but I'm overdue at the station."

Courtney moved to a table next to the window, worrying about what to say next. The scent of chocolate wafting up from her plate was making her mouth water. She was so out of practice. What did people talk about? For the last year, she'd spent her days with third graders and her evenings with her grandparents and their friends. Her palms felt greasy as she pulled a chair out and sat.

"So what's really behind those doors beneath the stage?"

"Pardon?" Courtney asked, confused.

"You know, those weird little doors under the stage. I spent every assembly wondering what was under there. I don't think I ever listened to the presentation."

Courtney laughed. "Really? That explains a lot about a few of the students in my class, actually. Sadly, it isn't very interesting. Choir risers and extra tables, last I checked."

"Bummer. I had my hopes pinned on a door to another dimension."

With one hand, Courtney peeled off the top of the cupcake with its thick icing and then lifted the little cylinder of naked cake to her lips with the other, realizing halfway that Josh was staring at her. "What?"

Josh shook his head. "I forgot how you ate cupcakes. Weirdo."

"I'm saving the best for last!" Courtney said, face glowing. He always made things so fun. When was the last time she'd had fun?

"I'm seriously reconsidering my snack choice watching you enjoy that cupcake."

"I think you could probably work the calories off pretty easily. You should go get one."

"Old habits, I guess. I'm sort of in training."

"How can you sort of train? Isn't it an either-or thing?" Courtney popped the rest of the cake into her mouth.

Josh cocked his head to the side. "You're right. It is. I am in training for a whitewater competition in September."

"That's awesome," Courtney said, swallowing. She lifted the icing-covered cupcake top and started to nibble.

"How about you? Still race?"

Courtney put down the cupcake, her mouth turning to dust. "No. I gave it up about six years ago."

"Sorry to hear that. I loved watching you race. You always looked so happy. Did you get injured?"

Courtney's heart began to thrum, and her face and neck felt impossibly hot. She looked down at the discarded cupcake on her plate. "Um, no. Sadly, I gave it up for a guy."

Josh's eyes grew round, and he looked like he was going to say something, but he pursed his lips.

Great. He was judging her. Was that disappointment on his face?

They sat in awkward silence for a few moments, Courtney poking at the leftover cake, breaking it into icing-topped clods on the paper plate. She'd always been happy when she raced. When she'd known Josh, it had been her greatest passion. She prayed Josh wouldn't ask for more details; now was not the time to get into the whole drama surrounding her ill-advised decision to give it up.

Josh's cell phone chimed.

"Shoot. I've got to go. He stood, picking up his now-empty plate. "Hey, would you like to go for a paddle with me and Russell sometime?"

Courtney looked up at him, and her heart squeezed. He looked so earnest. So hopeful. Friendly. As she'd mingled with him, she'd remembered how much fun he was to spend time with. She *could* use a friend. There was no harm in going for a paddle. They should get out and enjoy the area before it was spoiled by logging and perhaps a giant resort. "Um, sure. I'm slammed with placement meetings and marking the rest of the week, but maybe this weekend?"

Josh's smile was the sun breaking out from behind storm clouds. "Awesome. I'll text you."

Courtney quirked an eyebrow. "I didn't give you my number."

Josh ran a hand over the back of his neck, turning back into the skinny thirteen-year-old she'd once known." No. Your grandmother did."

"Of course she did."

Josh shrugged and offered her a sweet smile. "See you later."

Courtney waved as Josh wound his way to the library door. This being friendly thing was harder than she thought it would be.

CHAPTER 8

Friday after school, Courtney headed out to help her grandmother with the massive manor garden. As she crouched to pinch spent petunias from the front beds, Courtney worked up the courage to ask the question that had been like the whine of a mosquito in her ear all week.

"So, any news about the protests? You and Gramps planning to go up again?"

Gram, cutting some roses to take into the house, paused to look at Courtney. "You know we will. It's important to both of us. As for when. I think sometime next week, last I heard. Some negotiations are going on amongst the elders. The protest is causing delays on the road to the cultural centre, and some of the band want them to move off Pacheedaaht land altogether."

"That's no good. I hope they're able to sort it out," Courtney said, ignoring Gram's attempt to change the subject. "I worry about you and Gramps going out there. What happens if you get arrested again?"

Gram stepped over to Courtney and extended her hand to help her to stand. "It's a risk we're willing to take." She cupped Courtney's cheek. "Don't worry about us so much, love. We're tough old birds. Maybe when school is over, you can join us."

Before Courtney could answer, her phone dinged.

Forecast looks great. Up for a paddle tomorrow morning? Maybe lunch after?

Her grandmother looked over in interest. "Who's that, love?"

Courtney rolled her eyes at her grandmother's question, as if she didn't hope it was Josh. She swallowed before she answered, attempting to keep any emotion Gram could use against her out of her voice. "Just Josh."

Courtney stood and concentrated on deadheading the hanging baskets while her heart sped up in her chest. She scolded it. Josh was her friend.

Period. She wasn't looking for anything else. After the turmoil of Nathan, both the relationship and the breakup, she wasn't ready for anything else. Could she trust Josh? She'd trusted Nathan, and he'd cheated on her, even as he made her totally dependent on him. He'd promised her a future and snatched it away, leaving her alone and a stranger to herself. At first, she could hardly pick out cereal at the grocery store, so used to always getting what Nathan liked. It had taken a bit of experimentation, but she decided she didn't actually like cereal, preferring granola and yogurt instead. She liked the life she was building for herself. Would she drop it again, like she had when she met Nathan? She considered Josh's proposal for the day. Definitely yes for paddling. Would staying after for lunch make it too much like a date? Her fingers froze above the screen. Why was she making this so hard?

"Are you going to answer him, Court?" Gram asked, starting the hose. The water hissed and then splashed onto the leaves of the rhododendrons with a soft patter.

"Gram," Courtney warned, looking over her shoulder. "I have a lot of work to finish."

"You can afford a few hours for fun," her grandmother said, her eyebrow quirked like they did when she was determined to make her point. "You work too hard. Go. Have fun. You're not an old lady. Stop acting like one. I think Josh would be the perfect antidote to that ass, Nathan. And it is just an outing, not a proposal." Gram turned, aiming at the rhododendrons to her left.

Courtney sighed. She would not win this argument mostly because Gram was right. She pulled her phone from the back pocket of her shorts.

A paddle sounds great, thanks!

Lunch could happen organically, or she'd have an excuse to leave if things got weird. Courtney nodded her approval of her plan.

Awesome! Meet me at the Cedar Sands Cottages at 9? Sorry for the early start. Tide's best then.

Courtney snorted. She'd be up at 6:30 despite the fact it was Saturday. She was a lark. Always had been.

See you then.

Courtney stood and moved to tie up the drooping blue Himalayan poppies, refusing to acknowledge the satisfied smile on Gram's face.

The weather was glorious the next morning. It was clear, and the air was soft with the promise of summer heat later in the day. Courtney slept in till 7:00, surprising herself, and rushed to fit in a thirty-minute run, breakfast, and a hasty shower. She jumped in the car, smoothie in hand, wet hair piled into a messy bun. Halfway to the cabins, she remembered she'd forgotten to put on sunscreen. She arrived, harried, at five minutes to nine and tossed back the rest of her breakfast, hands shaking slightly.

"Get a grip, Court," she told her reflection, her distinctive hazel eyes accentuated with a bit of mascara. "It isn't a date."

A woof next to her car caused her to jump. "Russell! Don't sneak up on me like that!" She laughed as Russell wiggled with excitement next to her car. She opened the door and crouched down to say hi, Russell promptly rolling onto his back for belly rubs.

"Wow, he likes you," Josh said. "Get up, you big flirt." Russell twisted up and headed over to sit next to his person.

Courtney stood, holding in a gasp at the sight of Josh, clad in short trunks and a training singlet that exposed his toned, tattooed arms. So strange that the face she remembered so well was now sitting atop such an athletic body. Reality was not jibing with her memories. She forced herself to look at just his face.

"Sorry I'm late," she said, closing her car door and locking it with a beep.

"Only you would say being five minutes early was late," Josh said, his face lighting with a smile. "Want a coffee before we head out?"

Courtney looked out at the azure bay, calculating how fast she'd require a bathroom if she had a coffee.

"Maybe after? I'm good for now."

"A keener. Let's get going then."

Josh offered to leave her keys in his cabin for her. She stood awkwardly on the small front deck as he disappeared inside. She wondered what the inside looked like. Was he messy like he used to be, or had becoming an RCMP officer trained him out of that? She felt like she was intruding on his life somehow. Instead, she contemplated the water and open sky, reveling in the sun dancing on the small waves in the bay stretching out before her—her hometown at the best time of the year. The pebbly beaches were spectacular, secluded, and wild. Eagles and osprey soared overhead. Grey whales, and even the occasional orca, could be found in the waters off the coast. Bear and cougars roamed the towering cedar forest. Better than anywhere in the world, in her opinion. She closed her eyes and breathed in softly, grateful.

"It is the most beautiful spot in the world, in my opinion," Josh said softly, startling her from her reverie.

"I was just thinking the same thing. Is that why you named your dog Russell?" Courtney asked, and Josh nodded, smiling bashfully. "How did you end up staying here at Cedar Sands?"

"This resort is getting a little run down, but you can't beat the location. I always wanted to stay here when I was a kid, so I thought since this assignment is currently temporary, I'd fulfill my wish on the RCMP's dime."

Right, he was only back temporarily. Courtney ignored the bloom of disapointment in her abdomen. Good thing she was only hoping to be his friend. She noticed the wear now that Josh had pointed it out. The stain was peeling from the small deck, and a few of the spindles were crumbling with rot.

"Yeah. Dan has a great spot, though I like our little beach better—sandier, and the water is calmer."

"It is a pretty fine beach," Josh conceded. He thrust out a paddling jacket to Courtney. "You wear this one. You can adjust it to fit. I've got my competition one."

Courtney put the thin profile PFD on, zipping it shut. It was ridiculously large on her, and she twisted to adjust the straps to tighten it.

"Here, let me."

Courtney froze as Josh's hand brushed her hip. When she stiffened, he looked up, his ocean-coloured eyes inches from her. She could count his lashes and noted the faint dusting of fine freckles across his cheeks and above his trim dark-brown beard.

He blushed, taking a step back. "Sorry. That was presumptuous."

Courtney's side tingled where Josh had touched it. She laughed, hoping to break the tension. "No worries. I can manage."

With their feet crunching on the gravel beach, he led her to a pair of kayaks: the red one from the other day and a second one, bright yellow. These were definitely the fancy kayaks, an upgrade from the plastic leisure ones she'd paddled in the past. Jumping excitedly, Russell raced to the water's edge and then back to them.

"Calm," Josh said, voice soft and low. Russell shook and then sat.

"Aw, what a good boy." Courtney smiled.

"We're working on it," Josh said, handing Courtney a paddle. "He's a smart guy. He just needs more practice. After you, my lady," Josh said, gesturing to the yellow kayak.

It was peaceful on the water, the air clean and salty. The sun was warm, but a small breeze wafted over, keeping them from getting too hot. In the distance, they spied a trio of grey whales feeding, tails glistening in the morning sun, and watched as a raven looped lazily over the warming water, the sun gleaming off its blue-black feathers. Russell, wearing his bright green PFD, sat on the prow of Josh's kayak like a furry figurehead, and Courtney fished her phone out of the waterproof sleeve to take a photo.

This was nice. Just hanging out with Josh again, enjoying the natural wonder of Port Russell. Her hands were rubbed raw in places, and her arms were going to complain later, but Courtney smiled, truly happy for the first time in months. Courtney, her paddle resting across her kayak, lowered her fingers to the chilly water, running them back in forth in a lazy figure eight over the rippling surface. She recalled a canoe trip with her dad and Gramps on Gnome Lake before she'd left for university. Would she get the chance to paddle there before the chainsaws started?

"Uh oh," Josh said when he brought his kayak parallel to hers, startling her from her thoughts, "you look like you've gotten some sun, Court. Maybe we should head back?"

Courtney lifted her cold fingers to her cheek, the heat of her sunburn warming them. Shoot! Why didn't she put sunscreen on? "Yeah, I guess we better go in."

They paddled for the beach, Courtney ahead of Josh, and her kayak glided to a stop on the fine gravel with a scraping crunch. Courtney noted a figure watching them from the deck of Josh's cabin, and she lifted a hand to shield her eyes, trying to discern who it was. She could only make out that it was a man dressed more for the board room than the beach.

"Who's that?" she asked, drawing Josh's attention to the figure as his kayak slid to a stop.

"Shit," Josh said, causing Courtney to look at him in alarm. He lifted his sunglasses and scowled at the figure. "It's my brother."

CHAPTER 9

It was an impressive suit; it looked like a million dollars and probably cost almost as much. The red Porsche Cayenne SUV, double parked behind her green Subaru, certainly had. All Justin needed now was a mustache to twirl, Courtney mused, raising a hand to cover her smile. From the stiff set of Josh's shoulders and clenched fists, Courtney surmised he was not happy to see his brother. Russell emitted a low growl at Justin, who gave the copper-coated dog the side eye. Not friends, Courtney gathered. She followed Josh closer to his cabin and his douchebag brother.

"The dynamic duo, back again," Justin said, sneering, standing up from the deck chair he'd been lounging in, removing his sunglasses and nestling them into his stylishly coifed, deep-brown hair.

Courtney rolled her eyes. He'd always called them that in high school. Did he really think it was an insult? Honestly, though, they were adults now. What a ridiculous thing to say.

"What are you doing here, Justin?" Josh said, unclenching his balled fists slowly as he spoke. His voice had an edge to it, one she rarely heard. Russell was hanging back, his ruff raised slightly. Josh placed a hand on his head to calm him. The hair on the back of her own neck lifted.

"Whoa, bro, I come in peace." Justin smiled, but it didn't reach his grey eyes. "Look at you, Merrick, all grown up."

Justin raked his eyes over her body, from her toes to her messy bun, and Courtney was ashamed by the wave of fear that passed over her, gluing her to the beach. She felt violated and remembered all the times he'd leered at her when they'd been teenagers. He'd always been able to make her feel so small.

Josh vibrated with rage, taking a step toward his brother. "Don't look at her like that," Josh said through clenched teeth, his fists balling once again.

"What you going to do, beat me up?" Justin taunted, laughing. "Not sure that will look very good on your spotless record, bro."

This broke the spell that had frozen her, and Courtney stepped forward to put her hand on Josh's forearm. She couldn't let this escalate. "He isn't worth it, Josh."

"What are you doing here, Justin, besides being a class A jerk?"

"Me? I'm staying in this hell hole, just like you. I have to make sure the local RCMP are protecting the interests of the largest employer in town, thanks to your dear old grandpa."

At this, Courtney had to put her hands into the pocket of her shorts to quell the overwhelming urge to deck Justin. How dare he brag about tricking her grandfather!

Justin continued, emboldened by Courtney and Josh's anger. Saw you out on the water. Thought I'd say hi to my baby brother." He put his sunglasses back on and buttoned his suit jacket, a satisfied smirk on his fashionably stubbly face. "Can't stay to chat, I'm afraid. I've got to get going. I have an important meeting with a group who are going to help us get what we really want. I just wanted to let you two lovers know I'm back in town." He stalked past them to his gleaming Porsche SUV. He opened his door and slid into the driver's seat, lifting his shades, waggling his brows suggestively. "Don't do anything I wouldn't do, little bro."

With a vicious smile, Justin pulled his door closed and sped out of the parking lot toward downtown Port Russell.

Courtney realized her hands were shaking and took a deep breath to calm herself. Not only had Justin dredged up memories of how he'd treated both of them in high school and insulted her grandfather, his body language and sense of entitlement had reminded her of Nathan. How had she ever been attracted to someone like that?

"Douchebag," Courtney said once she was calmer. She glanced over at Josh, who had his eyes closed, fingers pinching the bridge of his nose. Not for the first time, marvelling over how Josh and Justin had been raised in the same house. "You okay?"

Josh's eyes popped open. "I should be asking you that."

Courtney waved him off. "It's okay,"

"No. No, it's not okay. Justin has never been okay. I'm so sorry."

"Honestly, Josh, you don't have to apologize for him. Justin's a grown man. He needs to own his behaviour." Courtney smiled. "It kind of feels like old times."

Josh gave a half smile. "Except now, thanks to Dad, he has the resources to do some real damage. Who do you think he's meeting? He's up to something. I can feel it."

"In your policeman bones?" Courtney asked, stifling a laugh.

Josh looked at her, and after a long heartbeat, his face lit up with a genuine smile. "Yeah. Standard RCMP issue. Like Wolverine." They laughed, and Josh gestured to the seats on the deck.

"Do you really think he'd do something serious?" Courtney asked, settling into the bright blue Adirondack nestled in the shade, glad to be resting after the exercise, too much sun, and the confrontation.

"I can't really get into it, but his name has come up a couple of times surrounding some shady business deals. My father's too. I'd like to think Justin wouldn't get involved in anything illegal, but he's ambitious and cutthroat. I just feel like I should look into it. I feel responsible."

Courtney recalled all the times her grandmother had encouraged her to listen to her inner voice. She hadn't, especially with Nathan, and had come to regret it. "I've recently learned it's best to listen to that little voice. Anything I can do to help?"

Josh quirked a brow but didn't comment on her admission. "Thanks for the offer. I might take you up on it at some point," Josh said, rifling a hand through his sunkissed brown hair.

Courtney turned her attention to the water lapping the beach to keep herself from staring.

"Hey, I promised you coffee. Still want one?"

Courtney glanced at her watch. Almost eleven. She had a pile of report cards waiting for her in her cottage. But, the morning had been so fantastic, despite Justin, and she was loath to leave. Staying would only be friendly, right?

"Sounds good, thanks. Can I help?"

"Nah, I got it. Cream and sugar?"

"Just milk if you have it," Courtney answered.

"Got it. Back in a flash," Josh said, stepping over Courtney and disappearing into the cottage.

Russell wandered over and rested his hand on Courtney's lap, begging for pets. As she ran her fingers over his velvety soft ears, Courtney realized that for the first time since she'd come back to Port Russell, it felt like it used to. Like home. She grinned, and Josh appeared with two mugs in one hand and a full French press in the other.

"What's that smile for?" he asked, setting the mug with a finger of milk in it on the arm of Courtney's chair and filling the rest of the mug with coffee from the french press.

The aroma of the dark roast coffee wafted up, rich and earthy, and Courtney's mouth watered. "Just such a great day. Sunshine, water, good company." Courtney pointed at Russell, his head still resting on her lap.

"You're shameless," Josh said to his dog, the other chair creaking beneath his weight as he settled into it. "I know what you mean, though. Despite my vile brother, I can't remember the last time I felt so relaxed. So at home. You know?"

"Yeah," Courtney said, her stomach fluttering. "I know exactly what you mean." She wished she could shake the sense of unease Justin had ignited as easily.

CHAPTER 10

The rest of the weekend passed in a flash, Courtney often thinking of coffee and conversation with Josh as she toiled on, marking and writing her year-end report cards. She'd had to stay up way past her bedtime to make up for the time she'd spent with Josh on Saturday, but it had been worth it.

On Monday morning, Danielle knocked as she bustled around her classroom, preparing for the day.

"Wow, you look chipper for the last Monday of the school year. Are you drunk?"

Courtney laughed. "Of course not. Just happy."

"That's a pleasant change of pace for you," Danielle said, stepping into the room.

Courtney turned to look at her colleague and opened her mouth to protest.

"No. Don't tell me you've been happy all along. I know you, remember? It doesn't matter why. I'm just relieved to see you're finally more yourself. I've been worried."

Courtney blushed, fidgeting with a stack of permission slips piled on her desk for the day's field trip. "So, ready for today?"

Danielle smiled and changed the subject. "No. But I'll have to be. Did you get the first aid kit out of the office already?"

Courtney nodded. "Yes. I also phoned Ray at the bus company when I arrived to confirm that he'll be here at 8:45."

The traditional year-end field trip to the Pacheedaaht Cultural Centre was the highlight of the year for Port Russell Elementary. It signaled the start of summer. Caught up in the logistics required to take three hundred kids on a field trip—bus bookings, letters for parents, and itinerary decisions—Courtney had been dreading it. But she found, now the day was here, she was looking forward to it. The elders would take them out into the woods and impart the local legends and Indigenous history of Port Russell. They might get to see the artist in residence work on his latest carving. It had been a magical day when she was a kid, and Courtney was looking forward to sharing the experience with her students.

When the morning bell went, her students' excitement was palpable as she opened the door to greet them for the day.

"Good morning!" she said to each student as they filed past. "Take your backpacks to your desk today, please. We'll be lining up for the bus once attendance and announcements are finished."

"Hi, Ms. Merrick," Tyson said, thrusting a small bouquet of roses, stems wrapped in a wet paper towel and aluminum foil, at her. They were gorgeous, salmon-coloured roses, as big as tea saucers and slightly peach scented. "My mom says she wants you to have these."

"These are beautiful, Tyson. I love them!"

Tyson smiled, two pink spots blooming on his freckled cheeks.

Courtney bent to breathe in the perfume of the roses, trying to remember the last time someone had given her flowers, but coming up short. Nathan had always thought flowers were a waste of money.

The last student jogged to the door as the second bell rang. Courtney pulled an old jar out of the cabinet beneath the classroom sink and put the lovely bouquet on her desk as her students chatted. Once the Grade 7 students finished with the announcements, the principal, Sandy Munro, came on to give them instructions on how they were going to board the buses. Courtney lined up her students, counting to make sure she had everyone—no small feat as they were vibrating with excitement. Then she walked them to their waiting bus, one of six parked along the curb in front of the school in single file.

"Isabelle, watch where you're going. Graham, hands to yourself," she admonished on the way.

Danielle caught her eye as they filed past and grimaced, her own students jostling with each other in their now-ragged line.

It was going to be a long day, but Courtney was thrilled to see how excited her students were. That made the work worth it. She watched as each student climbed aboard, stepping in to help a few of the smaller ones mount the steep steps. Once all the kids were loaded, she climbed on herself, greeting Ray, the bus driver. She counted again, then slid into the seat behind Ray. Once Danielle's class was also on board, she slumped onto the seat next to Courtney.

"We'll survive the ride as long as no one sings," Danielle said.

The ride to the longhouse would take about thirty minutes, winding through the old-growth forest, past Gnome Lake. Courtney marveled at the soaring green cedars and dancing sword ferns lining the sinuous gravel road. They were so lucky to have such a beautiful place to call home. How much longer would these trees be standing? Would this be the one and only time she'd be able to bring a class up here to enjoy the pristine forest? Sadness seeped in, tinging the day with grey. Giggling from the back of the bus drew her attention from the view for a moment, and after she surmised it was harmless, she turned forward as Ray lurched to a stop behind the bus they'd been following.

"What's going on?" Courtney asked, bracing herself against the seat.

"Not sure," Ray said, lifting the handset from his radio.

There was no cell service once you got a kilometre out of the townsite. Behind them, the kids were getting restless, so Danielle stood to remind them to be quiet, and Courtney missed the response. Ray twisted to look at her as Danielle got the kids to start singing to keep them out of trouble.

"Protestors," Ray said, pitching his voice loud enough for Courtney to hear over the increasingly raucous rendition of "Something to Sing About," a song they'd learned in social studies earlier in the year. "Apparently, they had the road blocked with some logs, but Gus, the driver ahead, says they're moving them for us."

The tension in Courtney's shoulders let up a smidge. Danielle returned to her seat, the kids continuing to sing, and Courtney relayed the information.

"Thank God. Can you imagine how disappointed these kids would be if they didn't get to go to the cultural centre? These protests are getting out of hand, if you ask me. They shouldn't be blocking people from travelling freely," Danielle said.

Courtney hoped they wouldn't see her grandparents when they drove past. She was beginning to come around to their way of thinking but wasn't sure how Danielle or any of her other colleagues would feel about it, especially now that the protest was directly impacting the field trip. The bus moved forward, swaying slightly as they drove over the rutted road, the kids letting out a cheer. As they proceeded slowly, Courtney noted an assortment of people, mostly university-aged kids, rain gear clad. One girl sported bright pink dreadlocks. They waved handpainted banners with slogans like *Respect Existence or Expect Resistance,* and someone shouted, "Climate change is real, kids. The planet is dying," through a bull horn at the caravan of yellow buses trundling by. Courtney heaved a sigh of relief when she didn't see her grandparents. She recognized a handful of protestors, Stan's nephew Alex one of them, but there were a lot of unfamiliar faces.

"Who are those people?" she asked as Ray braked to a stop again.

"I heard there's an environmental group from the mainland, call themselves Old Growth Guardians, camping on site now," Danielle said.

"Really?" Gram and Gramps hadn't mentioned anything about outside protestors. Courtney twisted in the seat and looked out the rear door window, seeing a sea of colourful signs as the protestors surrounded the buses and continued to shout. "Long way to come for a protest."

"Yeah, it is. I don't think it's a good sign. Things always go pear-shaped when outsiders get involved."

She'd have to have a conversation with her grandparents. Courtney righted herself and looked out the front window again. Ray's radio crackled, and he leaned to pick up, his brow crinkled in concern. The kids launched into some song from a cartoon they all liked and drowned out Ray's conversation. He put the handset back into the cradle and shifted in his seat, beckoning Danielle and Courtney closer...

"We have a problem, ladies. The leader of the Old Growth Guardians has decided not to let us through, after all."

CHAPTER 11

"Gram? Gramps?" Courtney called as she rounded the corner of the house at 4:00 p.m., searching for her grandparents. Now that the light showers that had fallen earlier in the day had cleared, they were likely outside.

"Back here, love," Gram answered.

Courtney was relieved to see her grandparents enjoying a pre-dinner drink on the back patio. The protestors had held them up at the blockade for a tense half an hour, shouting climate change facts over the bullhorn. Some of her students had been scared, though some were thrilled. Nothing this exciting ever happened in Port Russell, and the atmosphere on the bus had been chaotic. After Sandy Munro had gotten off the bus and spoken to the leader, they agreed to let them drive only as far as a roadside turnout to turn the buses around. When the kids realized they weren't going to get to the cultural centre, after all, the mood on the bus shifted, and some of the kids started to cry. Back at school, Sandy called the cultural centre to arrange for an in-school visit by a carver and sent staff to buy the popsicles for the kids.

It wasn't the magical day any of them had been hoping for.

After school, there had been an impromptu meeting to fill the parents in, teachers contacting any parents that hadn't been at pick-up. It had cast a pall over the end of the year, and sadly, the experience at the blockade would overshadow the stories and activities the elders had come to present at the school instead. Courtney was exhausted.

"You look like you've had a day," Gramps said, getting out of his chair. "Glass of wine?"

"Yes, please," Courtney said, sinking into the outdoor sofa, facing her grandmother over the decorative fire table. Her grandfather arrived with a large glass of pale pink rosé, and Courtney accepted it with a smile.

"How was the cultural centre? Did your students enjoy it?" Gram asked as Courtney sipped.

Gramps caressed Gram's shoulder as he walked behind her and settled back into his armchair. Her grandparents loved sitting out on the patio. Courtney and her parents had surprised them with new patio furniture at Christmas. Gram had initially refused to use it, saying it was "too fancy." Courtney was grateful she'd changed her mind. They were out there most nights, enjoying the garden and surrounding forest.

"We didn't actually make it up there," Courtney said, trying to relax into her chair.

"What happened?" Gram asked.

"The Old Growth Guardians, the new group that joined the protest, wouldn't let the buses past their blockade. Sandy Munro arranged for a few elders to come to the school to present, but it just wasn't the same," Courtney said. "The kids were really disappointed and a bit scared when they held us up. They surrounded the bus and shouted slogans over a bullhorn."

"They what? That's ridiculous!" Gramps said, leaning forward to set his beer down. "How is harrassing a bunch of kids going to help stop a logging company?"

"Did you know about this group? Gary Joseph, do you remember him? He came and did a carving demonstration. He said that the band is split on the decision to include the outside protestors. Some are for it, but many are against it. They agreed to let them have access to the road, but I don't think they realized they were going to blockade it."

"What a mess!" Gram said, glancing at Gramps. "We were told that a group from the mainland, with more resources, was interested in joining the protest. At the time, we thought it might help attract the media. Raise awareness of the issue. Bolster the number of protestors. Neither of us realized it was splitting opinion amongst band members or that they were going to start a blockade."

"There were a lot of people up there I didn't recognize," Courtney said, fiddling with the stem of her wineglass. Her stomach, in knots all day, twisted once again. She wished she could beg them to stay away, maybe find a different way to stop CFI, but realized she didn't have the right to force the issue. "You'll be careful if you decide to go up again? Some of these organized protest groups use extreme tactics."

"We'll be fine, Courtney," Gramps said. "I told you, I feel responsible for this. I have to do something to help. The future of Port Russell is on the line."

Gram leaned over and squeezed his arm. "I agree with Charlie. We have an obligation to our community and to future generations." Gram gestured to the forest. "We want this to be here for your children's children, Courtney."

Courtney's stomach swooped. How could Gram be so sure there would be grandkids? She'd wasted so many years on Nathan, and he'd done such a number on her that she had no idea how long it would take to heal. Courtney recalled her dream featuring her exploration of a shirtless Josh and blushed—so different from the ones she had about Nathan. Get your head in the game, Court, she admonished, shaking her lustful thoughts loose.

Courtney focused on her grandparents' determined faces and sighed. They were right to fight for Gnome Lake. It was a special place. And she understood the sense of duty they felt. It was why she'd chosen a career in education, after all. "Okay. But promise me you'll be careful and get out if it gets dangerous?"

"You know we will," Gramps said, picking up his beer again. "I'll make some calls before we go up again. How is Gary?"

"He's good. He's my student Annie's grandfather. She was beyond excited to have him demonstrate his carving at school. Did you know that Gary Joseph is the carver in residence at the cultural centre now?"

Her grandfather nodded, taking a sip of his beer. "Yeah. He retired in the fall and hoped he'd get on there."

"He is an amazing carver. I had no idea. He's working on a reconciliation totem pole that will be placed at the legislature in Victoria when it's done."

"He comes from a long line of talented carvers," Gram said. "His great-grandfather carved the totem in front of the municipal offices. You know, the one with the otter holding the shell you liked so much when you were little."

"Wow, I didn't know." Courtney made a mental note to approach Gary to ask if he could carve a mask or maybe a paddle for Gram and Gramps's upcoming fiftieth wedding anniversary. Her parents had put her in charge since they wouldn't finish teaching the term at the University of Adelaide until mid-August.

She lifted her chilled glass to her lips, taking a sip of wine, a hint of strawberries filling her mouth as she swallowed the tangy-sweet liquid. Some of the end-of-the-day tension began to slip away. "I hope my kids remember the great stuff they did with the elders at school today instead of our disastrous trip. We had to have an emergency meeting with the parents at pick-up, and then I had to call all the ones not there to explain the situation. It was not the fun day any of us had planned for. I'm not sure the Old Growth Guardians have done any favours for the cause. There were some pretty irate parents at pick-up."

"It's bound to be a contentious issue, with people on both sides of the issue. Port Russell loves the forest but also earns its living from it. We want to make sure both can happen in a fair and sustainable way," Gram said. "The kids learned a lot today, and knowing what a wonderful teacher you are, I'm sure they had fun."

Courtney blushed. "Thanks, Gram. It was just a long, emotional day."

"It'll all look better in the morning," Gramps said, putting a hand on the armrest of his chair and standing. "My turn to cook, ladies. Hungry?"

Courtney's stomach grumbled, and her head seemed to be floating several inches above her shoulders. "Yes. Need a hand?"

"Nope. I've got it. You two enjoy the patio." Gramps leaned over to kiss Gram's head and went to the kitchen.

"I didn't know Gramps could cook," Courtney said, setting her wine down. She'd be sloshed long before dinner if she finished the whole glass. She'd only ever seen her grandfather do things like carve roasts or stir dishes her grandmother had put together.

"He can't really," Gram said with a mischievous smile, "but he's determined to learn—a retirement goal, he said. I left him a straightforward recipe."

Gramps appeared with a bowl of chips and a shallow dish of salsa. "Um, I think it may take a bit longer than I thought. These should help tide you over."

Courtney moved to get up, and her grandfather held out a hand. "No. I can do it. Really. Just let me get on with it."

Courtney settled back in her chair. You never discouraged a determined student. "Fair enough. Shout if you need me, though."

Gram leaned forward to dip a chip, a wide smile bringing out the wrinkles around her eyes. "Find yourself a man brave enough to learn new things, Courtney."

Courtney's stomach clenched. Why couldn't it just be quiet for once? It wouldn't help this particular situation. Who knew when, if ever, she would be emotionally ready to be in a serious relationship? Her heart was so battered. She grabbed a handful of chips. Her grandmother was listing off more husband-worthy qualities, so Courtney nibbled a chip and just nodded, as she always did when her grandmother extolled the virtues of marriage.

Courtney didn't expect to find a man in Port Russell, let alone one like her grandfather, despite Gram's determination. Josh said he was only here temporarily, and she was happy to be friends with him again. She had her career. She shouldn't need a relationship to be fulfilled. Chips finished, Courtney retrieved her wine and settled into her chair, pushing aside the niggling worry that if she didn't find a way to heal, she might be alone forever.

CHAPTER 12

The last day of school came, a bittersweet day, as always. She was really going to miss her kids and was both looking forward to, and worried about, a break from the grind. She had planned on a quiet summer of gardening and mystery novels, partly because her bank account was still rebounding after the break-up and move, but was second-guessing herself as colleagues shared their summer plans at the end-of-the-year staff meeting. A trip would be nice. Maybe she'd head to Vancouver for a weekend getaway at some point and shop for some new clothes and school supplies. As Courtney was straightening the classroom, boxing up the mountain of year-end gifts, the usual mugs, and *many* bottles of wine (were the parents trying to tell her something?), her phone dinged.

"Shit!" she said out loud.

"Young lady! Language," Danielle said from the doorway, her own box of gifts in her arms. "I might have to call your mother."

"Maybe she can help," Courtney said wryly, gathering her planner, phone, and water bottle off her desk and shoving them into her bag. "My grandparents have been arrested. Again."

"What do you mean again? What are Mr. And Mrs. Merrick doing that's getting them in trouble with the law?"

Courtney slung the strap of her bag over her head and lifted the box off her desk. "They were out at the protest again today. They were released without being charged last time, but they might not get so lucky today." Courtney looked at all the jobs she still had to do in her classroom. "I have so much to do here. Is the school open tomorrow, do you know?"

"Yeah. Sandy said the office would be open tomorrow."

They exited the classroom and headed toward the office to sign out for the day.

"You told them what happened on the field trip, right?" Danielle asked as she shouldered the staff room door open.

The room was empty, save for Joanne Howe, the Grade 6 teacher, cleaning the staffroom fridge out for the summer. The smell of sour milk hung over the room, making Courtney screw up her nose.

"Getting out of dodge?" Joanne asked, chucking a handful of soy sauce packets into the garbage can she'd placed next to the fridge.

"Yeah. You leaving soon?" Courtney asked, shooting a warning look at Danielle. Joanne was the school gossip. All of Port Russell would know by dinner if she heard about Courtney's grandparents.

"The second this is finished," Joanne said. "Have a great summer." She grabbed the soapy sponge from the nearby bucket and started wiping out the inside of the fridge.

"You too."

Courtney set her box down and initialed next to her name in the sign-in book, handing the pen to Danielle. Once they exited the staff room doors, she answered Danielle's question.

"I did tell them about the swarming. They promised they'd be careful but refused to stop going out there. My grandfather feels responsible for this mess. He feels if he hadn't sold to CFI, they wouldn't have opened the door to developers."

"That's nonsense. No one blames him. He had no way of knowing they were planning to log Gnome Lake. I really feel for him, but I hope after today they find a less dangerous way of helping out. I'd hate for them to get hurt."

Courtney nodded, tearing up. "The threat to Gnome Lake is real, and I'm proud of them for standing up, but I'm worried about them."

Danielle transferred her box to her hip.

"Hey, it'll be okay," Danielle said, pulling Courtney into a side hug. "Look on the bright side. Maybe you'll get to see that hunky Constable Cameron at the station when you pick them up." Danielle waggled her auburn eyebrows suggestively.

Courtney laughed. She looked so ridiculous. She was grateful for the distraction. "If you want, I've got his number."

Danielle laughed. "Not sure Mr. O'Halloran would like that very much. Don't worry, Courtney. It'll work out. I'll let you get on with it. Please, let me know if you need any help."

"Thanks, Danielle. Have a great summer." Waving, Danielle walked to her car while Courtney walked to hers.

Courtney arrived at the RCMP detachment without remembering the drive and chastised herself as she pulled into the last free spot in the parking lot. She knew better. The last thing she needed was a car accident. She glanced at herself in the mirror, rolling her eyes at her unnecessary vanity. It wasn't as if she could do anything about her unwashed hair, pulled back into a pony this morning out of desperation. She headed in. Constable Huong was staffing the front desk.

"Hey Courtney, long time no see," she joked. "Can I get you to sign in here before I take you back? We are getting more visitors these days, and we have some officers from out of town helping out. They won't recognize everyone like I do." She indicated the log book on the counter, and once Courtney signed, the door buzzed, and Courtney walked through.

The detachment was humming, every desk filled with an officer, many Courtney didn't recognize.

"Wow, full house," she said to Emmy.

"It's all hands on deck. After the incident with the school buses, we brought in officers from North Cowichan and Sooke. There's been more clashes out at the protest site. Some pushing and shoving and some unusual tactics, like sits and people chaining themselves to trees and stuff." Emmy sighed. "We're supposed to be getting a few more in from the mainland to help out, though I'm not sure where we're going to put them. Just sit at that desk along the back wall. I'll go get Norma and Charles. They were facing a long walk home with their car towed and all."

A few other protesters were talking to officers in the cubicles Courtney passed, all of them much younger and only a handful Indigenous. Maybe the outside protesters were keeping some of the Pacheedaaht away? Judging by the raised voices and word choices, the new detainees were surlier than her grandparents. The situation had definitely escalated. No more friendly games of chess.

She sat at the desk Constable Huong had indicated and waited, her stomach clenching slightly. Damn Justin Cameron. Why did he destroy everything he touched?

Finally, her grandparents arrived, escorted by Josh rather than Emmy. Courtney stood. "Are you guys okay?"

Gram pulled Courtney in for a brief hug. "We're just fine, love."

As Courtney pulled away, she noticed a large, raw scrape on her grandfather's cheek, blood oozing through a layer of antiseptic ointment. The skin below his eye was beginning to discolour, and Courtney was sure he'd wake with a shiner tomorrow. "Gramps, you don't look fine."

"It's fine, Courtney. Please don't fuss. The paramedics already did that."

Josh cut in. "Hey, Merricks, can we take this outside?" he asked, pitching his voice low.

Alarm bells rang in Courtney's head, and she opened her mouth to ask one of the million questions bubbling in her brain, but her grandfather shook his head slightly. "I'd just like to get our vehicle and then go home, if you don't mind."

Courtney narrowed her eyes but nodded. "Of course."

"I'll buzz you out," Josh said loud enough for the other officers to hear.

They walked back to the front entrance, Gram squeezing Courtney's hand to reassure her.

The second they were outside, Courtney turned to Josh.

"What is going on?" She looked at Josh, then her grandparents. What was with all the cloak and dagger?

"I can't get into it here. There are a lot of members in there I don't know." A police van full of protesters pulled into the parking lot. "I'm due a dinner break. Meet me at the Russell Pub?"

Her grandfather and Josh shared a look Courtney couldn't decipher. "Can't you just tell us here?" she asked.

"I think we need a bit more privacy," Gramps said, and Courtney's eyes widened. "We'll try and get a quiet table."

Josh nodded and then walked over to the van to help bring the detained protesters into the detachment.

She unlocked her car for her grandparents, waiting until the doors were closed before turning to them. "So, who's going to tell me what the hell is going on?"

CHAPTER 13

After a frustratingly silent ride to the pub, her grandparents asking her to wait until Josh arrived before they answered her questions, they found a table on the deck of the Russell Pub. It was the lull between the lunch rush and before happy hour, so they had the deck to themselves. The pub was a town institution, the deck the place to be as it angled over the water and had spectacular views of Port San Juan. The afternoon held the hint of the upcoming July heat, and Courtney angled the umbrella over the table to create a puddle of shade. They ordered beer for Courtney and her grandfather, a cider for Gram, and a coke for Josh, still on duty. He arrived just as the server was delivering the beverages.

"Could you bring me a burger when you have a chance?" Josh asked, stepping over the picnic table bench and settling in next to Courtney. The bench sagged under his bulk, and Courtney inched slightly away, afraid she might end up brushing against his side. She was aware of his muscular leg just inches from her own, his warmth creating electricity on her bare thigh.

In the daylight, Gramps's face looked even worse than it had in the detachment, the scrape more vivid, the purple bruise blooming. Anger bubbled up behind Courtney's sternum. "So, spill. What happened today?"

Gramps took a long pull on his beer, the sharp scent of hops floating on the breeze, and Gram squeezed his forearm resting on the silvered surface of the picnic table in support. "There was a score of new protesters there, brought in by The Old Growth Guardians. The Pacheedaaht elders, leery of the protests, especially after the debacle with the field trip, counselled against attending today, so there were fewer of the original group there.

"The defacto leader of the Old Growth Guardian contingent, a young gal with bright-pink hair and a chip on her shoulder, calling herself Dissidence, had a bunch of her crew take down some trees to build a permanent blockade. When I spoke up, saying we couldn't block the road into the cultural centre and that cutting the trees was counter-productive given our goal of protecting them, she took exception, and she got in my face." Gramps paused and looked at Gram, who nodded.

"Some locals that did go up today, Brad Joseph, Gary's nephew, and a few others who've worked for me, got into a shoving match with Dissidence's people. I got bumped and fell down the road embankment."

"That's when we intervened," Josh said. "Arrested those involved with the disturbance, though the group's lawyer has already filed a complaint. I have a feeling that the court won't approve any of the charges we put forward." Josh let out a sigh, rubbing the condensation off his glass with his finger.

"Gramps, you could have been really hurt," Courtney said, reaching across to take his hand. "Please tell me you'll find a different way to fight against CFI. It sounds like these Old Growth Guardians are going to continue to escalate things. First, the bus blockade, now cutting down trees and creating permanent blockades? Why are they even here? Why do they care if the area gets logged?"

"The group is an organized protest group, Mr. and Mrs. Merrick." Josh caught Courtney's eye. "This Dissidence has popped up all over British Columbia, protesting everything from homelessness to pipelines. She has some anarchist training, and when she arrives, there is usually an escalation in techniques and clashes with police. The group has a bunch of high-powered lawyers, and charges rarely stick, though they do flood the courts, one of their stated goals.

"We've been told that CFI has applied for an injunction, which means the RCMP will have to enforce it. It's only going to get worse out there. I'm with Courtney. I think you two should stay away from Gnome Lake until things cool down."

Josh's meal arrived, the smell of hot oil wafting up from the steaming fries piled on the plate, and they paused while the server was within earshot. Josh picked up his burger and looked at it like he'd been trapped on a desert island.

"Sorry. I haven't eaten since the power bar I had this morning on the way out to the blockade."

"I appreciate your concern, you two, but this is a local issue," Gramps said as Josh took a big bite of his burger. "We can't just sit back and let this outside group dictate how things will change in Port Russell."

Gram, quiet until then, set her glass down on the table with a thump. "For goodness sake, Charles. You are not single-handedly responsible for what is happening at Gnome Lake. When you fell down that embankment"—Gram stopped, her voice breaking, and Courtney's eyes welled up, hearing the emotion in her grandmother's voice. "You promised me once that you would always listen to me if I got a bad feeling about something. I am having one right now. This is beyond us, Charlie. I love this town, and this forest is the home of my heart and soul, but I won't sacrifice you for them."

"Norma, I'm sorry. I didn't realize." Gramps put his arm around his wife, and she rested her head on his shoulder. He sighed, running his other hand over his chin. "Okay. We won't go out there anymore. The municipal council had asked me if I'd represent Port Russell in the government meetings around the new logging restrictions being held this summer ahead of the legislature's fall session. I was hesitant to be away from home, but maybe I can be of more use in Victoria."

"You didn't tell me they'd asked you to do that, Gramps," Courtney said. "I think you'd be an excellent voice for Port Russell. You have so much experience and an inside understanding of the industry. Why don't you go with him, Gram, make a bit of a holiday out of it?"

"It's a great honour that they've asked you, Charlie. Why didn't you say anything before?" She fixed her husband with a glare, and he had the good sense to look chagrined. "Going to Victoria is the safer option. You won't mind if I go, Courtney? We'd be leaving you with the garden maintenance and the house to mind. We just finished building those new raised beds, and I've got a load of soil scheduled to arrive in a couple of days," Gram asked, her face hopeful.

"I'm on summer vacation now. It'll give me something to do." Courtney said, smiling. She had thought she might join the protest but was reconsidering, given the altercation today and the abrasive leader in charge. Who knew what may happen if they kept using their extreme tactics?

Josh wiped his mouth with his napkin, his beard rasping, sending a shiver up Courtney's spine. "I can help Courtney. I don't really garden, but I can work a shovel. Russell loves outings."

Gram caught Courtney's eye and smiled widely. "Thank you, dear. I'll rest better knowing Courtney has you to help out."

Courtney shifted on the bench, breaking eye contact with her grandmother by looking out at the sun dancing on the water. Trust her Gram to turn this into a matchmaking endeavor.

Josh looked at this watch. "I've got to get back. My break's over." He reached into his back pocket to get out his wallet. Gramps held up his hand.

"We'll take care of your bill. It's the least we can do after your help today." Gramps stood and held out his hand, and the two men shook as Courtney's throat grew thick.

"I'm glad I was there. Good luck in Victoria." Josh smiled at Courtney. "Russell and I look forward to hearing from you."

Courtney returned his smile, praying she didn't look demented.

As Courtney got distracted admiring Josh's broad back disappearing around the corner of the deck, Gram lifted her cider, a look of satisfaction written all over her wrinkled face.

"Such a nice young man, don't you agree, Courtney?"

Yes, he was, but definitely out of her league, given her current tattered state. She'd love to play along with Gram's plans, but she also didn't want to disappoint her. Nothing was going to happen. Courtney rolled her eyes—at herself or her grandmother, she wasn't sure—and took a long drink of her cold beer, partly to quench the fire that had started to smolder deep within.

CHAPTER 14

The next day, Courtney finished cleaning up her classroom while her grandparents prepared for their trip. It had thrilled the council when Gramps agreed to help them out. While Gramps met with the other delegates to plan, Gram packed. Courtney returned from school to find her fretting over whether there was enough food in the fridge for Courtney.

"Maybe I should pop to town and stock up for you," Gram said, surveying the contents of her well-stocked fridge.

"Gram, I can buy groceries for myself," Courtney said, gently closing the fridge door.

Gram twisted her hands and then turned to grab the dishcloth, wiping her spotless counters.

Courtney was tired just looking at her. "Gram, please don't worry about me. Just focus on your trip."

Gram rinsed the cloth and hung it over the curved tap. "You know me, Courtney. I'm a homebody. I'm excited but also dreading being away. The garden is just blooming so nicely, and the weather is supposed to be hot and dry the next while. It'll need constant watering."

"Why don't you walk me through the to-do list? It'll help get your mind off things."

Gram's shoulders dropped a smidge. "Yes. Let's go. I wanted to check on the hostas, anyway. I put out some diatomaceous earth to keep the slugs at bay—darn things were shredding them up."

The lingering warmth of the day hung over the yard, a light breeze chasing away the mosquitoes as Gram and Courtney crossed the thick carpet of grass to the bed of hostas. Gram had planted them under the graceful branches of a crimson-leafed Japanese maple, purchased as a Mother's Day gift when Courtney had been in elementary school.

Gram crouched and inspected the broad-leafed plants, lime green and vibrant, sighing. "I know they just need to eat, but I sure wish the darn slugs would eat something other than these hostas. They're a hard-to-find variety."

"Only the best for the manor slugs," Courtney joked. "Do you want me to lay down more diatomaceous earth?"

Gram stood, only creaking slightly, and Courtney marveled at how spry she was for her age. "No. I'm the only one who's going to crouch down and look for imperfections. Let the slugs have their fancy feast." Gram laced her arm through Courtney's, strolling across the lawn. "Let me walk you through your list of chores. I've made sure there's lots to do, so Josh has to spend plenty of time here." Gram quirked an eyebrow at Courtney.

"Gram! You are incorrigible! He's busy and not your errand boy. I *can* manage without him."

"Are you sure about that?" Gram asked, eyes twinkling. "We just want you to be happy, love. He was a great kid, and now he's an upstanding guy—handsome to boot. What do you have to lose?"

Too much, Courtney thought, turning her face away from Gram's. If Josh broke her barely put-together heart, she didn't think she'd survive this time.

Her grandparents left early the next morning, a Thursday, and after a glorious run, Courtney allowed herself the rest of the day off to lounge on the deck, read a trashy romance, and drink beer. It was her gift to herself after a busy school year. When she got to the steamy part of the romance, she got lost in the hot fantasy, imagining Josh doing to her what the hero was doing to the heroine. She put the novel aside and contemplated a cold shower, sure she'd blush madly the next time she saw Josh. She made an enormous plate of pasta for dinner with brownies and ice cream for dessert and sat on the deck watching the sunset, soaking in the beauty and serenity of the dusky forest.

Friday, she woke renewed and ready for a day in the garden. She had an enormous pile of soil to move and a lot of watering ahead of her. After slathering herself with sunscreen, Courtney opened the door to her cottage, coffee in hand, just as a blue Toyota Tacoma pulled up with kayaks strapped to the roof rack. Josh. Her stomach fluttered, and her cheeks burned as she pushed away a replay of her fantasy.

He parked next to Courtney's Subaru, letting Russell out of the cab before him. "Morning! Mrs. Merrick called yesterday and said the soil had been delivered. I'm only available today, as I've got to attend a meeting in Victoria, so I thought I'd pop by. Hope that's okay?" He stepped tentatively onto the driveway, keeping one hand on the truck's door.

A meeting in Victoria. With whom? A girlfriend? Courtney shook the jealous thought from her head, reminding herself that Josh was just a friend. She glanced at the mountain of rich black soil sitting on a tarp next to the workshop. "That was kind of Gram. Thanks for coming over on your day off. I'd be at it for days if I had to do it on my own," Courtney said, leaning over to ruffle Russell's soft ears.

"I'm still not great with gardening," Josh said, and Courtney remembered teenage Josh "helpfully" digging up Gram's dormant tulip bulbs, thinking they were dead, and she bit her lip to keep from smiling. "But I'm very coachable," he continued.

"Okay, fair warning, there's a lot to do. There's the soil but all the daily chores too, like watering. I didn't realize how involved the garden was, to be honest. I don't know where Gram gets the energy to manage it. If you help, I might get to do more than just chores today."

Josh's face lit up as he smiled. "If we get everything done, maybe we can go for a paddle afterward? I thought I'd head up to Lizard Lake, try something new."

Courtney glanced at the kayaks. "I didn't realize Russell needed his own boat," she said, raising an eyebrow.

Josh looked at his feet, scuffing his sneaker over the driveway's blacktop, his face flushing petunia pink beneath his short beard. "I was just hoping you'd say yes. Be prepared, and all that."

"I thought you were a Mountie, not a Boy Scout," Courtney teased, then immediately worried if she'd gone too far. One night on her own was bliss, but eventually, she'd get lonely. She was done with that. She'd promised to be friendly and try to get out a bit more. Even if she wasn't ready to date, it was time to build some sort of social life. She'd let the chaos Nathan had created hold her back long enough. She took a deep breath and studied Josh's face. He seemed to be okay with her teasing. He was smiling, and his body language was relaxed. "Want a coffee before we get started?"

Josh straightened his shoulders and closed the truck door. "No, I'm good. Maybe later? What do you want me to start with?"

"Let's tackle the soil. I might as well put those muscles of yours to work." Courtney kicked herself when she saw the look in Josh's eyes.

"You like my muscles?" Josh said, moving toward Courtney, too close for her comfort.

"Josh," she warned, taking a step back, her heart thrumming fast enough that Josh could likely hear it. "I'm sorry, I shouldn't have said that. It crossed the line."

He furrowed his brow. "What line?"

He was standing near enough that Courtney could smell the warm spice of his soap. "The friend line."

"The friend line," he repeated, mouth turning into a frown.

"Yes. Friends. I'm not looking to date anyone right now. And, you're only here temporarily."

"Not necessarily," Josh began, and Courtney tamped down the trill of hope that began to crescendo upon hearing he might stay in Port Russell. He studied her face and was quiet for a heartbeat, a million thoughts crossing his face in the silence. Was he angry? Would he be okay with keeping it as just friends? Courtney realized she was holding her breath. "Friends it is then. Sorry if I misunderstood."

Hope plunged into disappointment, and Courtney felt her shoulders tightening as the awkwardness of the misunderstanding bloomed between them.

"Court, I can go if you want," Josh offered, turning toward his truck.

She eyed the waiting mountain of soil and sighed. "No. Please don't. I really could use your help with moving all that dirt."

"Okay, point me in the direction of a shovel, and let's get moving."

They spent the rest of the morning filling wheelbarrows with soil and trundling it down to the new raised beds Gram had built along the south edge of the yard, as she'd run out of space for new plants and had a wish list of perennials she wanted to add. Courtney was thankful there was little time for conversation, still embarrassed over her reaction this morning. Should she have let whatever was going to happen just happen? Would it be so bad to be more than friends with Josh? She was certainly attracted to him, and he had put the moves on her.

Russell followed them from pile to bed for a while, but once the sun climbed in the sky and the temperature rose, he found a shady spot and collapsed in the cool grass, eventually falling asleep. Courtney longed to join him.

After two hours of hard labour, Courtney needed a break. It looked like they'd hardly made a dent in Mount Blacksoil.

"It's time for a break. Feel like a coffee?"

"That'd be awesome. I'll fit in a few more loads while you're making that. Why does it feel like this pile is growing, not shrinking?"

Courtney laughed. "Meet me on the deck in fifteen." Russell was right on her heels when she mounted the steps to the deck. "Come on, buddy, help me make coffee."

Courtney putzed in the kitchen after starting the coffee pot, tamping down the worry that things would be awkward with Josh over coffee. Russell collapsed on the cool tile in the kitchen, watching her pace with open curiosity.

"It'll be okay, right?" she asked the dog. In response, he thumped his tail against the floor. Courtney laughed. "I'll take it as a yes."

Once the coffee had finished brewing, she poured out two mugs, then opened the door with her elbow just as Josh was rounding the corner onto the patio. Russell sprang up to follow her, wagging his tail slowly, then sniffing Josh's dirt-covered sneakers.

"Perfect timing," Courtney said. "You take it black, right?"

"Yeah. Thanks. Wow. I forgot how big this yard was. Does your grandmother still do all the work on her own?"

Courtney settled into one of the armchairs, and after he'd brushed loose dirt off himself, Josh settled into the other. "Most of it. Gramps mows and does any grunt work, like digging or moving heavy pots. They manage for now, but they're starting to slow down. It's one of the reasons I moved back. They won't hire anyone, but they don't turn down free labour."

Josh laughed. "Remember that time your grandpa had me go up on the roof to help with the Christmas lights? I still have nightmares about being up there, slowly sliding down the shingles, him calling out, 'If you fall, just grab onto the gutter.'" Josh shuddered.

"Oh my god, I completely forgot about that." Courtney laughed. "Gram was furious with him for taking you up there."

Josh walked to the banister, raising his mug to take a sip as he admired the view from the hill the manor sat on. Courtney noticed he had some dirt on the back of his khaki cargo shorts and wrapped her hands around her mug to keep herself from brushing it off. Friends did not feel up their friends' behinds. She had to abide by her own rule.

"This is a gorgeous spot. Bet sunsets are a treat to watch out here."

Courtney refocused on the conversation and recalled the spectacular show she'd watched the night before, a riot of hot pink and mauve dancing over the glittering Pacific just visible over the jagged treetops of the forest behind the manor. "Yeah, best show in town."

Josh's phone binged, and he dug it out of the pocket of his shorts. "Damn," he said, scowling.

"Oh no. Bad news?" Courtney hoped he wasn't being called into work. Despite the awkwardness first thing, they made a good team. It felt right working alongside Josh.

"Justin," Josh said, setting his coffee down and rubbing a hand over his beard. "I called a friend in the Victoria PD to see if his name had ever popped up. Apparently, it has."

Courtney scowled. She didn't put it past Justin to be known to police. He'd never been a rule-follower or respectful of authority. She was distressed to see Josh having to deal with it. It must be hard to be related to selfish dirtbags, particularly when you were a policeman. How two kids who grew up in the same house ended up taking such disparate paths was beyond her. There were some benefits to being an only child, chief among them not having to deal with siblings and their issues.

"What for?" she asked.

"I guess there have been some shady business deals. Allegations of fraud. Some talk of insider trading. He and Dad have been seen with some 'unsavoury' characters. Never enough to be arrested, but enough that they're on police radar. 'Not exactly law-abiding,' is the way my friend described it."

Josh sat back down, and Courtney could see the tension in his shoulders as he lifted his coffee mug off the table.

"Sorry," Courtney said. "It must make it hard for you."

"Thanks to dear old Dad and his constant comparisons growing up, we don't have a lot to do with each other, but he is my brother, and if he does do something, it'll cast suspicion on me. That's hard to shake sometimes when you're in law enforcement. We have our issues, but I don't want to see him end up in prison. Justin is doing what he's doing out of a misplaced sense of duty to our father. Dad's the one that deserves to go to jail."

"You don't see any of your family? Not even your mom?" Courtney asked.

"Not really. Mom came to see me graduate, and we talk on the phone once in a while. Justin invites me to things, and I avoid going whenever possible. I cut my father out of my life as soon as high school was over, and I haven't spoken to him since."

Courtney was surprised by the venom in Josh's voice and saddened to hear he was estranged from his family. She couldn't imagine being without the support of family. She'd never really liked Mr. Cameron. He'd been loud and overbearing when she'd known him, always critical of Josh. She knew Josh had probably made the right decision but hated to think of Josh all alone. "Sorry to hear about your family, Josh. That must be lonely."

Josh shrugged. "I've gotten used to being on my own. As my therapist reminds me, it's better than being involved in a toxic relationship."

Russell roused himself from his nap in a pool of sunshine to check on his master, and Josh absently ran a hand through his red fur.

"This news from my buddy confirms my worries about Justin's involvement here in Port Russell. If he's skirting the law in Victoria, he's doing the same here. Port Russell is a special place. I want it to stay that way. If this project goes forward, I'm worried it will change it for the worse."

It surprised Courtney to hear he felt the same way she did."Where do you even start with an investigation?"

"I can't actually start an investigation, not a legitimate one. A hunch isn't enough. The intel from my friend is a lead, but I'll have to check some things out while I'm in Victoria for my meeting." Josh fell silent, and Courtney glanced at him. His brow was creased, his jaw clenched.

As Courtney sipped her coffee, letting him think, his eyes lit up like her students did when they understood what she was teaching them. "Want to come to Victoria with me, do a little digging? I have the next three days off, and you're on vacation." Josh leaned toward her, fingers tracing the rim of his coffee cup.

Courtney's mouth grew dry and the hand holding her mug trembled. She wrapped the other hand around the side of the mug. Just the two of them on a road trip? Was he crazy? That was more than friendly, wasn't it? "I don't know, Josh. I mean, I promised Gram I'd water the pots." It sounded lame, even to her.

"I could really use your help. I can't poke around CFI too much. I'm known, and there are limits to what I can look into regarding his life without getting in trouble with the superintendent."

"Maybe we should just wait until a formal investigation is started then. It isn't worth your career, Josh."

"It'll be too late. You got a taste of Justin back in high school. He was a bully then, and now he has resources to back him. I don't want to wait until he does something that can't be undone. I have a bad feeling about this protest."

Courtney bit her lip and studied the light-brown surface of the coffee in her mug. They shared similar thoughts about the protest, too, then.

"You know your grandparents are concerned about this and are determined to help. What if they come back from the meetings and get sucked back into the protests? Things are going to get violent out there—the top brass has put us on high alert, and there's talk of involving ERT. Those guys don't mess around."

Courtney looked up and met Josh's eyes. He was right; Gramps had been persuaded to help by going to the hearings for now, but when they returned, he might insist on heading back out to protest. Didn't she owe it to her grandparents and to her community to help prevent things from spiraling out of control? But would going to Victoria give Josh the wrong idea? Was she ready for this? Courtney traced the faux wicker on the arm of her chair.

Josh cleared his throat. "It'll give us an opportunity to really talk. I'm curious about what you've been up to this year. C'mon, it's the road trip we always talked about taking when we were in high school. And bonus, now

I can actually drive. The friend line will be strictly observed, I promise." He looked so hopeful. Courtney hated to let him down. She'd have all summer in Port Russell, and with Josh only here for as long as he was needed with the protests, they might not get another opportunity to spend so much time together. When would she get an offer like this again? And he was doing it to help her grandparents and the town. They had a common goal.

"Um, sure. I can help you."

Josh's eyes crinkled as he broke into a wide smile.

"It is contingent on me finding someone to water Gram's garden, though. If it suffers, she'll never put me in charge again."

CHAPTER 15

Courtney had to bribe Marilyn with a bottle of wine and a bridge game to convince her to look after the garden. She had half hoped Marilyn would refuse, giving her an out from this trip. As she'd packed Friday night, she'd picked up her phone at least three times to text Josh to back out. Each time, she'd talked herself out of it. It was just two old friends on a road trip, she told herself. They were there to look into Justin and figure out what he was up to. He'd promised to respect the friend line. It had been hard to figure out what to pack. Would she need a dress? Business attire? Summer casual? She ended up throwing all of it in her suitcase, just in case.

Josh offered to drive, so on Saturday morning, she hauled her overstuffed roller bag out to the driveway, making a loop of the manor to ensure all the doors and windows were secure as she waited. As she rounded the corner of the house back to the driveway, he was loading her suitcase into the rear of his Tacoma.

"What do you have in here, rocks?" he teased.

Courtney's cheeks bloomed pink. "I wasn't sure what I'd need to wear. I've never been on an investigation before."

"Not an investigation, remember? Just two friends going on a Canada Day road trip."

Josh had explained what they would and wouldn't be able to do, so he didn't cross any lines. He was worried about his brother, and Courtney sensed he wanted to help Justin avoid trouble, if possible, though she wasn't entirely sure why. It was also clear he wanted to make sure any future charges brought against their father would stick, his anger palpable every time the topic of his dad came up. Courtney hoped they'd be able to talk about it a bit more throughout the weekend.

"Here, let me." Josh leaned past her to open the passenger door, his hand brushing Courtney's. The hair on her arm rose, and she smoothed it down with her opposite hand. The subtle cedar spice of his aftershave drifted over her, and she pursed her lips. Yum.

Courtney slid into the seat and closed the door as Josh jogged around to the driver's side. She noticed something missing.

"Hey, where's Russell?"

"I couldn't find a pet-friendly hotel in Victoria, so Emmy said she'd have him for a few days. Russell was very excited to discover he'd be spending his time with a couple of energetic boys—he didn't even say goodbye."

"Aw, poor Dad," Courtney said. The Huong boys, Oliver and Hudson, were great kids who'd been lobbying for a dog for ages. Courtney knew they were in heaven.

"You booked me my own room?" Her stomach was doing a rhumba. She'd insisted on separate rooms when she agreed to the road trip. Nathan would have discounted her wishes. Would Josh listen?

"Yes. Separate rooms booked, just as we discussed." He slid his sunglasses back on and smiled at her. "Ready?"

The dance in her midsection slowed, and Courtney managed a smile in return. She was as ready as she could be.

Josh headed for the Juan de Fuca highway, which wound along the Salish Sea coast through Jordan River, Sooke, and then onto Victoria. The late June morning was flawless, the wide sapphire sky clear but for some high diaphanous cloud above the blue-grey sea. It would be hot by midday, especially away from the beach breeze. Josh rolled down his window.

"Do you mind if we leave the air-con for later? The air is so fresh this morning, and I just want to enjoy it while I can."

Courtney smiled. She'd been thinking the same thing. "Sounds good." She pushed the button on her window, the air rushing into the cab, tossing her dark-brown hair around her face. Courtney tucked an errant lock behind her ear, closed her eyes, and took a deep breath. She lived in the most beautiful place in the world. Well, that is until hordes of tourists descended, drawn by a luxury development. Ugh. She hoped it didn't come to that. Maybe they'd find something in Victoria to stop Justin and his stupid plan.

Besides the fresh air, having the windows open made it difficult to speak, and Courtney was relieved. She wasn't sure how she would navigate two hours in the car with Josh without having to talk about what they'd been up to the last few years. Courtney wrapped her arms around herself, focusing on the view. She squirmed in her seat when she imagined telling Josh about all the mistakes she'd made with Nathan, how he'd made her into something small and unrecognizable. He'd be so disappointed in her. Maybe agreeing to this road trip had been a mistake?

They alternated between driving through green tunnels of towering conifers and open stretches where pebbled beaches descended to the ocean waves. Between Jordan River and Sooke, Courtney started sweating and picked her shirt off her chest to cool off.

"Time for the AC," Josh said, noticing. He leaned over to turn it on, and Courtney reluctantly rolled her window shut. Cool air began blowing from the vents, and she angled the one near the window toward her.

"Hey, I found this great playlist the other day." Josh turned the stereo on, and "Boom Boom Pow" by the Black Eyed Peas blared. "Remember this?"

Courtney laughed. It had been the number one song the summer Josh had left Port Russell. "You hated this song! You changed the station every time it came on."

"Absence makes the heart grow fonder, I guess. This playlist is full of all our favourites." Fergie sang, and a rhythmic electronic beat started. Josh wiggled his head in time to the music, looking absolutely ridiculous. Courtney laughed out loud. Josh started singing, badly off-key.

Courtney wiped tears from her eyes. She'd forgotten how hard he could make her laugh. They sang along with quite a few oldies as the highway moved from the coast and began to wind through the more urban areas of Sooke and Langford. After a year in Port Russell, Courtney was overwhelmed with the busyness of the road, grateful Josh had volunteered to drive. Driving in a town without any stoplights and a maximum speed of fifty kilometres an hour had changed her driving. Courtney couldn't believe she used to drive these freeways everyday, clogged with traffic and busy with shops lining either side. She preferred the pace in Port Russell.

They drove into downtown Victoria, behind the Empress, and then along the inner harbour. The legislature building was set up for the Canada Day celebrations, and the sidewalks were crowded with tourists dressed in a dizzying array of colours and carrying shopping bags emblazoned with maple leaves from the tourist shops clustered along Government street. As they neared their destination, her stomach began to dance again. She decided to ignore it.

"Wow, it's busy," Courtney remarked. "No wonder you couldn't find a pet-friendly hotel."

"Actually, I was lucky to find a hotel at all," Josh said, driving toward Laurel Point. "I have a confession to make."

Courtney's chest grew tight. "A confession?" Her stomach roared to life again.

"I had to book us rooms at the Inn at Laurel Point. I used their special first responder discount, though, so it's almost the same price as some of the mid-range hotels. It was either them or the Empress, which was totally out of range. Sorry."

"It's okay," she said, the tempo in her stomach slowing. As long as there were two rooms, she'd pay whatever she had to.

The Inn at Laurel Point sat right on the inner harbour with views toward downtown Victoria and the grand Empress hotel at the apex of the U-shaped harbour. The inn was a five-star hotel and a place Courtney had only dreamed about staying at. She normally went for the budget hotels on her teacher's salary, but splurging just this once wouldn't bankrupt her.

Josh turned onto the curved drive leading to the glass-awning-covered front entrance, the valet stepping out from behind a podium next to the door to greet them.

Courtney's stomach fizzed as if full of pop rocks. Her stupid gut just wouldn't leave her alone today. The glass doors to the hotel slid open, and a bride, glowing in a floor-length sheath of ivory lace, an enormous bouquet of frothy pink peonies in her hand, stepped out. Her face radiant, she extended her free hand toward her tuxedo-clad groom. A photographer pointed toward the manicured garden to the right of the doors. When the bride noticed Josh and Courtney, she nodded, as if acknowledging Josh and Courtney were a happy couple too.

This was a mistake.

She wasn't ready. She should have stayed home. The happy couple reminded her of what she wanted for herself—what Nathan had taken away from her and was still preventing her from going after. Courtney swayed, suddenly dizzy, forcing herself to suck in a big breath.

Josh appeared on her side of the truck and lifted her suitcase from the back, startling Courtney out of her inner turmoil.

"Hey! Congratulations," Josh called to the couple as they drifted past; the groom lifted a hand in thanks. Courtney hoped the smile she had plastered on her face looked halfway convincing.

"Josh, I don't know about this," she managed to spit out, her hands trembling.

Josh noted her hands. He stepped up on the curb, her suitcase still in his hand. "Please, trust me? We have our own rooms, and this is a convenient spot because Justin's condo is just past Fisherman's Wharf, about two blocks west of here." He held out his hand.

Therein lay the problem, Courtney thought. She didn't trust Josh. Honestly, since Nathan, she didn't trust anyone other than her immediate family. Especially herself. Yet, she'd trusted Josh completely when they were kids. He hadn't changed that much, and now he was a police officer. That had to make him inherently trustworthy, didn't it? She slid out of the truck, wrapping both hands around the strap of her purse.

Josh smiled and lowered his hand.

The lobby of the hotel was all polished granite and modern furnishings. Courtney hadn't seen that much glass or so many shiny surfaces since she'd been in Port Russell. The local decorating ascetic was mostly earthy colours and cured cedar. This room was blinding.

Josh walked toward the front desk, his sneakers squeaking on the polished granite, and Courtney trailed behind him, marveling at the view of the harbour out the bank of windows on the north side of the lobby.

"Good afternoon, sir. Welcome to Laurel Point Inn. Are you and your partner checking in?" the concierge and silver-haired man in a neat black blazer and tie said.

"We're not partners," they said at the same time.

"My apologies. Last names?" the clerk asked smoothly.

"The reservation is under Cameron. There should be two rooms."

The sound of clacking computer keys echoed off the sleek walls, taking a little longer than usual.

"I'm sorry, sir, but I can only find one room under Cameron."

Josh shot her a nervous smile.

A wave of panic washed over Courtney. Had he done this on purpose?

"No, I'm sure I booked two. Do you still have two rooms? It doesn't matter if I don't get the special rate." Josh leaned over the narrow desk, pitching his voice lower. "I promised my friend separate rooms."

"Unfortunately, we're booked solid for the holiday, Mr. Cameron. This is our last available room. You'll find rooms hard to come by in the city this weekend—lots of weddings, the Canada Day celebrations, and the labour congress hearings have us hopping."

Josh turned to look at her expectantly. "I'm sorry, Court. I understand if you don't want to stay. We can just check the CFI offices and head back."

Courtney fought back tears as the clerk looked at her and then pointedly at the couple in line behind them. Tension knotted her shoulders, and she longed to see if she still had a roll of antacids shifting around the bottom of her purse. She'd come this far. If she went home, she'd end up watering the hanging pots and watching Netflix for the rest of the summer. Maybe, for the rest of her life. Of all things, Gram's voice rang in Courtney's head. *"He's such a nice young man, and you deserve to have some fun, love."* She could handle this. It was a weekend away, not a proposal. She'd set clear boundaries. She took a deep breath.

"No, it's okay. We can stay."

Relief washed over Josh's face, and he turned to give the desk clerk his credit card. They got their key cards and headed to the fourth floor to their room. Courtney used hers as Josh's hands were full with the luggage. When she swung the door open, she gasped.

The view was spectacular. The far wall was dominated by sliding glass doors, with a patio that overlooked the harbour. Definitely not a standard room. It was dominated by a king-sized bed, immaculately made up with smooth white bedding. A brown velvet brocade runner lay across the foot of the bed, and two striped cylindrical pillows rested before each of the gigantic pillows at the head of the bed. A small chocolate-coloured love seat was angled against the wall opposite.

There was only one bed.

Josh set the luggage down, jaw clenching, and walked toward the phone on the desk.

"Hello? I just checked into room 408. Would it be possible to have a cot sent up?" Courtney watched as Josh's face fell. "Oh. Um, no. That's okay. Thanks." He turned to look at Courtney. "They don't have any cots left."

Courtney approached him and placed a hand on his arm. "It's okay, Josh. This is the last room they have. We're both adults. We can figure out how to share. I can sleep on the chaise." Courtney marveled at the sinewy warmth of Josh's arm beneath hers, and two hot spots appeared on each of her cheeks.

Josh rested his hand over hers and looked at her, his long-lashed blue eyes suddenly the only thing to look at in the room. "I feel terrible about this. You probably think I planned the whole thing. I can't say I'm unhappy about the mix-up, but I want you to know that I didn't have any ulterior motives when I asked you to come with me."

Like melting ice, Courtney's heart shifted suddenly in her chest, a familiar warmth spreading over her body. "I believe you," she whispered, frozen to the spot. Josh angled his head toward her, and her lips began to tingle, anticipating his mouth on hers. Would his beard tickle?

A sharp knock at the door caused her to jump, and the spell was broken. Clearly irritated, Josh pulled the door open with a bit more force than necessary. Courtney reprimanded herself for almost crossing the line she'd set.

The concierge was standing outside with a tray of chocolate-covered strawberries and a condensation-bespeckled bucket containing a bottle of champagne.

"As an apology for the room mix-up, please accept this little treat, Mr. Cameron," he said. He bustled into the room and set the tray on the desk next to the TV. "Enjoy."

The concierge looked directly at Courtney as he said this, and she wondered if the guy had X-ray vision and had seen what was about to happen before he knocked. Her head was spinning, so Courtney strode to the patio door and made her escape as Josh shook the man's hand and tipped him. What would have happened if he hadn't interrupted them? Courtney shivered. Was she disappointed? Did that mean she was ready for more with Josh? This was harder than she thought it would be. Being so close to him was confusing.

Josh appeared a moment later with two glasses of bubbly and the plate of strawberries. "I hate to waste a good bottle of champagne." He held out a glass to Courtney. "Here's to adventures with old friends." He offered his glass as a toast, and Courtney tapped it with hers, pushing aside the heavy blanket of disappointment that descended with Josh's words. Friendship was what she came for. Nothing more.

CHAPTER 16

"Right, I need to get out of this chair and get moving, or I'm going to be down for the count," Josh said, standing and extending a hand for Courtney. She glanced at her watch and was surprised to see they'd spent two hours talking, enjoying the summer air, and it was now mid-afternoon. It was just like old times, easy and fun. Courtney took Josh's hand, ignoring the spark that rippled up her arm when their skin made contact. When she stood, the world spun, and when she opened her eyes, Josh had his hands wrapped around her waist, steadying her. Courtney stepped back, admiring the turquoise-coloured button-up that hugged his biceps and shoulders.

"Little dizzy from the champagne. I don't think the strawberries soaked up any of the alcohol." She giggled, placing a hand on Josh's chest. "Did I mention I like this whole beard and muscles thing you've got going on?" Courtney blushed and resisted the urge to clap a hand over her mouth. How could she have said that out loud?

Josh cleared his throat and smoothed the khaki fabric of his shorts. "Let's get some food into you. Fancy a walk to Fisherman's Wharf?"

They rode down in the elevator, avoiding each other's eyes in the mirrored interior of the car. Courtney caught her reflection in the polished chrome, glad she'd worn her favourite floral top and the cute navy shorts that made her legs look a million miles long. She smiled at herself.

The elevator opened, and she followed Josh, the heels of her sandals clicking on the lobby's sleek stone floor. They exited the door opposite where they entered, a sidewalk leading down to the walking path surrounding the point and the inn. There was a marina in the small cove where modest sailboats moored, their aluminum masts jutting into the sky, white hulls shining in the summer sun. Sea gulls swooped overhead, and Courtney noted the harbour taxi stopping on the central jetty of the marina, a family with two elementary-aged children getting off to explore Laurel Point.

Courtney felt like she was floating as they strolled along the asphalt walking path, which skirted the marina. A crowd of tourists with their cameras out caught her eye, drawing her attention to a trio of river otters sliding in and out of the water, their sinewy wet bodies glinting in the bright sunshine when they popped out onto the rocks. The next cove, a larger marina, hosted a dozen brightly coloured houseboats, several takeout restaurants, and rows of picnic tables.

"Fisherman's Wharf," Josh said. "We can get something to eat before we poke around Justin's place. Maybe see if we can get any info about his coming and goings from the concierge." Josh pointed to a humongous building of dark gray stone, separated from the wharf by a small parking lot.

A condo building with aspirations of being a castle, Courtney thought, with its crenelations and stonework. It was at least twelve stories high, a hulking behemoth.

"Justin likes to brag there's a helicopter pad on the roof," Josh said, rolling his eyes.

Courtney laughed. "Yep, sounds like Justin's kind of place."

They clattered down the metal jetty to the wharf, Courtney holding onto the railing for dear life, champagne still coursing through her veins. They stopped at the bottom to get their bearings.

"What do you fancy?"

Courtney checked out the restaurants' names, the smell of frying fish making her mouth water. "Ooh, fish tacos, please."

"I was hoping you'd say that. They're my favourite. Find a seat, and I'll order."

Josh returned with two halibut fish tacos each, and Courtney's mouth watered as the scent of chipotle and lime drifted on the air. "This is a great seat, and we can see Justin's place from here. Fifth floor—the one with the extra large deck. See it?"

Courtney shielded her eyes with her hand and looked up. "How does he afford a place with a harbour view?"

"Between you and me, I think he over-extended himself. He made sure to invite me to his housewarming, probably so he could brag about how successful he is. I didn't attend."

A harbour view condo and a flashy car—Justin had gotten exactly what he said he wanted when they were kids. As Courtney chewed her delicate halibut, perfectly seasoned and fried to perfection, she looked at Josh to get a sense of how he felt about his brother's success. He had a giant blob of mayo on his chin.

Courtney stood slightly and extended a napkin. "You have mayo," she said, blotting Josh's chin without thinking. He widened his eyes in surprise, and she froze. "Sorry, occupational habit." No more day drinking for her.

"No, it's okay. Friends don't let friends walk around with mayo all over their face," Josh said, wiping his napkin over his beard, his eyes a deep, dark blue. Pupils dilated.

Mortified, Courtney took a swig of her water, looking up at Justin's condo again. That's when she spotted an Asian woman sporting bright pink dreadlocks walking down the jetty at the other end of the wharf. Trailing behind her was Justin, wearing a black short-sleeved dress shirt, crisp Bermuda shorts, and, *ugh,* soft loafers with no socks. Did you get a uniform when you decided to become rich and snobby?

"Josh, look."

Josh turned his head, knitting his brows. "Should we move?"

"No, he's not expecting us to be here. He likely won't even see us. Just avoid looking their way as they pass."

Courtney's heart thumped in her chest, and she focused on looking at Josh. He was calm and composed, lifting his water bottle to his mouth and drinking. In her peripheral vision, Courtney was shocked to see the pink-haired woman reach out for Justin's hand. Laughing, he leaned over and kissed her. They made an odd couple, Justin looking like a model out of a Polo ad and the woman with her unconventional hair and battered Birkenstock sandals. They moved right past them, oblivious to Courtney and Josh's attention.

Josh lifted his phone and took a few shots of the strange couple as they walked toward the fish and chip restaurant at the opposite end of the wharf. What was Justin getting out of the relationship? They didn't look like they had much in common.

Courtney made the connection. "Is that the pink-haired protester Gramps was talking about?"

"Yes, it is. I think we know how Justin is connected to what's going on at Gnome Lake. Now we just have to figure out what angle he's playing."

As they walked back to the hotel, Josh decided there was no point in digging around at CFI now that they knew Justin was in a relationship with Dissidence, the leader of The Old Growth Guardians.

"Seeing him in public was helpful. We didn't have to do anything questionable to get the information, so I can share it with my commander."

"Maybe we should head home then," Courtney said, opening the gate to the path leading to the hotel entrance.

Josh licked his lips. "We paid for the hotel room. No sense in heading home before Monday. We should enjoy the sights. I was hoping maybe I could take you out to dinner tonight? The restaurant here in the hotel is supposed to be spectacular."

Courtney bit her lip. This sounded very much like a date, especially since they'd finished their "investigation." He looked so hopeful, though, and it felt good to hang out with him. He was easy to talk to, and he made her laugh. She felt like his equal, valued for who she was. Nathan always made her feel as if spending time with her was a chore. He'd called her the "old ball and chain."

She was still a bit shocked that Josh's family had imploded and was worried he hadn't entirely worked through his anger toward his father, in particular. But Josh was a good friend. She was enjoying spending time with him. As Gram told her constantly, she should enjoy being young and have some fun. "Uh, sure. That sounds good."

Josh exhaled. "Great. I'll make reservations for 7:00. Sound good?"

Courtney glanced at her watch. How was it already 4:00 p.m.?

"I've got to head into division and drop off some files, meet with the commander. I'll be back around 6:30." He flashed her a wide smile, and Courtney felt that zip of electricity dance up her spine again. Josh walked to the front desk while Courtney pushed the button to call the elevator, hoping she wasn't making a huge mistake.

While Josh was away, Courtney showered and pulled a sweet butter yellow sun dress made of soft linen out of her suitcase, glad she'd been so indecisive when she'd packed. She applied mascara and lip-gloss and carefully combed out her shoulder-length hair so it would dry in soft waves. The day she forgot to wear sunscreen while kayaking had worked out in her favour, her face now kissed with summer colour.

She grabbed the cozy mystery she'd brought and settled into the deck chair on their balcony, trying and failing to get into it. She kept attempting to figure out how Justin and the protester were working together. What were they planning? How deep did the conspiracy go? At 6:30, Josh called out through the open patio doors, startling her from her drifting thoughts.

"Just going to hop in the shower, be out in a minute."

Courtney's stomach fluttered as if it had a butterfly farm in it. She bookmarked her place in the novel and ran her fingers through her mostly dry hair. She looked out over the harbour, refusing to think about Josh, naked and wet, mere feet away.

Fifteen minutes later, Josh poked his head, dark brown hair curling damply onto his forehead. The spicy cedar aroma of his aftershave drifted on the summer air, turning her core molten.

"Ready?" Josh asked.

Courtney took a deep breath and stood, smoothing her dress.

"Wow, you look beautiful," Josh said, his voice oddly husky. Josh had swapped out his cargo shorts for some slim chinos, his loose summer button-up shirt with a more formal navy blue one.

A warm wave washed over Courtney. "Um, thanks. I packed it just in case."

The hostess seated them at a table on the deck overlooking the water, with a clear view of the white wings of the Johnson street bridge and the boat traffic in the harbour. The menu was amazing, West Coast modern, featuring local fish and produce. They shared a bottle of excellent south Okanagan pinot noir with notes of berries and herbs. Courtney ordered spot prawns and a salad of local greens, while Josh indulged in a steak served with foraged mushrooms and new potatoes grown in the Cowichan Valley.

"Did you know the Pacheedaaht are starting to forage for mushrooms around Gnome Lake? It's big business, local food," Courtney said, piercing a prawn with her fork.

"Really? Cool." Josh cut into his steak. "I hope that my brother, or should I say my dad, is stopped. It's madness to log a place as pristine as Gnome Lake." He loaded his fork with steak and one of the mushrooms.

"Do you think the protesters will be successful?"

Josh grimaced. "Probably not. The injunction is pretty tight, and most rulings go in the favour of the companies. I think your grandpa and the delegations lobbying will have a more lasting impact. Get the protections enshrined in law so crooked businessmen like my dad can't game the system like they do now.

"He probably convinced Justin to woo that poor woman. The commander I met with today—she's in charge of the white-collar crime division—mentioned Dad has been meeting with the local MLA. I wonder if that's linked to the protests somehow? I wouldn't put it past my father to bribe government officials to get what he wants." Josh's voice was hard and hateful.

"Let's hope that's not the case," Courtney said, brow creasing in concern.

The conversations drifted onto sunnier topics, and by the end of the meal, Courtney's stomach ached from laughing so much. They reminisced about people they knew, talked about the places they'd travelled to, and their favourite movies. Courtney was relieved the conversation stayed light. Telling Josh about Nathan tonight would put a definite damper on the fun and flirty evening.

As they lingered over their wine, the lights strung over the patio came on, transforming the beautiful space into something out of a fairy tale. Courtney, head floating on a sea of red wine, found herself staring at Josh's mouth, wondering what it would be like if he kissed her, as he almost had earlier this afternoon. She shook the thought loose. Friends, Courtney, just friends. That's best for everyone right now.

They split the bill and drifted back upstairs, the king-size bed looming ominously when they entered the room.

"I'll take the couch," Josh said, opening the closet and looking for extra linens.

"It's hardly a couch. How are you going to fit on there?" They were adults. Should she suggest they share the bed? Would that be weird?

"I got us into this mess. It's the least I can do."

Courtney noted the set of his shoulders as he reached for the plastic-covered bundle of linens. She wouldn't win this argument. Josh wanted to be the gentleman. "Okay. Thanks," she said, limbs heavy.

They took turns in the bathroom and said their awkward "goodnights." As Courtney lay in bed, watching the twinkling lights of Victoria, Josh just feet from her, she allowed her mind to wander, dreaming about how the night might have ended if Josh was more than just her friend.

Courtney woke up at 6:30 the next morning, her body not getting the memo about summer vacation. Josh was snoring lightly on the love seat with his feet hanging over the edge. Hopefully, he'd be able to get up off the thing when he woke. It looked really uncomfortable. Restless, Courtney crept out of bed and took her running clothes into the bathroom, taking care to hold the lever down until the door was pulled close so the click wouldn't wake Josh. It would be good to get out for a run. Her mind always worked better when her feet were pounding a solid rhythm.

When she exited the bathroom, Josh was sitting up on his makeshift bed, rubbing his hands over his face. Courtney could hear the rasp of his beard in the early morning quiet.

"Morning," he said, yawning. "Headed out for a run? Mind if I join you? If I don't move my body, I think I'll be a pretzel permanently."

The sharp stab of guilt twinged between Courtney's shoulder blades. There would be no thinking if Josh was next to her. They'd essentially been on a date the night before, and Courtney was less happy with the friend line she'd set for them. She needed to sort out what she was feeling. God, he didn't run shirtless like when he kayaked?

"Um, sure. You looked so peaceful. I didn't want to wake you."

Josh snorted. "Peaceful, huh? Give me a sec. I'll be ready in a flash."

Courtney nodded awkwardly and wandered over to look out the patio door at the waking city as Josh occupied the bathroom. Had the sound of her peeing woken him up? God, the walls were thin. Thankfully, Josh was wearing a teal blue Dri-fit shirt and black running shorts when he came out of the bathroom, although the shirt still revealed his sculpted shoulders and pecs. Courtney fidgeted with the hem of her bright-pink Lululemon shirt and readjusted her Dri-fit cap, eager to focus on anything else.

They exited the lobby into the perfect summer morning, the cool night dew sublimating in the strong July sunshine. Despite the early hour, there were plenty of people out already, the city humming because it was Canada Day. They ran along David Foster Way, passing dog walkers and families strolling with early-rising young children, past Fisherman's Wharf, and around Justin's hideous building.

"Don't worry. He probably only went to bed a few hours ago. Definitely not a morning person," Josh said as Courtney looked up at Justin's balcony as they ran by. She could do without a run-in with Justin.

The day promised to be a hot one, and Courtney was glad she'd worn her running cap, or the sweat would be pouring unattractively down her face and into her eyes. It was easy to run with Josh. She didn't have to hold back because he was in good shape. She found she enjoyed sharing this part of herself with Josh, and it surprised her.

"Do you run a lot?" she asked as they passed the naval base. When she'd known him before, he only ran if he was being chased.

Josh laughed. "Turns out you were right. Running is good for you. In university, my coaches made me do dry land training, and then when I entered depot to train for the RCMP, there was a lot of running. I guess I got hooked without even realizing it. I'd still rather paddle, but I try to go for a run a couple times a week."

Imagining runs with him in the future, Courtney smiled as she looked forward to it.

They ran out to the end of the breakwater at Ogden point, the sun dancing on the grey-blue water on either side. The mountains of the Olympic peninsula were a smudge in the distance through the warming air.

When they got to the end, they paused for a water break. Courtney lifted the hem of her shirt to mop her face. A breeze off the water tickled her bare stomach, causing her skin to turn into gooseflesh. It felt glorious.

Josh poured water over his head. “I know I’m being a bit of a wimp, but it’s getting too warm for me. I think I might have to call it quits,” Josh said, wiping water off his face.

Courtney glanced at her watch. They’d barely done three kilometres—she easily did ten—but it was rather hot. She missed the cool shade and damp moss on her usual forest route. “Let’s run back to the shore, get one more kilometre in, and then we can walk back to the hotel as our cool down.”

“I say yes to running back along the breakwater, but how about I buy you an iced coffee at the restaurant we passed before we walk back.”

“You’ve already paid for too much, Josh. How about we race, and the loser picks up the tab?” Courtney said. Josh nodded, and Courtney dashed toward the shore.

“Hey, no fair!” Josh shouted from behind as she put her foot on the gas.

She beat him easily, and he jogged up, chest heaving, hands on hips, a few beats after she’d stopped. “I. Forgot. How. Fast. You. Are,” Josh said, gulping air.

Courtney felt bad. “Have a seat on the bench, and I’ll get you some cold water.”

“No. Loser buys. Those are the rules. Never mind this,” he pointed at his red face. “It looks worse than it feels. Remember, I’m a blusher—it’s one of the reasons I grew this damn beard. I was tired of people asking if I was okay all the time.”

Courtney laughed. “Deal. I did beat you rather soundly.”

Courtney sat on a bench facing the Salish Sea, noticing a dad and his son on the beach trying to launch a kite shaped like a dragon. She closed her eyes and soaked in the sun. She hadn’t felt this much like herself in over a year. Probably longer. When she opened her eyes after what felt like mere minutes later, she was startled to see Josh standing a few steps from her, an odd dreamy look on his face.

“How long have you been standing there?” Courtney’s face tingled as she blushed.

“Sorry. You looked so beautiful that I didn’t want the magic to end.”

Beautiful? She was sticky with sweat and wearing well-loved running clothes that were older than her students. Her stomach gave a slow flop when she recognized the look in Josh's eye. Desire. For her.

Josh sat, setting the coffees onto the bench.

Courtney stiffened involuntarily, even though her heart was beginning to thrum in her chest.

Josh reached slowly, like he was trying to catch a butterfly, and took her hand. "Court, I have a confession to make."

Courtney's mouth ran dry, and she heard her heart beating over the sound of the waves and the breeze. She forced herself to take a slow, even breath.

"I came back to Port Russell partly because I wanted to reconnect with you. When the posting came up in Port Russell, I jumped at the chance. I've always wanted to come back. It was my happy place. I mean, I named my dog Russell, for god's sake. I also fully admit that I hoped you were there, hoped maybe we could start up what we once had. I've never gotten over you, my first love, and I've always felt bad about how things ended between us."

Josh looked at her, and something within melted into a pool deep in her abdomen.

"This trip, the time we've spent together? I feel as if I've found myself again."

"Me too," Courtney whispered, catching her bottom lip between her teeth.

Josh leaned over. "I really want to kiss you. Is that okay?"

Courtney's stomach did a slow roll. Was she actually going to do this? Was this a good idea? She took a deep breath. Yes, yes, she was going to do this. She managed a nod, and he set his lips, surprisingly smooth and warm, onto hers, setting off fireworks in her brain that tumbled and zapped all the way to the base of her spine. Exactly the same way her body had reacted when he'd first kissed her that day so long ago in the treehouse.

He lifted a hand, still cool from the coffee, and cupped her jaw, his long fingers curving around her neck. "You're sticky," he said, smiling before placing his lips on hers again, sucking in slightly.

Courtney smiled, her core on fire. If she didn't stop kissing him right now, they'd get censured for indecent public acts. She pulled away slowly, looking into Josh's luminous blue eyes. "I, I need to slow down a bit." This is not how she saw this morning, or this trip, going.

"Okay," Josh said, leaning back on the bench. "I can go slow." He gave her a wicked smile and handed her a coffee.

The friend line may have just been obliterated.

CHAPTER 17

While watering the hanging pots back at home Tuesday morning, Courtney smiled, remembering her weekend away with Josh. After the kiss and his startling confession, they'd stopped at a cute bakery across from Fisherman's Wharf Park, lingering over breakfast. She'd dreaded facing the king-sized bed again, not sure she'd make the best decision in the heat of his revelation. Luckily, the hotel had found another room and offered it to them when they'd wandered back in.

If the move to separate rooms had disappointed Josh, he hadn't pushed, taking it slow, just like she'd requested. He'd asked to hold her hand and made sure she was comfortable if he put a hand around her waist. They'd gone to the Canada Day festival on the legislature grounds and then out to dinner again, this time at Bin 4 Burgers, lacing his fingers through hers as they'd wandered the streets of Victoria.

They'd discussed Justin's motives for dating Dissidence and how it could impact the outcome of the protests. Josh was convinced Justin was the manipulator rather than the co-conspirator, admitting to Courtney that he felt sorry for Dissidence, having been impressed by her intelligence and integrity. At the end of the night, he'd sent her back to her room with a toe-curling goodnight kiss that made falling asleep a challenge.

Courtney moved to the next pot and marvelled at how easy it had been to be with Josh. She felt safe and loved when she was with him. But he was still her friend. That was the best part. Would he remain her friend if they took this further? What would happen if they broke up? Her stomach clenched, and she overwatered a pot, which leaked all over her running shoe.

"Get a grip, Courtney. It was one kiss," she said to herself, shaking excess water off her shoe.

With Josh, there were none of the stifling expectations she'd had to navigate with Nathan. No landmines she had to avoid. Josh considered her thoughts and feelings and treated her with respect. She was looking forward to hanging out with him this summer. It would be fun and light. Possibly hot. It wasn't forever, but maybe that was exactly what she needed now—someone to date, not a long-term relationship.

Her phone, tucked into the back of her jean shorts, binged. She turned off the hose and slid the phone from her pocket.

Have a great day, beautiful.

Courtney's breath hitched when she saw he'd added a red heart emoji. Uh-oh. Her heart giddy-upped in her chest. That wasn't light. Hadn't she been clear about her expectations? Courtney's legs itched to move, to hit the pavement and just keep running. Maybe she'd let things go too far with Josh. She enjoyed the dates and the kiss, but she wasn't ready for serious yet. Was she? Her fingers hovered over the keyboard, her mind spinning with all the things she wanted to say, settling on nothing. Chicken. She turned her phone off and slipped it back into her pocket.

Her fridge was empty, and the mail hadn't been picked up in a week, so Courtney pushed aside the restlessness and drove into town. She'd go for a run later. She had trouble finding parking in the small lot next to Agnew's Market, the grocery store. It was packed with unfamiliar cars and camper vans. As she walked to the entrance, she passed lots of university-aged kids loading their vehicles with supplies and one with a map spread out over the hood of their car.

"You just drive up this road here," a young man with his long hair tied up in a top-knot explained to a pair of young women wearing hiking boots and backpacks, one sporting a Greenpeace patch. "Just let Dissidence know you spoke with Owen in town. She'll let you past the blockade. We're so glad you've come all this way to join us."

Old Growth Guardians. So they were actively recruiting more people to the protest.

The trio turned to look at Courtney as she passed. She attempted a friendly smile but was afraid it came off more as a grimace.

The grocery store was busy, and Courtney had difficulty finding a few items.

"Hey, Paul," she said as the produce manager hustled by. "Do you have any more bananas or red peppers?"

"Sorry, Courtney. We've had a bit of a run on items that don't have to be cooked." He looked pointedly at a couple picking up tofu from the cold case. "We're expecting a shipment later today."

Courtney sighed. She should have gone for the run. She bought what she could, then walked across the parking lot to the post office. While the local businesses would benefit from the increased traffic created by the protesters, it felt strange to see so many unknown people in her quiet little town.

As she pulled open the door to the post office, the bells attached to the hinge jingling, a news van from a mainland TV station pulled into the parking lot. If the news was here, it was only going to get more complicated. Locals always bristled a bit when outsiders took over. It would definitely create more tension in town and at the protest site. Gram and Gramps were safe in Victoria for at least the next week. What about when they came back? Courtney wondered if it would be safe for anyone now.

She waved at Marilyn and headed to the bank of silver mailboxes located on the wall adjacent to the main desk. She opened the box she shared with her grandparents and pulled out a stack of envelopes. As she sorted through them to see what was hers, Marilyn called her over.

"There's a package for you, Courtney. Just give me a second."

Courtney leaned against the desk and fished out a postcard featuring the Taj Mahal from one of her former students hiding in the stack of bills and advertisements. She appreciated how much their handwriting and sentences had improved in the year and a half since she'd last seen them. Courtney smiled.

"You look happy," Josh said from behind, causing her to jump. He was on duty and wore a patrol jacket and heavy-duty belt complete with service revolver and a radio attached to the front of his vest.

While there were plenty of advantages to living in a small town, there were plenty of downsides too. Figures after leaving him on read this morning she'd run into him. Would he be upset she hadn't replied? Cheeks pinking, Courtney gave him an awkward smile, praying he wouldn't expect her to kiss him here. If Marilyn saw, the whole town would know by dinner.

"Did you get my text this morning?"

Courtney fumbled with her stack of mail. "You sent me a text? Hmm, I didn't get it." She bit her lip, praying he wouldn't call her out on her lie. Cell phone coverage was notoriously spotty in Port Russell, after all.

"I'll wait till you see it then," Josh said, winking. Courtney heaved a sigh of relief.

Marilyn plunked a medium-sized box on the counter. "Weighs a ton. Cost a fortune to send this."

Curious, Courtney noted the neat black letters of her name, blocky and cramped, then the return address. It was from Nathan. Anger flared in her chest, and her hands trembled, knocking the stack of mail and her student's postcard onto the floor. Why did she let him have such power over her?

"You okay, Court?" Josh asked, immediately bending to retrieve her envelopes.

Courtney made eye contact with Marilyn, willing her not to say anything. The last thing Josh needed was to hear the sordid story of her failed relationship from someone other than her.

"Yeah, yeah. I'm fine. Just didn't drink enough water this morning." Courtney accepted the stack of mail from Josh, keeping her eyes on the shiny toes of his boots.

"How can I help you, Constable Cameron?" Marilyn said.

"We're expecting a registered letter?" Josh asked.

"I've got it here in the back." Marilyn disappeared into the storage room behind the desk.

Courtney lifted the box off the counter. It did weigh a ton, and relief flooded her. It must be the books she'd been begging him to send her for the last year. Jerk kept them just to gall her, likely. Her legs twitched to get moving again, and a ravine-sized gulf, no, make that a Nathan-sized gulf, seemed to have opened between her and Josh. She started moving to the door.

"Let me help you with that," Josh said, approaching to take the box from her.

Courtney angled her body away, and his eyes widened in surprise. "Um, it's all good. I've got to run, unfortunately. Meeting Danielle for lunch." Her mouth tasted like she'd been licking pennies. She hadn't lied this much in more than a year.

"That's nice. Say hi for me," Josh said, turning briefly to accept the letter from Marilyn.

Courtney pushed the door open with her hip, setting the bells off again.

"Hey, um, want to meet for a paddle later?" Josh said

"Sounds great. Text me!"

Marilyn flashed Courtney a puzzled look before the door swung shut behind her.

Courtney speed walked to her car, her arms burning beneath the weight of the box.

CHAPTER 18

After staring at the box all afternoon, hands shaking, Courtney worked up the courage to open it, relieved to find it contained the books she'd asked for and a note with all of two sentences.

Here are the books you asked for. Hope you're well. N.

It surprised her to discover she felt nothing—not anger or, worse, longing. Something had shifted within. He didn't have any power over her anymore. All her anxiety was a waste of time. Courtney laughed, and her eyes filled with tears.

He was still an asshole, though.

She'd given him over six years of her life. Let him take her away from Port Russell and her family, and worst of all, she'd stepped away from her track career because he didn't like it. Her success had made him feel small. The tsunami of regret and guilt she'd battled all year swelled again, threatening to take her under. How could she have let him drag her so low? Make her less? Fill her with such self-loathing?

No. She would not let herself slide back down in the mire. She'd returned home to come back to herself. Now things had shifted. She couldn't let him have that power back. Over the last year, she'd worked hard to regain it.

She glanced over to the postcard she'd propped against the fruit bowl on her counter, where her student had declared her the best teacher ever, and smiled. She'd made a difference in her students' lives and returned to her family and community. She was valued in Port Russell. Now, her weekend with Josh in Victoria had unlocked the last door, freeing her from her self-imposed social isolation. Courtney dumped the books onto her bed and, empty box in hand, opened her cabin door to fling it onto the driveway.

"Good riddance, asshole!" She shouted, hitting Josh square in the chest with the box.

"Oh, my god! I didn't see you there," Courtney said, hands flying to her mouth.

"Interesting recycling technique," Josh said, bending to pick up the box where it had landed at his feet. He was out of uniform now, sporting red swim trunks, a grey tank top, and a pair of ancient TEVA sandals.

Courtney wanted to snatch the box back from him, but Russell bounded over, demanding pets. As she ruffled rusty velvet ears, Josh read the name on the box, scowling.

"This is your ex, right?"

Courtney raised her eyebrows. "How do you know about him?"

Josh walked the box over to the large recycling bin sitting next to Courtney's cottage door. "I met him once." The lid shut with a plastic thump.

"What? You met Nathan?"

"I came to see you run the first year you ran for U Vic at the university championships."

Courtney remembered it well. She'd run a personal best in the 1500 metre. Josh had been there?

"I was at Simon Fraser university, but I happened to see a news story about the strong track team at U Vic, and I knew you'd be there. So I hopped on the ferry and headed to the island for the weekend."

Russell spotted a squirrel and charged off, barking wildly. Courtney gestured to the wicker chairs on her small porch and perched uneasily on the one nearest the door.

"I was standing trackside as you huddled with your team after the medal ceremony. This brash Aussie pointed you out and said you were his girlfriend. That it was serious, and he was thinking of asking you to marry him."

Courtney closed her eyes briefly. Sounded like Nathan. Deluded and possessive. At that point, they'd only been dating for a few weeks. He'd never asked her to marry him.

"I felt so guilty about leaving Port Russell and not contacting you. I realized I'd made a huge mistake. You'd moved on." The hurt was evident in Josh's voice. "Marilyn let slip he's the reason you stopped running competitively. Is that true?"

Courtney's stomach clenched painfully. "Yeah. He was the reason I stopped doing a lot of things."

"Were you going to marry him?"

Courtney laughed, not out of joy. "No. He told other guys that because he was a possessive dick. We lived together for a few years. I gave up running for him. I gave up who I was for him. I lived where he wanted to live, did what he wanted to do, and saw who he wanted to see. I thought he wasn't the marrying type and made my peace with it, but it turned out he didn't want to marry *me*. He met someone else about eighteen months ago. They got married this last New Year's Eve." Courtney glanced over at Josh and took in his clenched jaw and fists.

"First, he treated you like garbage, and then he cheated on you? Asshole. I wish I'd decked him that day at the track," Josh said, voice steely.

"Me too," she said, shifting in her chair, the wicker creaking beneath her. "In the end, I should thank her for taking him off my hands. I came home because of it. Port Russell is home. This is where I belong." Courtney surprised herself. It rang with truth for the first time since she'd been back. "I'm so sorry we didn't connect that day."

Josh looked over at Courtney as Russell hopped up onto the porch after his unsuccessful attempt to catch the squirrel, collapsing with a sigh at Courtney's feet. "Better late than never," Josh said, his wide smile lighting up his eyes as he reached for Courtney's hand.

CHAPTER 19

On a whim, as she prepared dinner for herself the following night, Courtney tuned into the evening news on the network the news van was from. As she chopped, half listening, she heard the anchor say something about Gnome Lake. Setting down her knife, Courtney snatched the remote from the coffee table and turned up the sound, perching on the arm of the couch. It was an interview from the protest site, and Dissidence, with her bright-pink hair, acted as spokesperson.

"What do you hope to achieve with this blockade?" the young reporter asked.

"The Old Growth Guardians speak for the spirits of the trees."

At this, Courtney rolled her eyes. Who was she, the Lorax?

"We will not rest until the provincial government declares a moratorium on the harvesting of old-growth forests throughout the province of British Columbia."

Courtney raised her eyebrows. So, they hadn't really agreed to join to save Gnome Lake but to further their own political agenda. True, it might protect Gnome Lake, but only if they were successful soon.

The protesters gathered around her let out a loud cheer at this statement, launching into chants accompanied by drumming. Courtney spied one or two familiar faces. The rest were new to her. With this dramatic backdrop, the young reporter signed off.

Courtney finished making her salad and sat at her small dining table, spearing a forkful of lettuce and cherry tomato, ruminating as she crunched. What was Justin's angle on this? There was very little protection for the old growth in the province. When her grandfather's company had been logging the area, they had stayed away from Gnome Lake out of respect for the Pacheedaaht and the belief that it would hurt Port Russell in the long run. In addition to being culturally significant for the local Indigenous groups, old-growth forests are carbon sinks and necessary for a healthy ecosystem able to withstand the coming climate changes.

Gramps refused to log the local old growth, even though it hurt him financially, out of duty to his community and his belief in sustainable forestry. Justin, if his outward appearance and prior track record of behaviour were an indication, would likely have no qualms about harvesting the old stands in the area. They were worth more money. He'd only be interested in saving them if something were in it for him. Or his father, if Josh's hunch was correct.

Courtney finished her salad and got up from the table to put her dishes in the sink. As she ran the water, the final report of the show came on, a fluff piece about the projected increase in tourism expected on the west coast of Vancouver Island. Ugh! There were too many tourists as it were, in her opinion. Apparently, the area had made some Top 10 List in some hoity-toity tourist magazine. They'd called the Salish Sea coastline the "St. Tropez" of Canada. Sure, if you liked to wear a turtleneck to the beach most of the year, Courtney thought to herself, putting her dish in the drying rack. She prayed it came to nothing. She loved Port Russell just the way it was.

Newscast over, Courtney flicked off the TV, grabbed her current read, the latest mystery by her favourite author, and a glass of wine, heading out to sit on her porch. Gram had read it first and said it was the best one in the series so far. The spice of warm cedar filled the air as the sun-warmed siding of her cottage had cooled down now that the sun had dipped to the top of the trees. Courtney curled into her chair, sipping her cold glass of rosé, enjoying the quiet summer evening. She opened her book and tried to read, but her brain refused to focus on the words, picking away instead at the problem of Justin's involvement with Dissidence.

Maybe he's just sleeping with her, Courtney thought but discarded it just as quickly. While she wouldn't put that past Justin, she'd known plenty of women like Dissidence in university. She would be a passionate feminist as well as an environmentalist. She wouldn't be involved with Justin unless she wanted to be. So, something had thrown them together. Josh had mentioned that Dissidence was a professional protester—maybe Justin hired her? Had she created a diversion while the crooked MLA pushed through the necessary paperwork so they could break ground on the resort as soon as the trees were cut?

Courtney read the same paragraph three times and looked away from her book in disgust. *Okay brain, you win.* She marked her place, set the paperback down on the table, and picked up her wine. She glanced at the cover of her book, recalling why she'd been excited to read this new novel. Her favourite detective was going to go undercover in the criminal gang she'd been tracking for the last three books and finally, hopefully, catch the person who'd killed their partner two and a half books back.

Courtney sat very straight in her chair, sloshing her wine onto her shirt.

"Oh my god. It's so obvious," she said out loud.

If she wanted to figure out what Justin was up to, joining the protest and getting to know Dissidence was the way to do it. Josh had rules to follow, but she had every right to join the protestors. It would be dangerous, sure, but if she could link Justin to the protests and maybe even to a possible backroom deal, it would be more than worth it. She might be the key to getting CFI away from Gnome Lake before it was too late.

She needed to go undercover.

It didn't take Courtney long to find a way in with the local protest group, just one call to Marilyn. As always happened in Port Russell, where the ties that bind were more like a spider web, Stan's nephew Alex was the local Pacheedaaht organizer and was thrilled to have one more Port Russell resident involved. If this undercover thing worked, hopefully she'd be able to give Josh the information he'd need to get Justin, and this Dissidence, to move on. He'd told her he wanted Gnome Lake saved and his father stopped. She was sure he wouldn't mind using unusual methods to do so.

Alex swung by to pick Courtney up the next morning.

"Hey. So glad you've joined us," Alex said as Courtney climbed into the cab of his battered pickup truck, setting the pack of supplies that he suggested she bring by her feet. "Lost a ton of people once these mainlanders showed up." He was a few years younger than her, and it surprised Courtney to see a grown man rather than the shaggy-haired kid she saw at family barbecues growing up. Marilyn proudly told her he'd left Port Russell to attend university, gaining a degree in environmental science. Alex navigated the manor driveway with just his right hand on the wheel, taking a swig from the giant travel mug he held in his left hand, the comforting smell of dark roast filling the truck's cab.

"Now that school's over for the summer, I finally have the time to dedicate to the cause. Gram and Gramps are very passionate about it." Courtney had told Alex she wanted to make up for her grandparent's absence and support the community. "You've got to step up when things are this important."

"True that," Alex said, stopping at the T-intersection leading to the highway as low cloud gathered around the tops of the trees across the highway. "Getting intense out there. You brought the stuff I told you to?"

Courtney half lifted her pack. "Yes."

Alex had instructed her to wear sturdy boots, long pants, and sleeves and to pack a thick old coat, rain gear, a change of clothes, work gloves, a toque, several bandannas, and swim goggles, as well as plenty of water, power bars and copies of important documents like her driver's license and birth certificate, in case she got arrested. Her backpack barely zipped shut.

"I'm a bit confused about why I need some of the stuff."

"This isn't just standing around with placards and shouting slogans, as I explained last night. We are actively engaging in blockading the road, and Dissidence has some plans for acts of civil disobedience. CFI has applied for an injunction, and the RCMP presence has swelled in the past few days. It could get hairy out there today. That's where the bandannas and goggles come in."

Courtney's stomach clenched. "I'm afraid to ask."

"Lots of pushing and shoving. Sometimes tear gas. Water canons. Standard anti-protest procedures." Alex glanced over at her. "Don't worry. I got you. The cops wouldn't dare hurt us, now that the press is watching, anyway. You got copies of your documents? There's a good chance you'll be arrested."

Her mouth turned into a dry riverbed. She knew she wouldn't get fired for being arrested for civil disobedience, just a conviction—she'd checked her collective agreement last night, just to be sure—but it would likely give some parents pause in the future to find out their child's teacher had been arrested. It would come up at some point. This was a small town, and not everyone agreed with the protest, especially now that mainlanders were involved. But if her grandparents could do it, so could she.

Justin, in his ridiculous car, a perma-smirk on his face popped into Courtney's head. Josh thought he was up to something. Courtney was intimately aware of the damage he caused when he wasn't rich and the CEO of the largest employer in town, and she didn't doubt that what he was up to would lead to heartache and pain for those she loved. The forest around Port Russell was special and deserved to be protected. Climate change was real, and the old growth played an integral role in the health of the planet. She owed this to her grandparents, her students, and herself. Port Russell was her home. She wasn't just going to sit back and see it suffer. She'd sat on the sidelines long enough.

Alex turned onto the Gnome Lake road, the shoulder lined with vehicles. "Damn. Problem number one—some of these cars aren't pulled far enough onto the shoulder. Gonna get towed for sure."

There had to be thirty vehicles lining the narrow logging road, though Courtney remembered it was wider near the intersection than closer to the blockade. There were a lot of shiny hybrids and SUVs favoured by weekend warriors, as the locals liked to call them. Some battered camper vans and used hybrids sporting university stickers too.

"They're gonna have to come back and move them. Lucky you, I got preferred parking." Alex chuckled darkly. "Got supplies for Dissidence in the back, so we get to drive right to the blockade."

They pulled up to a makeshift gate fashioned out of a narrow log resting on X-shaped logs on either end, lashed together with bright yellow rope. The gate was manned by a pair of large men with red bandannas covering the lower half of their faces. One approached the truck while the other prepared to lift the log blocking the road and pivot it out of the way.

Alex rolled down his window. "Morning, Duane," Courtney started, recognizing one of the men who'd been a supervisor at her grandfather's company, also Pacheedaaht.

"Courtney! Great to see you here. When's your granddad coming back?" Duane said, leaning into the window.

"Next week sometime, I think. The meetings are over on Saturday, but Gram and Gramps are going to take a bit of a vacation before they head home."

Duane nodded. "See any cops?"

"They aren't here yet?" Alex asked.

"Just the two cars that were here overnight. Just wondered when the rest of them would decide to show up."

"How many are usually here?" Courtney asked.

"Yesterday, at midday, when the press was here, there were at least a dozen cars. Some drove in from Victoria, just for the afternoon. Dissidence figures that will become the standard, or even increase, if CFI is successful in getting their injunction," Duane said.

"You got a radio?" Alex asked. "The vehicles down the road are gonna get towed if they aren't pulled further off the road. Don't want a repeat of yesterday."

"Yesterday?" Courtney asked.

"Bunch of cars got accidentally smashed as they were being towed," Duane said, making air quotes around accidentally. "Prick cops. Aren't from here and don't care about anything. Bad enough we have to put up with these mainlanders. Liked it better when it was just us locals."

The hair on the back of Courtney's neck prickled, and she said a prayer of thanks that she'd managed to convince her grandparents to stay away for another week. She'd done it to avoid having to explain her sudden decision to join the protest—she'd never been able to lie to Gram—but she was grateful they wouldn't be caught in the escalating conflict.

Alex reached back into the extended cab of his truck and pulled out a couple of chocolate bars, handing them to Duane, whose face lit up. "Little treat for you, bro. Stay strong."

"You too, man," Duane said, nodding at the guy at the gate to let them through.

Alex rolled forward, the truck rocking on the pot-holed surface of the road. He waved as they passed. Courtney took a deep breath. There was no going back now.

CHAPTER 20

"Come meet Dissidence," Alex said as he yanked his truck into park.

Courtney heaved an inward sigh of relief. She'd been scrambling for an excuse to meet Dissidence that wouldn't have raised alarm bells for Alex. No one in Port Russell would accuse her of being a social butterfly, even before Nathan.

The activist was easy to spot with her cotton candy hair, and Courtney just about gave herself away by walking toward her without Alex. He was busy unloading a metal pipe, curiously the diameter of a human arm, from the bed of his truck and didn't notice. After hefting the pipe onto his shoulder, he pointed out where they had to walk with his chin.

"Can't miss Dissidence. She's the one with the crazy pink hair," Alex said. "Says she'll help me do mine when things quiet down."

"You're going to go pink?" Courtney asked, looking at Alex's long black braids.

"Maybe not pink. Was thinking bright blue, maybe neon green."

"That'll be popular with the elders."

Alex laughed. "You'd be surprised. Uncle Bill asked Dissidence to do his."

"Elder Bill is here?" Courtney hadn't heard that some of the Pacheedaaht elders were involved.

"Bill and George Joseph are. The other elders are supporting other methods of protest, sending delegates to the talks in Victoria and even trying to get the feds to weigh in, especially now that the Old Growth Guardians are involved."

Courtney flushed a little, embarrassed she was so uninformed. "I hadn't heard it was causing a rift. Sorry to hear that."

Alex shrugged. "Is what it is—no bad tempers, just differences in opinion. Here we are." Alex reached out and touched Dissidence's sleeve. "Your armlock, fearless leader."

Dissidence turned around, and Courtney was finally able to see more than just her bright pink hair. She was a bit older than she'd appeared before, in her late twenties, shorter than Courtney, maybe five foot two in hiking boots. Her skin was a lovely gold, the summer sun creating a constellation of freckles over each of her high cheekbones. Her eyes, the colour of black coffee, shone with intelligence and determination. She smiled at Alex's news, her eyes nearly disappearing as her cheekbones lifted.

"Awesome! Just in time, I got word that the injunction was passed." Dissidence turned her gaze toward Courtney. "Who do we have here?"

It was friendly but buried beneath the surface cordiality was an edge of suspicion and steel. Courtney decided she'd better make an effort to get on her good side, pronto.

"Hi, I'm Courtney Merrick." She extended a hand, and Dissidence grasped it with a handshake far stronger than her size would indicate.

"She's a family friend. Charles and Norma's granddaughter." Alex vouched for her.

Dissidence's face lit up again. "Charles told me all about you. So glad you could join us."

"Sorry I couldn't be here sooner. End of a school year is always a mad rush."

"Tell me about it. I'm on sabbatical, but I normally teach middle school social studies."

"Wow. Really? I had no idea you were a teacher."

"Have to pay the bills somehow, but my real passion is activism. Alex, were you able to get the central post fixed in the arm tube?"

"Yup. This is some of my best work yet,"

"What is it for, exactly?" Courtney asked. Her grandfather had always said people liked to answer questions about themselves, and she'd found this especially true of teachers.

"It's an armlock. Two protesters insert an arm in either end, and, thanks to Alex, this particular model has a central post that each protester can be locked to. When the police arrive to remove protesters from blocking a road or piece of equipment, it takes a long time to get the protesters out of the armlock. Civil disobedience 101: make things uncomfortable and cumbersome for authority. We'll use this in conjunction with the sit you guys strung up yesterday." Dissidence gestured toward a platform suspended about ten metres in the air above the road, just past where they were standing. "That ought to slow down the arrests in a suitably frustrating manner."

The sit had a platform just long enough for two protesters an armlock apart. Courtney worked out what Dissidence was proposing and decided to gain some brownie points. She pointedly ignored her clenched stomach. If she was serious about getting some dirt on Justin, she'd have to be bold. "If no one has volunteered to go up in the sit, I'll do it."

The activist's smooth, arched eyebrows rose, though Courtney wasn't sure whether it was in surprise or admiration. "Just want to warn you, if they take you out of the armlock, they will definitely arrest you."

Courtney's heart fluttered. In for a penny, she thought. She needed to get close to this woman. Being locked to her, potentially for hours alone in the sky, could provide a lot of time for chatting. That would give her a better chance of finding out something to help Josh. "I understand."

When Courtney looked Dissidence in the eye, she could see it was admiration, not surprise.

"Well, let the games begin."

Dissidence prepped Courtney on what to expect, and an hour later, sweating in the heavy old Carhartt jacket she'd found in the garage, Courtney shifted slightly in the tree-sit. The whole thing wobbled, and Courtney stiffened.

"That's normal," Dissidence said. "They sway, but it takes a lot to make one fall. We brought in rope experts to set up this sit. I've never been in one that's collapsed."

Courtney looked at the gravel surface of the road, at least two stories below, and nodded, her mouth dry. Dissidence had assured her it was safe. She had no choice but to trust it was true.

"Hey, fearless leader," Alex called from beneath them. "Cop convoy's on its way."

"Excellent," Dissidence said, face breaking into a manic smile. "I love this part."

Courtney's palms slicked. She understood on an intellectual level what she was getting into, but she'd never been in trouble with the law—not even a parking ticket. This was unfamiliar territory for her. Would Josh be responding today? Butterflies swirled in her stomach.

"Hey, don't worry," Dissidence said, squeezing Courtney's hand inside the armlock."Remember what I told you."

In another time, under more honest circumstances, Courtney would genuinely like to hang out with the radiant-haired activist. She was passionate, kind, and funny. They'd already swapped a few teaching horror stories, laughter coming easily. Too bad she had crap taste in men, Courtney mused, Justin in his slick suit popping into her head.

Dissidence had explained how things would likely go down. The police would arrive and read the injunction aloud, giving anyone who wanted to leave the chance to do so. Once they read the injunction a second time, they would likely arrest anyone remaining for contempt, as long as they remained non-violent and non-reactionary. Dissidence had explained that if things went pear-shaped, they would most likely be charged with mischief. She had advised Courtney to keep her muscles relaxed, make her body heavier, and keep her mouth shut if she didn't want to escalate things with the officers lifting her off the sit.

"I'll be insulting them enough for the both of us," she said with a wink.

Past the barricade, the first of the RCMP vehicles, a white truck with the iconic blue and red lights mounted on top, pulled up to the barricade. Courtney wondered how many protesters there were. Perched in her sky-seat, she had counted at least fifty, though it was hard to keep track of everyone as there were multiple barricades, and some had chained themselves to old growth trees on either side of the rutted logging road.

Behind the first police vehicle was a familiar red SUV. Courtney laughed. Justin drove his Porsche up here? Posturing douchebag. Just like him to ensure he had a front seat for any chaos he created. He'd probably want to make sure Dissidence was doing as he'd commanded. She'd only just met Dissidence, but Courtney suspected that the activist probably didn't know the whole story and was being played by Justin and his father.

Beside her, Dissidence was yelling the same slogan over and over. "Respect existence, or expect resistance!" If Dissidence had noticed Justin below, she had a great poker face.

The police were stopped by Alex and Duane, still manning the first set of gates, the former yelling loud enough for everyone to hear. Dissidence had explained this was necessary so witnesses could testify as to what they'd heard if it came to it.

"We know our rights—you gotta read the injunction. We are gathered here in peaceful protest as is our democratic right as citizens and keepers of this land," Alex shouted.

Courtney was impressed with the resolve in his voice. These people were walking the walk, not just talking about saving the forest but actually stepping up and putting themselves on the line for the good of the whole planet. Courtney found herself humbled by their courage despite her own terror.

The officer speaking to Alex, an inspector based on the insignia on her shoulder, was not from the local detachment. The crowd linked arm in arm behind Alex and Duane, on the road, and those scattered in the trees quieted down to listen.

"I am here to inform you that you are gathering here in contravention of a court injunction," she read out loud.

Courtney understood very little of the legalese.

"All those wanting to leave should gather their things and leave immediately. We will enter the site in fifteen minutes and arrest anyone remaining for contempt of court."

An officer behind her made a show of setting a digital timer, flashing it toward the crowd who were now booing and shouting, "Go home," "Shame on you," and many other things Courtney was frankly shocked to hear coming out of people she ran into at the grocery store.

A bead of sweat trickled down her back, and she shifted, setting the sit swaying. Dissidence squeezed her hand even as she shouted, "Go home, pigs!" at the RCMP officers. Courtney scanned their faces, skipping over the smirking face of Justin, leaning nonchalantly against his over-priced ride. Was Josh here? Honestly, she was more nervous about seeing him than being arrested. Well, maybe equally as nervous. Alex and Dissidence's advice about her rights and responsibilities if she was arrested whirled in her brain. Her hands were trembling. What were the officers below thinking? Were they nervous too?

The protesters on the ground began singing a song Courtney wasn't familiar with, accompanied by the beat of a single drum. Courtney's heart skipped in her chest when she spotted Josh, his brow furrowed in concern at the scene around him. When he saw her in the tree-sit, locked to Dissidence ten metres in the air, his posture stiffened. His mouth, usually relaxed and smiling, became a slash on his face. He was mad.

At that moment, Justin pushed himself off his car, following his brother's line of sight, and realized who his girlfriend was chained to for the first time. His face shifted to a sadistic smile. Courtney empathized with all the ants he'd probably scorched as a kid. Remembering why she came in the first place, she stole a glance at Dissidence. What did she think about her boyfriend standing with the police here to arrest them? Her golden face was smooth, though she was studiously avoiding looking at Justin directly, her eyes focused on a spot a few cars down the line. How was she so calm?

The timer went off, and the officer flashed it toward the woman who'd spoken to them earlier. She immediately launched into a second reading of the injunction. The crowd increased in volume, the quiet hush of the forest transforming into a cacophony of shouts and drumbeats, an indecipherable roar. When the inspector was finished, she signaled to officers behind her, and in pairs, they moved forward to arrest Alex, who immediately went limp, dropping to the ground like a sack of cement. Justin strolled over to speak to the inspector, the scowl on her face telling Courtney all she needed to know regarding the officer's opinion of his presence on site. The protesters sent up a cheer, their chants changing to advice and praise for Alex.

"Stay strong!"

"You got this, brother."

Courtney saw the lips of one officer moving as the other one leaned over, tying Alex's hands behind his back and his ankles to each other with huge black zip ties. The officer tested to see they were secure, and then he bent to pick Alex up with black-gloved hands under each arm while his partner grabbed Alex's work boot-garbed feet. They carted him past the barricade, and Courtney lost sight of him. Dissidence had told her they would arrest them, place them into a bus or paddy wagon, and transport them into Port Renfrew for processing at the detachment.

It took hours, even with the extra officers they'd brought in. Courtney counted at least a dozen officers, working in pairs, arresting protester after protester. In the midday heat, Courtney was slicked in sweat, swaddled in the thick jacket. Her hair was plastered against her neck, and she had to pee desperately while being thirsty at the same time. Dissidence had counseled her to ask for water straight away when the officers showed up, saying they were bound to give her some and it would slow the arrest protest down.

It was about 1:00 p.m. when they finally acted to remove Dissidence and Courtney from the sit. Courtney's stomach dropped like an untethered elevator when she looked down into Josh's blue eyes, more a stormy grey today beneath the dull cloud overhead, his brow crumpled in worry. The lips that had kissed her so gently on the beach only days ago scowled up at her. Courtney straightened her shoulders, reminding herself why she was there. She was doing this to get Josh the information he needed about Justin. She steeled her resolve, even though her gut wobbled like one of Gram's famous jello salads. Dissidence squeezed her hand and drew her attention.

"We got this, sister! Hold on."

As they were lowered out of the sky, everything slowed, as if she were watching the sports highlights in slow motion. Josh put a hand on either shoulder as the platform thumped to the ground, crouching down to whisper in her ear as he lowered a heavy blanket over her. They'd brought a gas-powered grinder and were trying to gain access to the arm lock, even though Dissidence was shouting for them to stop.

"What are you doing here?" Josh hissed into her ear.

"I'm trying to help," Courtney said, trembling as the vibration of the grinder transferred from the arm lock to the muscles of her arms. She grimaced in pain.

Josh stood. "Stop! You're hurting her," he shouted. He addressed Dissidence. "Please, get the key so we don't have to cut you out."

Courtney held her breath, hoping that Dissidence might give up, unsurprised when she shouted back.

"Never. We are here for Mother Earth. She takes precedence over all!"

Josh wiped a hand over his face, the muscles of his shoulders so tight Courtney could see them from her position on the road. Josh crouched again.

"This is going to be really uncomfortable. Are you okay?"

Courtney nodded. "I'm fine. I just really need to pee. Could I have some water?"

Josh chuckled, though there was no mirth behind it, and gestured for another officer to bring a water bottle over. "I hope you can hold it. This is going to take a while."

CHAPTER 21

In the end, it took half an hour to free them from the armlock using the grinder. Courtney thought her teeth were going to fall out from the vibration, and her arm was still numb. Once back at the detachment, it took four hours to be processed. But to her great surprise, once that was done, they released her. Both Dissidence and Alex, because they'd been arrested before, were charged and transferred to Victoria, where they would be held until they could be brought before a judge. With Gram and Gramps away, Courtney realized she had no one to drive her home. Josh instructed her to take a seat near his desk until he was free to take her home, as she'd refused his offer to call Marilyn to pick her up. Of course, the town would find out eventually, but if the town's biggest gossip had to come pick her up from jail, they'd know immediately. It was well past seven, and Courtney's stomach grumbled loudly.

Josh hadn't said a word to her since he'd told her to take a seat. Chewing her lip, Courtney watched him finish the reports on the arrests he'd made that day. He rubbed his eyes and face, belying his exhaustion. He was busy and didn't have the time to talk, she assured herself, sipping the green tea Constable Huong had brought her. Would Josh be like Nathan and forbid her from continuing her undercover operation? She didn't think he would once they had a chance to discuss things. Josh was a rational guy. Courtney prepared her arguments. She was a grown woman and didn't need his permission to do things. She had the interests of her community at heart. Her grandparents needed her to step up because they couldn't. While there was an element of truth in each explanation, she also knew Josh would be upset with her for not running it past him first. When they were kids, they'd promised each other they'd always be honest. A little voice inside reminded Courtney that even when they were kids, they'd both broken that promise. She by never telling him how she really felt and Josh when he'd left her. As the minutes ticked by and Josh didn't even look in her direction, quiet dread turned her stomach to cement.

Courtney rested her head on her crossed arms on the edge of Josh's desk and dozed off, her day having started at sunrise. A shadow fell across her, and Courtney started, eyes fluttering open to see Josh before her, service belt and duty vest removed.

"Let's go," he said, not looking her in the eye.

Courtney's gut twisted, his body language and tone of voice reminding her of Nathan.

Courtney stood, back creaking, waving goodbye to Constable Huong as she spoke to someone on the phone at her desk at the back of the room. She followed Josh through the side entrance and out into a gorgeous summer evening, the earlier cloud cover now gone and the sky a dusky violet with streaks of fuchsia. He unlocked his truck and headed for the driver's side. All hope Courtney had that he was preoccupied rather than angry flew out the window. Swallowing the giant lump in her throat, she opened the passenger side door and slid into the seat, her right arm protesting as she pulled the door closed with a quiet thud. She rubbed at her still-throbbing arm with her left hand. It was going to be black and blue in the morning, despite the padding of the now-destroyed Carhartt jacket. She could smell the day on her, acrid and sharp.

"Look, Josh," she began.

"Not now," he snapped, taking a deep breath before continuing. "Just, I need to think for a bit."

Courtney nodded, irritated with herself when she felt the stab of tears behind her eyes. Josh started the truck, rolling down both windows before maneuvering the truck out of the small lot. Courtney was grateful for the soft evening air streaming in as they drove through the quiet streets. She dashed the tears from her eyes before they fell. At the four-way stop at the edge of town, Josh turned toward his cottage instead of the manor. Courtney opened her mouth to protest but caught herself. Russell. Poor guy had been on his own all day. Of course Josh needed to see to him first.

Summer season was in full swing at Cedar Sands, the red neon "no vacancy" lit up on the resort's sign. Josh pulled into his assigned parking space, facing the beach, and slid out of the cab to rescue his dog. The distinctive smell of campfire wafted on the wind. Courtney saw several groups of vacationers clustered around the firepits set up on the beach, laughing and drinking beer. They were unaware of the war in the woods happening just kilometres away from where they sat, and Courtney envied them. She didn't think she could be that carefree again after this afternoon.

Russell shot out of Josh's cabin like a rocket, heading for the shrubs planted between the cabins and the beach to relieve himself. Courtney remembered how good it felt when she'd finally been able to pee earlier this afternoon. Josh pointed to the truck when Russell was done, and with tail wagging and face joyful, Russell bounded over to the cab and leapt onto the seat when Josh opened the door. He headed straight for Courtney, licking her ear and waggling so much the truck rocked slightly.

"Hi, Russell." Courtney laughed, ruffling his ear. At least someone was happy she was here.

Russell settled himself in the small backseat. They drove in silence out toward the manor, Courtney aware of waves of emotion pooling off of Josh. She bit her cheek to keep herself from saying anything. It had always taken him time to work through his emotions. After their first few arguments, she'd learned that it was better to let him process before talking. He hadn't changed that much. She empathized with him. It must be hard to arrest people you knew and liked. The officers that didn't live in Port Russell had moved with quiet efficiency and open irritation. From the sit, Courtney had watched the toll it was taking on Josh, especially as Justin had sat for at least an hour watching his brother, saying things to Josh as he passed that Courtney hadn't been able to make out from her aerial position with Dissidence.

Courtney stole a glance at Josh. His jaw was set, both hands gripping the steering wheel tightly. Was he going to continue with this silent treatment the whole way? Her stomach burned as they continued to drive. How much time did he need? How mad was he?

They turned onto the manor drive, the solar lights her grandfather had installed illuminating either side of the driveway up to the house. Courtney's own cottage was completely dark. Naively, she thought she'd be home long before dark and hadn't left the porch lights on when Alex had picked her up. Courtney raised a hand and scratched Russell's throat in farewell as Josh pulled up beside her parked Subaru. She twisted to unbuckle her seat belt, not sure Josh was ready to talk.

"Thanks for the ride, Josh," she said quietly, reaching for the door handle.

"Wait," Josh said, placing a hand on Courtney's forearm. She swiveled to look at him, surprised to see his eyes glassy, a film of tears coating his deep blue eyes in the dim interior light. "When I saw you up in that sit, my heart stopped. I was so afraid for you today."

The lump in Courtney's throat grew, and tears pooled in her eyes again. She hadn't meant to worry him. "I'm sorry. It seemed like the best way to get to know Dissidence."

Anger flared on Josh's face. "You shouldn't be out there. It's dangerous. *She's* dangerous."

He'd gone there. Full Nathan. A flicker of irritation, fueled by her empty belly and exhausted limbs, licked at the base of Courtney's neck, lighting a fuse. "I don't need your permission to do things, Josh. I'm an adult. You're the one who insisted I come to Victoria to investigate Justin. I figured Dissdence was an in."

Courtney struggled to take a deep breath, the all too familiar feeling of suffocation she'd tamped down the whole time she was with Nathan coming back in full force. "By the way, she is brave, not dangerous, and what they're doing out there is important. I might have gone out to spy on Dissidence, but I'll go back to support their cause." Courtney blinked. Holy crap—where did that come from?

Josh leaned back, dropping his hand from her arm and closing his eyes for a breath. "You're right. You don't need my permission," he said, his voice strained. He looked down at his hands, one thumb rubbing the back of his other hand, and continued in a voice barely above a whisper. "Arresting you was one of the hardest things I've had to do. I could tell the grinder was hurting you, and I wanted to make them stop. Walk away. Anything, so I didn't have to watch. But I didn't want to leave you. It may have been the longest half hour of my life. I wanted to wrap myself around you. Shield you from any pain or discomfort." His eyes locked with Courtney's, and she could see the spark of desire flickering in the dim light of the cab.

Russell whimpered as he stood half on the backseat and half on the console between the driver's and passenger seats. He licked his person's face, and Josh moved his hands to stroke either side of his companion's head.

Courtney's chest ached, her heart thudding, one beat, then two, before she lunged forward across the console, surprising Russell, who skittered into the backseat. She pulled Josh into a kiss, surprising everyone. After a heartbeat, Josh returned the kiss, deepening it, slipping his tongue past Courtney's lips, exploring, seeking, searching.

Russell, confused, let out a ruff, and Josh paused to open his door to let him out before resuming his kiss, weaving his hands into Courtney's hair. He tasted like coffee and sea salt.

"Come inside?" Courtney whispered in Josh's ear, planting kisses along his stubbled jaw.

Josh groaned, the vibration buzzing Courtney's lips. "You're sure?" he whispered, pulling back, his blue-grey eyes, swimming with desire, looked straight into her molten centre.

"I've never been more certain of anything in my whole life."

CHAPTER 22

Still on school time, Courtney awoke the next morning at 6:30, the soft yellow sunshine of the new summer morning streaming through the open blinds, illuminating Josh, still asleep. She was curled onto her side, and her eyes swept over his peaceful face, his criminally long lashes brushing his cheeks, the sun gilding his strong forehead and cheekbones. He was gorgeous. The events of the evening rushed in, and Courtney smiled. She had never felt as safe and cared for with Nathan. Josh treated her with tenderness, never pushing her or forcing her to do anything she wasn't ready for. He gave her the freedom and the power to choose, and Courtney was grateful, and something more she was afraid to even say in the silence of her mind. Behind her, Russell put his muzzle on the bed and whimpered, tail swishing in anticipation.

After rolling over as quietly as she could, Courtney got out of bed, putting a finger to her lips to remind Russell to be quiet, too. She pulled on her pajama bottoms, a tank top, and a hoodie she'd left on the chair in the corner of her room, grabbed some flip-flops, and tiptoed with Russell to the bedroom door, pulling it closed to let Josh sleep longer.

"Let's go for a walk," she whispered to Russell, who wiggled his butt in agreement as she pulled the flip-flops on.

Once the cabin door was open, Russell shot off to the tree line to take care of business while Courtney stood on her porch, stretching, soaking in the early morning glory of what would likely be a beautiful summer day. The sky was a clear cerulean. The dew hung in the air as a reminder of the magic night just past. A hummingbird zoomed up to the feeder hanging off the eave of her porch, his throat flashing rubies in the bright morning light. Courtney sighed. She hadn't been this happy, this peaceful, in as long as she could remember. Not since the summer she was sixteen. Not since before Josh left.

Russell bounded back over, and Courtney stepped off the porch to greet him, sinking her hands into his soft rust-coloured fur.

"Ready for that ramble now?" Russell actually hopped, he was so happy, and Courtney laughed out loud.

"That's a beautiful sound," Josh said from the open door behind her, pausing with his hand on the frame. He had a strange, wistful smile, and Courtney briefly wondered why he looked sad when she felt so happy. "I want to remember you in this moment forever. You are breathtaking."

Her breath caught for a moment, then she blushed, smoothing bed-ruffled hair behind her ear, her anxious thoughts evaporating like dew in the strong sunlight. "The only thing breathtaking is my morning breath."

Wearing his duty pants, a white undershirt, and no shoes, Josh stepped off the porch and put a hand on Courtney's hips and pulled her in for a long kiss before placing his forehead on hers. What was he thinking?

"You're right. Your breath is horrible," he said with a wide smile.

Courtney slapped at his arm. "You'd better step back then."

Josh wrapped his arms around her, and Courtney placed her head in the crook of his neck. "No. I don't think I will."

Russell barked impatiently, reminding Courtney of her promise. "I told him I'd take him for a walk."

"You're stuck now. He never forgets about the 'W' word, do you, Russ?" Josh stepped back, taking Courtney's hand and winding his fingers through hers. "I have an hour or so before I'm back on duty. Mind if I tag along?"

"I guess so," Courtney said, tugging on Josh's hand. "Um, you might want something on your feet, however."

Josh dug a pair of flip-flops out of his truck, and then Russell took off for the beach path, pausing every so often to look back to ensure his slow people were still following him.

"Sorry about the early morning. Russell is an early bird."

"I was already awake. Still on school time." Courtney considered that statement. "Actually, I'm an early bird myself. I never sleep in much past eight, even in the height of summer break."

"Me too," Josh said, raising their entwined hands to kiss the back of Courtney's. "Seems we're well suited to each other."

Courtney's heart took off like a quarter horse at the races. She took a deep breath as she looked down the path at Russell's foxlike tail poking above the deep green ferns rather than at Josh's open face and adoring eyes. This was a lot. And fast. Maybe they should have waited. "So. Where do we go from here?"

"I think we just continue down this path, following Russell," Josh said, the tone of his voice oddly light.

Courtney turned to look at Josh, quirking a brow. "That's not what I was asking."

Josh stopped on the path, squeezing her hand lightly. "I know, Court. I'm just afraid to say it out loud as if it might evaporate in the light of day."

Courtney's heart squeezed. "I'm not that flaky."

"No. I know you're not." Josh looked down at the ground for a moment, then back up at Courtney.

His face was so open, so vulnerable. It took Courtney's breath away. Did she feel the same way about him? What if he wanted more than she could give?

"Court, I've wanted this with you since I was sixteen. It feels fragile at the moment, like you're a butterfly perched on a flower that will alight if I get too close. I'm afraid that I'll ruin things again."

Courtney could hear her heart beating in the hush of the forest. Fear gripped her, and she felt nauseous. She needed to move and started walking, Josh gripping her hand so she wouldn't slip away. They walked in silence, Courtney's mind reeling. She wanted Josh too but was also realizing that she needed to be her own person too. Nathan had forced her to bury that girl, and this year in Port Russell, especially yesterday, she'd slowly, shovel by shovel, begun to uncover herself. If she got involved with Josh, would she lose herself again? They entered the clearing with their tree house, and the answer crystallized in her mind.

She walked to the bottom of the ladder and gently pulled her hand out of Josh's grip, turning to face him. He looked like someone readying himself to face the firing squad.

"It's not so bad as that," Courtney reassured him, and he let out the breath he was holding.

"But it isn't what I want to hear, either."

"Maybe, maybe not. I don't really know what you have in mind."

At this, Josh quirked an eyebrow. "I thought I demonstrated quite clearly what I wanted last night."

"I agree. It was a clear and amazing demonstration, by the way. I'm talking about all the rest of it. The relationship part," Courtney said.

Josh nodded, moving to lean against the tree trunk next to her.

"You are my best friend, still, after all these years. I've never felt as easy with anyone else in my whole life. I don't want to lose that."

"Me neither, Court," Josh said, reaching for her hand again. "Friends first and always."

Courtney chewed her lip, deciding how much she wanted to tell Josh. His clear blue gaze convinced her. "I told you a bit about Nathan. But, it was worse than I let on." Courtney felt Josh stiffen. "It was an emotionally abusive relationship. I thought I came home because he cheated on me, but once I got some distance from him, I began to see how he'd eroded my sense of self. I lost myself, Josh. I don't want to do that again."

"I won't let you, Court. I love you."

Courtney's stomach did a slow roll. He loved her? Was she ready to say the same to him?

"I don't want to change you. I want us to be partners. To collaborate on our relationship."

Courtney nodded, struggling to take a breath. "I know. I trust you. I just don't trust myself."

"If I ever get my hands on Nathan," Josh said, a fierce grimace on his face, and Courtney felt a surge of love for him.

"I want to be in a place where I'm the one who gets her hands on him, do you understand?"

Josh studied her, reaching over a hand to tuck a stray hair behind her ear. "I do. I know you'll get there. Can you trust me to walk with you?"

Courtney's heart stopped, then started with a thud. "Yes," she whispered. "But, we'll have to take it slow, okay? Well, slower," she said, her lips quirking in a crooked smile.

Joy, like the sun rising over the horizon, bloomed on Josh's face. "Slower. You got it." He leaned over and kissed her soundly, sending electricity dancing up and down her spine.

They called for Russell and walked back to the cottage, hand in hand. Courtney made Josh a to-go mug of coffee and rustled up a protein bar for him while he jumped in the shower.

"Are you sure I can't make you a real breakfast," she said, handing them to Josh. "I can't see how you can function on this alone."

"It's okay. I have to get Russell back to my place before I head over to the detachment. I'll grab something more substantial later."

"Russell can stay here with me," Courtney said, and Russell, napping on the mat in front of her sink, opened one eye to peer at her.

"Really? That would be great. I hate leaving him on his own." Josh leaned over and smooched Courtney. "Russell, be a good boy." Russell answered by thumping his tail on the floor twice. "Court, I don't want to put a damper on the morning."

"Damper?"

"Please, at least for today, stay away from the protest site."

Courtney's eyebrows raised in surprise.

"I want to have a conversation with you about it. Until then, could you stay away?"

Irritation flared briefly, but Courtney considered what he was asking. He'd asked her to collaborate. That meant compromise. "Okay. I'll stay away today, and I'll have that conversation, but I don't think I want to stay away indefinitely."

Josh nodded. "Thanks." He squeezed her hand. "See you later?"

Courtney smiled. "It's a date."

CHAPTER 23

Courtney leaned over the fire table on the deck and lit the last candle, the effect somewhat dimmed by the sun hanging out above the trees. It was too warm to light the fire, so she thought the romantic flickering of candles would create a nice ambience in the dusky evening light. Effervescent nerves were bubbling up in her stomach as she looked at her watch again. She smoothed back wisps of her wavy brunette hair in a loose braid because of the heat and checked her reflection in the patio door as she went into the manor to finish the salad. She had a deep purple bruise blooming on her right arm, but it was way too warm for long sleeves. Maybe the dress, a cute little floral minidress, was too much? She checked out her toned legs in the glass and smiled.

"What do you think, Russell? Dress or shorts?"

Russell lifted his head off his paws for a moment but slumped back down immediately.

"You're no help."

Courtney decided she'd be more comfortable in shorts and made it to the mudroom door when she heard a vehicle pull up. Shoot. She'd dithered too long. She opened the door and called out to Josh, who was walking over to her cottage.

"We're in the big house tonight—Gram has a better kitchen."

Josh pivoted and doubled back, his face lighting up when his gaze landed on Courtney. When he got closer, Courtney saw his hair was damp, and he had a brown-paper-wrapped bottle in his hand. He leaned in for a kiss.

"Mmm, I've been thinking about kissing you all day," he rumbled. "You look amazing."

"Thanks, so do you." Courtney could smell eucalyptus and mint, likely Josh's soap, over his natural salt-sea musk. A fire ignited, low in her belly, thinking about running her hands over his chest and through his damp curls. "Russell and I prepared dinner."

"Russell helped you? That'd be a first." Josh chuckled as he stroked her hand with a thumb as they walked hand in hand to the kitchen.

"We had a great day, didn't we?" Courtney asked her furry companion, who was wiggling a welcome for his person. Josh let go of her hand and set the bottle on the counter so he could crouch down and give his dog a belly rub. "We watered, weeded, and went for a run. He helped in the kitchen by taking a nap."

"Lucky boy," Josh said, standing to retrieve the bottle. "I brought you some wine. I was hoping to bring flowers, but the flower shop was closed by the time I got off duty."

"Aww, thanks." Courtney pulled the bottle out of the bag. "Champagne?"

"I wanted to celebrate. I hope it goes with dinner."

Courtney laughed. "I'm sure it will. Can you open it? I don't have the knack."

Josh worked on peeling the foil and metal cage around the cork then twisted until a small pop and fizz signaled the release of the cork as Courtney retrieved some flutes out of the china cabinet.

"I'm impressed. I'd probably have sent that thing ricocheting around the room." She handed him the glasses. "You head out to the patio. I'll be right out with dinner."

Courtney retrieved the salad out of the fridge and set it on the tray with the chips, plates, and condiments, carrying everything out and setting it on the table. The sun had finally dipped below the trees, and the candlelight flickered romantically in the growing dusk.

"It's magical out here with the candles," Josh said, grabbing Courtney's hand. "Sit for a second. I want to make a toast."

Courtney's stomach flipped over, and she willed her stiff shoulders to relax. He said he'd take it slow. Fingers cold, she took the glass, focusing on the golden bubbles racing to the surface along the sides of the fine crystal flute.

"Here's to old friends and new journeys." Josh raised his glass.

Courtney let out the breath she'd been holding and raised her glass, hand shaking slightly, the glasses ringing a clear note when they tapped them together. Courtney took a sip. The bubbles tickled her nose and lips as the toast and citrus notes of the champagne danced on her tongue.

Josh lowered his glass. "Is something wrong? You're really quiet."

"No," Courtney said, leaning over to squeeze his hand. "I was a bit worried about what you were going to say."

"I promised I'd take it slow. You have to promise me you'll tell me if I'm pushing you too fast. Okay?"

Courtney met Josh's eyes, candlelight setting gold highlights in their sea of blue. "Okay." Courtney set her glass down. "Ready to eat?"

"God, yes. I'll be plastered if I drink any more of this without anything to soak it up."

"Help yourself to salad. I'll grab the main off the barbecue." She returned with a platter of hot dogs.

Josh laughed. "You remembered."

"Hard to forget. I think Gram went through two or three dozen packages of hot dogs a week that summer. She was worried for you."

"They are still my kryptonite, though I ration myself a bit more these days."

"I even splashed out for the gourmet all beef dogs," Courtney said, waggling her eyebrows. "Only the best for my man." As soon as it was out of her mouth, she regretted it. Way to take it slow, Courtney.

Josh ignored the comment and asked her to pass the mustard, and Courtney was grateful. They ate and laughed, and Russell showed off his best tricks for a couple of pieces of hot dog. The sun set, and the Edison bulb lights flicked on overhead, reminding Courtney of their dinner in Victoria. Her head buzzed after multiple glasses of champagne, and Josh invited her to snuggle with him on the love seat.

"Only if you want to," he added, his eyes reminding her a lot of Russell's as he'd watched them eating.

"I am getting a bit chilly." She curled up next to Josh. He draped his arm over her shoulders, his warmth radiating through her thin summer dress. She closed her eyes to soak in the delicious moment.

After a few blissful minutes of silence, Josh cleared his throat, causing Courtney to stiffen again. "Hey, don't worry, I'm not making another toast." He paused for a breath. "I saw Justin again today." She felt the rumble of his voice.

"Oh. Where?"

"At Cedar Sands. I had to run over to get a clean uniform shirt, and he was sitting on the porch of his unit at the opposite end from mine."

"I can't believe he's staying there. I'd have thought it was beneath him."

"Probably not his first choice. The extra press, police, and protesters from the mainland have created a bit of an accommodation crunch in town."

"Aren't the protesters sleeping in their vans and camping?" Courtney remembered all the vehicles parked in the grocery store lot and the no-vacancy signs up on the local campgrounds.

"Some, but there's been an influx of new protesters, mostly retired people, to bolster the main group the Old Growth Guardians have in place."

"Did you hear anything more about the hearings for Dissidence and Alex?"

"They go before the judge first thing Monday morning. I imagine they'll be back in town by early afternoon."

"Really? Even Alex?"

"The Guardians have their own legal counsel on staff. She's a bit of a pit bull, I've been told. They'll be released on bail. It'll take months for the charges to wind their way through court, and if they plead guilty, the judge will move directly to sentencing. That's when the fun really begins."

"Fun? What do you mean?"

"They will be given strict instructions to stay off the site, so if they show up, we'll have to arrest them every single time." Josh sounded weary.

"Why all these games? It seems a stupid waste of resources. No one, especially the Pacheedaaht, wants the old growth logged. I don't understand why the government hasn't changed the laws to better reflect what people want. Gramps said there were some changes after the Clayoquot Sound protests in the nineties, but it didn't really go far enough. Why push through a project so many people are opposed to?"

"Money." Josh sighed. "I didn't just see Justin. He saw me and ambushed me in the parking lot."

Courtney turned her head to look at Josh, his eyes sad. He absently stroked her arm, raising goosebumps everywhere he touched. "You know how he always liked to gloat about how much better than me he is. He still believes he's the golden child. He let slip Dad's made him CEO, so all the profits are in his name. But, it also means he's the one Dad will leave holding the bag if things go south."

Courtney sat up. "What profits? I thought the development was just in the planning phase?"

"They're openly advertising a luxury resort along the shore of Gnome Lake—an exclusive gated hotel with a hundred units and a gourmet restaurant. My friend in white-collar crime received a tip and is investigating. They think Dad is involved in real estate fraud. Why am I related to such a douchebag?"

Courtney caught the singular. "So which one is the douchebag?"

"My Dad. Justin doesn't do anything of his own accord. Justin is doing this in a bid to impress Dad, as always. Get approval he's never going to get. My dad is a narcissist. He's only in it for himself. It took me a long time, and therapy, to come to terms with the way I was raised. Every day, I fight against the feeling I'll never measure up." Josh sighed, and Courtney squeezed his hand to show her support. "I feel guilty for getting out and leaving Mom and Justin behind. Dad is using Justin, and he can't, or won't, see it."

Courtney twisted out of Josh's arms to perch on the edge of the love seat, facing him, her mind calculating. "I know you're not a fan of me going to the protest site."

Josh's face turned to stone.

"Hear me out." Courtney raised a hand, and he softened slightly. "You can't investigate your brother or your dad until you have some solid evidence. Wouldn't an admission of a relationship between Justin and the leader of the group protesting give you probable cause to look into a conflict of interest?"

Josh pursed his lips. "It might."

"I don't really know why he's playing both sides, but I'm willing to bet Dissidence has no idea either. If she finds out, her anger may compel her to sick her pit bull lawyer on Justin's lying ass." Courtney gave a grim smile when the vision of Justin cowering against his stupid Porsche while a high-powered lawyer served him with papers popped into her head. "At the very least, we could make him uncomfortable. Make him think about his involvement. At best, I might find something out that could really help you get at the root of the problem."

Josh rubbed his hands over his face. "Court, I don't know. It's only going to get rougher out there. The Old Growth Guardians are known for their extreme protest tactics and the police response—" He stopped short, clearly skirting a line he couldn't cross professionally.

"I'm a big girl," Courtney reminded him. "I promise not to take any unnecessary risks. But I want to do this. For myself *and* for Port Russell. "

"I hate this part of my job sometimes, Court. I don't want guys like my dad and Justin to win, but I have a professional duty to uphold the law."

"I know," Courtney said, taking his hand.

"I have one condition," Josh said, looking her directly in the eye. "If I find out all hell is going to break loose, you have to promise me you'll leave, no questions asked."

Courtney swallowed, a flicker of fear igniting in her chest. "Wouldn't that information be confidential? I don't want to get you in trouble."

"I don't want to see you get hurt." The flicker grew to a steady flame when Courtney saw the fear in Josh's eyes.

"I promise. If you tell me to leave, I'll leave."

CHAPTER 24

Josh spent a second night with Courtney, cuddling this time, then helped her weed and water the vegetable garden before leaving for work. As they worked, joking and chatting just like they did when they were kids, it struck Courtney how similar they were to her grandparents when they worked in the garden together. Gramps would tease Gram, and they always had lots to talk about. They enjoyed each other's company, even after fifty-plus years together. Courtney told herself not to get ahead of herself. Despite their newfound extra-curricular activities, she and Josh were still friends, and Courtney wanted it to stay that way. Josh was too important to her to lose. She'd asked him to take it slow. She had to abide by that, too.

She tidied her cottage, taking some laundry over to the manor house and reading on the patio as she waited for the load to finish in the washer so she could hang it out to dry. She found she missed Russell's presence. Glancing at her watch, she grabbed her phone and dialed Gram, swinging her legs over the arm of the love seat and settling back into the pillows, watching wispy white marine clouds scud across the bright blue sky.

"Courtney! Good morning, love," Gram answered. "What trouble have you scrounged up on this lovely July Monday?"

Courtney recalled the kiss Josh had planted on her before he left, her face flushing. "No trouble for me today, Gram, just chores. Got up early to water the garden. Now I'm doing some laundry."

"No hot date last night?" Gram teased.

Courtney scowled. Did someone see Josh drive out here? Did Gram suspect something, or was she just playing matchmaker again? Courtney's heart thumped in her chest. She wasn't ready to share her relationship status with anyone yet, if it was, in fact, anything other than friendship. It was too fragile. She took a deep breath. "You know I'm not that kind of girl, Gram."

Her grandmother harrumphed. "A grandma can hope. You haven't just been gardening and reading, I hope. Hey, how was your trip to Victoria? We were sorry we missed your call. It would have been nice to meet up with you and Josh."

Courtney had thought she might keep her road trip a secret from her grandparents, but when she chatted with her mother on the phone the night before she left, Jill had disabused her of that notion with one word. Marilyn. Gram would definitely hear it from her best friend, so Courtney had called her grandparents when she'd been waiting for Josh on the hotel balcony.

Recalling the romantic afternoons she'd spent with Josh, Courtney was glad they'd not been able to meet up. "Um, it was nice. We went to the legislature for the Canada Day festivities. Had fish tacos at Fisherman's Wharf. It was nice to have a little adventure."

"Speaking of adventure, a little birdie told me you've taken up a new cause."

"A little birdie called Marilyn?" Courtney asked, rolling her eyes.

"Who else?" Gram laughed. "She mentioned Alex took you up to the protest site the other day. How did that go?"

Did she really not know? "Um, I got arrested."

Gram laughed. "That a girl! Good for you!"

Courtney shook her head. Only her grandmother would find that a good thing.

"How are things going with the talks?"

Gram let out a sigh. "Slowly. If certain people would just butt out, it would go much faster."

"Who's causing the delay?"

"Ugh, Marc Welton, our esteemed MLA."

Courtney chuckled. "Is that sarcasm I detect?"

"Sarcasm from me? Never," Gram replied, her smile evident even over the phone. "He's just got a lot to say, most of it unhelpful."

"Huh, that's weird," Courtney said. "Isn't he supposed to be representing his constituents?"

Her cell phone binged, an unfamiliar number popping up on her screen. Scowling, Courtney tapped on the notification to open the text.

Hey Courtney, it's Dissidence. I got your number from Alex, hope you don't mind. I was wondering if you wanted to meet me for coffee tomorrow?

She heard Gramps's voice in the background but couldn't make out what he was saying. "Is that Gramps? Say hi for me."

"I will, love. He was letting me know he managed to make a ferry reservation. We're going to head into the Interior for a few days to visit some old friends. Can you manage the garden for a few days? Maybe invite Josh over to help and make him dinner?"

Courtney sighed. "Honestly, Gram, you're relentless! Yes, I can manage the garden. You two have fun. When do you think you'll be back?"

"Likely next Saturday. Promise me you'll at least try to have some fun?"

"I will," Courtney said, her nighttime endeavors over the last few days playing in her mind. She blushed. "Drive safe, Gram. Love you."

"Love you too, Courtney," Gram said, making a kissing sound into the phone before hanging up.

Courtney swung her legs over and sat straight, stretching. She re-read Dissidence's text and considered the invitation. It felt a bit out of the blue, but then, they had spent the better part of a day holding hands. I guess that made them friends? Courtney was pretty curious about how things had gone in court. She guessed Dissidence was out on bail if she'd texted. If they were friends, maybe she could ask about more personal things, like who Dissidence kissed when she wasn't busy protesting and how she managed to pay for things when she hadn't been teaching for a full year—solid links to fraud or collusion to take back to Josh. Courtney typed her response.

That'd be great. What time did you have in mind?

The dots blinked as Dissidence read and responded.

Two okay? Do you know a good place? I haven't spent much time in Port Russell proper.

Courtney laughed. That was an understatement. Though, she wasn't one to talk. Danielle must have invited her to go for coffee half a dozen times before she gave up on Courtney and stuck to chatting over the photocopier. Maybe going undercover as a gal pal was going to be tougher than she'd thought. Courtney pursed her lips. Yet another thing Nathan had managed to erode from her life. He'd always been jealous when she'd done things with her friends and not him. Eventually, she'd just stopped going to avoid his barbed comments and sulking, and ergo her lack of friends and friendship skills.

The White Raven Coffee House near the post office is nice. They roast their own coffee and have killer cinnamon buns. Meet you there?

"Or, so I've heard," Courtney muttered.

Dissidence responded with the thumbs-up emoji. She had a coffee date. The washer buzzed, so Courtney wandered in to retrieve the laundry. As she hung the load on the clothesline, she realized she was a little nervous. What should she wear? What would they talk about? It had been easy while they were protesting—this seemed so much harder somehow. How should she broach the subject of Justin? It's not like she could come out and ask if he was paying her to protest. She'd give herself away. Maybe she wasn't cut out to be a spy.

"Geesh, get a grip," Courtney said, snapping out a pillow case, the light scent of clean linen filling the air before Courtney draped it over the line and set clothespins on the corners. "It's supposed to be coffee, not the inquisition."

It was a few minutes past two when she parked the Subaru in a spot down the block from the coffeehouse. Damn. She'd dithered about what to wear—seriously, she was out of practice with this whole socializing thing—settling on a pair of ankle-length jeans and a soft green V-neck T-shirt. Her third outfit. It turned out she owned workout clothes and teacher clothes and not a lot in between. If she ended up going on dates with Josh, she was going to have to do some shopping. She pulled the door open, and the alarm chimed. Dissidence had grabbed a spot in the back, and she raised a hand in greeting.

Kelli Dunbar, the owner, gave a surprised wave and raised an eyebrow when Courtney sat down with the very conspicuous Dissidence but didn't say a thing when she came over to take Courtney's order.

"Hey, Courtney. Good to see you. How's your break so far?" A couple of years older than Courtney, Kelli was an active parent at the school, her twins just having finished Grade 1.

"Good, so far. How about you?"

"Counting the days till school's back in," Kelli said with a laugh.

Courtney smiled in commiseration. The twins were a handful, according to their teacher. "I'll take a London Fog and a cinnamon bun if you have them."

"You're in luck. There's a few left today." Kelli turned to Dissidence. "You okay? Need more hot water?"

Dissidence opened the lid to the small teapot, the earthy scent of green tea wafting across the table. "No, I'm good. If there's a second cinnamon bun, I'll take it."

Kelli nodded and hustled back behind the counter to work on the orders.

"I've been trying to convince myself to be good, but you've twisted my rubber arm."

"Sorry," Courtney said.

Dissidence laughed, the sound low and throaty. "I'm not."

Kelli arrived with their buns and Courtney's beverage. "Enjoy. Let me know if you need anything else."

Courtney tried to ignore Kelli's open stare of curiosity. She wasn't doing anything wrong. Not really. Before her mind dove into the rabbit warren of worry, barely buried by the thin veneer of lipgloss Courtney had put on to make it look like she'd made an effort, she cleared her throat.

"Sorry I was late."

"No worries. I don't have much else planned for today. Quiet day at the site, at least on our side, and the lawyers told me to lie low for a bit."

"So. How was court?"

Dissidence popped part of the outer rim of her cinnamon bun into her mouth and raised a finger, closing her eyes and moaning in ecstasy. Courtney's eyebrows shot up, and she peered around to see if anyone else was noticing Dissidence's reaction.

"That will be so worth the guilt." At Courtney's perplexed expression, she explained. "I've been vegan for the better part of the last year. This is so not vegan, and it shows."

Kelli poked her head over the bar, concerned, and Dissidence gave her the thumbs up. "This is the best cinnamon bun I think I've ever had. Bravo!"

Kelli waved her thanks and disappeared again.

Courtney pinched off a bit of bun and slipped it into her mouth. "Holy crap! You weren't kidding!" The bread was soft and yeasty, the cinnamon sugar heavy on the cinnamon and just the right amount of sweet. No wonder the whole staff at Port Russell elementary was so obsessed with this place. Courtney was mad at herself for not taking Danielle up on her many invitations. The two women unwound a bit more of their pastries and ate in silence, Courtney desperately trying to figure out how to steer the conversation in the right direction.

Dissidence pushed her plate away. "I want to pace myself." She poured herself some more tea, cupping her hands around the hand-thrown pottery tea cup. "Court was court. Our lawyer got me released on bail. It'll be months before I have to go face the judge again, though our legal team may decide to plead not guilty and draw out the process a bit."

"So what does that mean for you? I mean, do you have to stay away from the site now?"

Dissidence sipped her tea, chuckling after she'd swallowed. "Not a chance of that happening. Just means I'll likely be charged every time I'm arrested. Likely means more time in jail for me. But, that's what I signed up for."

Maybe that was what she was hired to do—divert attention away from the real estate shenanigans. Courtney took a sip of her creamy tea latte, the bergamot of the Earl Grey filling her nose and coating her tongue. "That must be hard on your loved ones."

A scowl, like the clouds obscuring the sun on a summer afternoon, passed over Dissidence's face before she schooled herself. "My parents and I don't really see eye to eye on a lot of things. Environmental activism isn't really seen as a great career in the eyes of Chinese parents. Heck, they'd only just gotten over me choosing to teach over becoming a lawyer. My boyfriend's cool with it, though."

Jackpot!

"Boyfriend?" Courtney prayed her voice was more girls-out-for-coffee than detective-interrogating-a-suspect. "What's he like? What's his name?"

A slow, dreamy smile transformed Dissidence's face again, her chocolate brown eyes twinkling with what Courtney hoped wasn't desire but feared definitely was. "He lives in Victoria. We're really different, but that's kind of what makes it hot, I think. It's pretty new. I should probably stop talking before I jinx it."

Dissidence had dodged her question regarding her boyfriend's name. Courtney's gut burbled with a stab of fear. She had to keep her talking. "Yeah. I know what you mean. I've just started seeing someone too."

Dissidence raised an eyebrow, suddenly interested. "Do tell."

Courtney was suddenly so glad she could tell someone about Josh. Even though, on the one hand, she was afraid, on the other, she wanted to shout out that she wasn't going to die an old maid after all.

"He's an old friend. We recently reconnected. It's pretty new."

"But pretty good, too. Right?" Dissidence smiled at Courtney over the rim of her mug.

"Yeah. It is." Courtney was surprised at how easy it was to admit. Dissidence was easy to talk to, she'd better be careful, or she was going to give too much away. God, she was a terrible spy. "I moved back to town this past fall after a bad breakup. It's nice to be with someone who values me. Is it like that with your guy?"

Dissidence tore off another tiny piece of cinnamon bun and placed it on her tongue like a communion wafer. "Yeah, I think so. He listens to what I have to say. We're collaborating on a project together."

Courtney choked a bit on the mouthful of London Fog and was just about to press Dissidence for details when the door chimed.

Dissidence hissed.

"Look, it's one of our friendly neighborhood RCMP officers. Hello Constable Cameron!" Dissidence called out, waving. Courtney, sitting with her back to the door, sensed Josh's eyes on her back and froze in place, her eyes firmly focused on her cinnamon bun. She silently willed Josh to ignore her.

"Ms. Liu," Josh said, continuing on to the counter.

Gratitude rolled off Courtney in waves. She heard him order a large Americano, then the whine of the espresso machine as Kelli pulled the shot for his order.

Dissidence pitched her voice low, leaning toward Courtney. "Must be super weird for you, being arrested by your local cops."

"You have no idea," Courtney said, burying her face in her latte.

The door chimed again as Josh left, and Courtney let out the breath she'd been holding.

"I have to come clean," Dissidence started, and hope inflated like a balloon in Courtney's chest. Maybe she was more convincing as a spy than she thought she was.

"Oh, why?"

"I was really hoping to convince you to come out again. I was super impressed with your moxie and conviction the other day. I could really use someone like you up there supporting me. What do you say? Will you come to the dark side? We have vegan chocolate-chip cookies. I'm also drowning in testosterone." Dissidence waggled her brows like a cartoon villain.

Courtney felt the hope deflate somewhat. She needed to be patient. It was an opportunity to spend more time with the professional protestor. Maybe she could get her talking about the project she and Justin were working on, wrangle a confession out of Dissidence. "Sure. I'd like to help out, but only if you bring me cinnamon buns. I don't do vegan cookies."

Dissidence laughed, holding out her hand. "Deal."

CHAPTER 25

Courtney agreed to head back to the blockade with Dissidence on Saturday, as the petite protestor planned on lying low for a few days with her mysterious boyfriend in Victoria. Sitting in her Subaru after her coffee date, Courtney texted Josh with all the information she'd gathered so far and was secretly pleased when he invited her over for dinner and a paddle. She'd realized as she talked to her mom the other day she was getting lonely, rattling around at the manor all by herself.

"Are you taking advantage of having the place to yourself?" Carolyn had asked, clearly fishing.

Memories of hot dogs on the patio with Josh popped up. They were friends. It wouldn't be weird to say he'd been over, but something had stopped Courtney. If she told her mom, there'd be no going back to "just friends."

"No. Just enjoying some people-free time, Mom."

Carolyn had sighed. *"Please don't spend the entire summer alone, Court."*

So she accepted Josh's invitation.

Cedar Sands was bustling, with several groups gathered on front porches and on the beach, making the most of the beautiful summer weather. Courtney couldn't remember the last time they'd gone without real rain in Port Russell for this long—two weeks and counting. She stepped up to Josh's door, hearing voices on the other side. She knocked, and Josh, phone to his ear, a harried look on his face, yanked the door open. He held up a finger as Russell waggled over for some love. Courtney crouched to give his downy head a kiss.

"Look, I can't talk right now." Josh gave a sigh of frustration, glancing over at Courtney. "Not now, Ash. I'll call you tomorrow." He paused. "Tomorrow," he declared, a strange edge to his voice.

Not a work call, then. Curious, Courtney raised her brow when Josh canceled the call. He seemed pretty upset with this Ash. Why was he acting so weird? "I can come back if you need to deal with something. Russell and I can go for a wander on the beach." Russell's ears perked at the "W" word.

"No. It can wait." Josh extended a hand and pulled Courtney to standing. "It is so good to see you." He leaned in for a kiss, his soft lips making Courtney's tingle with remembrance. She realized the door was still open and pulled away.

"Someone might see."

"So? You embarrassed to be seen with me?" Josh said, tone not quite as light as it should be.

Courtney flushed. Was she embarrassed? "No. I just don't want to blow my cover. You know how fast news travels in Port Russell."

Josh laughed. "Courtney the spy. I hate to tell you, but the whole town knows we're friends."

Courtney's flush deepened. "Sure, but they don't know about this." She spun her hand around, linking them together.

"Maybe they should."

Courtney's heart thumped in her chest, and her mouth drained itself dry. "Josh, I don't know." She found she couldn't look him in the eye, afraid to see hurt in their blue-gray depths, so she focused on his toned pecs, which only brought up the mental image of them sheened in sweat following their exertions the other day. Josh reached forward and lifted her chin with a light finger, sighing.

"Court, I promised we'd take it slow. I'm only proposing a date. In public. No public declarations of love. Is that too fast for you?"

The room spun for her, and she clutched his forearm to steady herself. There was that word again. Love. Anxiety burst like an angry thunderhead in her core. Russell whimpered at her feet and rubbed against her bare leg, a furry anchor. Bless his heart. Courtney forced herself to speak past her suddenly numb lips. "What kind of date?"

"One of my neighbours invited me to the beach for beers and a fire. Super casual, mostly out-of-towners. What do you think?"

Courtney made the mistake of looking at Josh, his face laid bare with hopeful anticipation. How could she disappoint him? Why was this so hard?

He was easy to spend time with. Gentle, kind, and patient. He knew her. The true, pre-Nathan her. Say yes, Courtney, she told herself sternly. It's just a beer, not an engagement. Courtney nodded, and Josh smiled, radiant in the early evening sun.

"Have a seat on the porch. I'm almost done prepping the salad."

"Salad? How did you get so buff eating salad?"

Josh laughed, cheeks growing pink at Courtney's compliment. "It's a necessary balance to all the crap I eat when I'm on duty. I'll be right out."

Josh disappeared into the cottage, closing the door to keep the bugs and Russell out of the kitchen.

Courtney sank into one of the deck chairs, legs still trembling following Josh's accidental declaration. If he was in love with her, maybe she should call it quits right now. He deserved someone who could love him freely—without baggage. She'd never forgive herself if he got hurt because she was such a mess. Lost in thought, she startled when she heard a voice come from the path to her left.

Justin.

Courtney rolled her eyes. Absolutely bloody perfect.

"Better be careful. You know this town is full of gossips," Justin said, the smirk on his face setting Courtney's blood boiling. "You seem to spend a lot of time with my dear little bro."

Courtney narrowed her eyes at Justin. Russell, ruff raised, was growling, a deep low buzzing sound. Justin had always been like this, pushing buttons and creating havoc in his wake. Courtney was irritated that he could still get her going. "Piss off, Justin. Don't you have some trees to cut down? It's okay, Russell." She laid a hand on Russell's bristling hackles.

Justin laughed without humour, glaring at Russell when the growling grew stronger. "Touchy, touchy. You'd think you'd be in a better mood, given your recent activities."

A bell rang in Courtney's head, clearing away some of the anger. She'd told exactly one person about Josh. Dissidence. Had Justin just confirmed their relationship? Had he meant to? Courtney schooled her face. She didn't want to give Justin any clue that she was onto him.

Justin placed his arms on the balustrade, leaning forward, and Russell let out a sharp warning bark that caused Justin to step back. "Word of advice from one old friend to another."

Courtney snorted at his description. Old friends, her ass.

"Little bro isn't as available as he makes himself out to be."

What the hell did that mean? She flashed back to the look on Josh's face when he'd answered the phone earlier, and her stomach squeezed. The door rattled open, and Justin stepped back as Josh exited.

"What the fuck are you doing here?" Josh growled, holding a giant bowl of salad in one hand and a bottle of wine in the other.

"Just shooting the breeze with Courtney here. So fun to be back in Port Russell. Mom made me promise I'd make nice. She wants you to come to the shareholders meeting next month, being a major stakeholder and all."

Josh still owned stock in CFI? The look of glee on Justin's trendily stubbled face turned the heat up on Courtney's anger again, making it simmer. Same old Justin, reveling in the chaos he created.

"Leave," Josh demanded, his anger, a heady spice, rolling off of him in waves. Courtney also saw guilt and hurt in his eyes. It would be so hard to have to deal with such a toxic family dynamic. Russell circled back to lean against Josh, whimpering.

Justin waggled his fingers. "Later, losers. Don't do anything I wouldn't do, little bro." Then, laughing, Justin disappeared behind the cottage.

Josh set the salad and wine down, his hands trembling, face stricken. "I forgot glasses," he said, pivoting and disappearing again, Russell glued to his heels.

"What the hell?" Courtney muttered. That was weird, even for the Cameron brothers. Questions swirled as she processed the little drama she'd just witnessed. What had Justin meant about Josh not being available? Was there someone else? Courtney recalled the phone call she'd walked in on. Was he talking to another woman? And why hadn't he said anything about his shares in the company?

Josh reappeared with two glasses and a corkscrew.

"Josh," Courtney started.

He held up a hand. "Can we not, just for now?" Josh's voice wavered. "I want to forget about him, just for tonight. Please."

Cold dread snaked down the back of Courtney's neck. Something was going on, she was sure, but Josh rarely asked her for anything. He was barely keeping it together, his trembling hands giving him away. He needed a friend right now, not a million questions. What was the harm in leaving it for one night?

"Okay," she said reluctantly, the words sour in her mouth. "But we'll talk about it, right?"

Relief washed over Josh's face. "Yes. I promise. I've got some stuff to sort out first."

She knew a thing or two about baggage. He'd asked her to collaborate. That meant give and take. "You sort, then we'll talk about it."

Josh opened the wine, the cork releasing with a pop, and poured Courtney a glass of the straw-coloured pinot grigio. He tapped her glass with his and then took a gulp himself. Russell settled with a sigh at Courtney's feet.

"Okay, back to date mode. Dig in, please."

Courtney swallowed her mouthful of crisp wine, the tang of cold tropical fruit sliding down her throat, and looked over to see two forks resting on the salad, a tantalizing mix of fresh greens, cucumber, dill, and salmon. "Um, this is an interesting way to serve a salad. You know it's customary to provide plates or bowls?"

"Why? We can share," Josh grinned at her and speared a piece of the dill-flavoured salmon.

"You have clearly been a bachelor for too long. Gram would die if she saw this." Courtney dug into the salad.

The sun sank closer to the horizon, the afternoon sun weakening to molten gold, and whispers of the coming sunset set whisps of marine cloud alight in shades of orange and pink. They ate in silence, Courtney not entirely able to slip into date mode until Josh's neighbour walked by, a case of beer under his arm, and several friends in tow.

"Heading down to light the fire. You still coming, mate?" he called, his accent outing him as Australian as he trudged on the beach in front of the cottage.

Josh looked at Courtney, his eyebrow quirking in question.

She nodded, relieved. It would be better to have other people around tonight. Justin's conversation and Josh's weird reaction were niggling her mind. She needed the distraction, or she'd end up pushing Josh, even though she'd promised him time to sort stuff out.

"Sounds great, man. Thanks for the invite. Be there in a few."

The Aussie waved and trudged toward the fire pit his friends had gathered around.

"He and his girlfriend are touring the coast after a season working at Big White. They're a cool couple," Josh explained, sipping his wine. "You're sure, you're sure?" he asked, nervously chewing at his upper lip. "We can go for a moonlit paddle or just hang out here if you want."

"No. I said I'd go," Courtney said, horrified at the tone of her voice. She took a breath and then smiled to remove some of the sting. "Gram will be proud of me—I have plans on a weeknight with people my own age."

Josh nodded, his mouth smiling while his eyes were guarded. They finished their dinner, Josh putting the remains of their shared salad in the cottage and returning with a six-pack of beer from the local brewery. "Never go to a party empty-handed. I learned that from your Gramps."

"Sounds about right," Courtney said.

Josh extended a hand, and slowly, Courtney took it, allowing Josh to pull her toward the beach. Butterflies fluttered among the salad, and her steps faltered. Josh looked back at her.

"Don't worry, Court. You can do this." He squeezed her hand.

Courtney straightened, schooling her anxiety. She could. While never the life of the party, at one point, she'd been friendly, outgoing even, when she wanted to be. She could be that again. She just needed more practice. Russell was back to his perky self, racing ahead of them toward the group knotted around a now blazing fire.

The Aussies, Lachlan and Fiona, the mainland couple staying in the cottage next to Josh, and a couple of young guys they'd befriended while hiking earlier that day, were delightful. Funny and conversational, they made it easy to enjoy their company, and Courtney laughed freely, marveling at how comfortable it was to be with Josh. Every once in a while, he'd take her hand or rub her back, letting her chat with the others without making demands of her attention or shooting her jealous looks like Nathan used to. She found herself relaxing, though she could sense the undercurrent of Justin's warning flowing through her subconscious.

The group broke up at about eleven, the Aussies and their young hiking friends planning to meet up for a hike in Sooke Potholes Provincial Park the next day on Courtney's recommendation. They exchanged numbers and said their good nights, heading to their cottage. Josh held out his hand and wound his fingers with Courtney's.

He cleared his throat. "You're welcome to stay with me tonight." He looked into her eyes, trying and failing to keep expectation off his face.

Courtney's stomach squeezed. She wanted to stay, but. But. Justin's warning, intended to create problems, rang in her head. Damn him. "I think I'm going to head home." She thought about lying to Josh, saying she had early plans with Dissidence, but changed her mind at the last minute.

Josh squeezed her hand. "Yes. Of course." He lifted their twinned hands and kissed the back of her hand. "I'm a little disappointed, not going to lie. But I get it. We'll walk you to your car." Josh called Russell, and they trudged through the sand to the parking lot. The clear sky above was an indigo carpet of stars, so close Courtney felt she might be able to reach up and brush the velvet of the milky way.

She opened her car door and turned toward Josh, standing on tiptoe to brush her lips against his. "Thanks. I had fun."

"I'm glad," he said, running his hands down her arms, leaving an electric trail in their wake. "Drive safe. Come on, Russ, time for bed."

Courtney slid into the driver's side and leaned over to slide her key into the ignition. When she looked up, she saw Justin sitting beneath the porch light of his cottage. He lifted his wine glass in an ironic toast, his face split with a mocking grin. Icy dread pooled at the base of Courtney's spine, the undercurrent of worry about whatever Josh wasn't saying swelling, threatening to overflow and wash out what they were building.

Courtney shook her head, uncertain if it was herself she was saying no to or Justin. Twisting to shoulder check, she backed out of her spot and made her way home, praying that her anxiety wouldn't pull her under.

Courtney shot a hand out and slapped the snooze button on her ancient clock radio with a groan. She'd been having a vivid sex dream starring Josh, and now with the abrupt wake-up call, it sublimated, leaving her dry and needy. Ugh! Why hadn't she just stayed with him last night?

Wide awake, she threw off the light coverlet and padded over to the window to open the blinds. The early morning summer sunlight bathed the cedars at the edge of the lawn in gold. It was the light that promised to turn into searing heat. A Stellar's Jay swooped through the yard as a fat, red squirrel scampered along the edge of the raised bed around her grandmother's prized rhododendrons, making the most of the relatively cool morning. Yawning, Courtney realized she'd better do the same, and she pulled on a faded T-shirt and a pair of old running shorts before wandering into the kitchen to make coffee. As she waited for the water to boil, she scooped some coffee into the French press and cranked open the window over the sink. The forest was alive with bird calls, and Courtney smiled. Summer mornings were the best.

Coffee in hand, Courtney slipped on her flip-flops and walked across the dew-damp grass to check on the vegetable patch. A sparrow, startled by her approach, careened through the wire walls Gramps had built around the precious veggies to keep the deer out. At least the sparrow was probably lending a hand by eating insects, but Courtney peered through the wire to inspect for damage. The tomatoes would need a good drink. The sun, just barely over the tree tops, already warmed her exposed skin. If she got everything done, maybe she could entice Josh to come over for a paddle or some other strenuous activity. She smiled, imagining his wicked grin as she suggested it. Maybe they could try the treehouse—it would fulfill a teenage fantasy. Sipping her coffee, Courtney strolled to the hose at the side of the house, switching the feed to the watering system Gramps had installed in the veggie garden. Justin's warning popped back into her head as she waited for the water to start hissing. What if Josh had been lying to her, and there was a woman in Port Hardy? Maybe a teacher? He seemed to know a lot about her job, more than most adults. Maybe he knew because his girlfriend is a teacher? But it was Josh. He wouldn't lie to her. Not about something so important. She dismissed it—after all, Justin lived to make her squirm. She'd let the water run while she ate breakfast, then she could work on soaking the hanging pots at the front of the house. Maybe Gram would appreciate another automatic watering system; keeping up with all the garden chores was exhausting. Courtney made a note to talk to her parents about going halvsies on pot-watering irrigation for Gram's birthday.

As Courtney plopped two pieces of bread into the toaster back in her cottage, her phone, still in its charger, pinged.

Morning, gorgeous!

Josh. Courtney's heart skipped a beat when she saw the heart-eyed emoji. She pictured him, shirtless, leaning against the counter in his tiny kitchen, hair damp from a shower. Need, hot and wet, gripped her lower half. Should she ask him to come over? Would that be weird, given her refusal last night? This thing, whatever it was, was so new—a delicate seedling. Hands shaking slightly, she responded.

Morning, you. Missed you last night.

Missed you...more.

Courtney's mouth watered as she typed.

Do you want to come over to play?

As soon as she pushed send, she regretted it. What a stupid thing to say. Way too fast. A deep flush crept up to her hairline. Her toast popped, and terrified of Josh's response, she set her phone down and busied herself with spreading peanut butter on the still-warm slices. She focussed completely on carefully slicing a banana and arranging the thin slices across the gooey surface, killing more time. Only once she was seated at her small bistro table did she work up the courage to read his response. It was Josh; he'd at least be kind when he let her down.

You have no idea how badly I want to come over to play.

Josh ended the sentence with a drooling emoji, and Courtney let out the breath she'd been holding.

Unfortunately, I'm on duty today. Can I see you tonight?

Cheeks warm, biting her lower lip, Courtney typed her response.

It's a date.

She sent him a kissing emoji and was light-headed when he sent her a single red heart. Holy cow—she had a boyfriend. Smiling, Courtney picked up her toast and bit into banana and peanut butter bliss. Her phone rang. She picked up without looking at the number.

"Can't wait till tonight, hot stuff?" Courtney said, around her mouthful of peanut butter.

"Hot stuff? Were you expecting someone else?" Her mother laughed

"Mom!" Courtney flushed madly. "Um, I thought you were someone else."

"Hmm, I gathered that. Anyone I know?"

A tsunami of nerves roiled in Courtney's stomach. She was torn. If she said it aloud, the tender new shoot might be trampled. But, then again, it could be just what it needed. Her parents, Carolyn and David, on exchange teaching at the University of Adelaide, were far, far away from the gossip chain in Port Russell.

"Yeah. Actually"—Courtney took a deep breath—"Josh. Josh Cameron?"

"Josh Cameron! What's he doing back in Port Russell?"

"He's been stationed here. He's an RCMP officer now."

"Really? Skinny little Josh?" Her mother laughed. "I hope he's bulked out."

Courtney's cheeks burned like coals. Her mom had no idea. "He's not sixteen anymore, Mom." It was time for a subject change. "I wasn't expecting your call till later this week. Isn't it crazy late for you?"

"I'm upgrading some papers, and I had a brainstorm about your grandparents' anniversary. Your dad and I think we should try to pull off a surprise party while we're there for our visit. What do you think?"

"You want to try and surprise Gram?"

"I know it's going to be tricky, but fifty years of marriage is a big deal, Court. It deserves to be celebrated."

"Yeah, I'm not against celebrating. I'm just not sure how we'll be able to surprise someone who knows everything all the time." Courtney shivered. When she was younger, she wondered if her grandmother could read minds.

"We'll have to have some help," Carolyn said.

Courtney sighed. "You mean Marilyn."

"Don't think we'll pull it off without her. Can you talk to her, ask her what she thinks? We were thinking of the Saturday of the Labour Day weekend. They won't be expecting a party so far away from their actual anniversary, and that way, Dad and I can be there. We won't be able to come home in October. That may help with the element of surprise."

Courtney pictured a glittering party here at the manor, with all of Gram and Gramps's family and friends celebrating the deserving couple. She imagined walking in holding Josh's hand, and a smile blossomed on her face, even as a peanut butter and banana tornado twisted in her stomach. Would she actually be ready to go to a public event with him, or would she freak out like she did last night? What if he didn't sort out his stuff? Could she be with someone who owned shares in the company threatening her home?

"It'll be wonderful, Mom, even if we don't pull off the surprise. I'll contact Marilyn."

"Okay, sweetie. Thanks." Courtney heard her dad's voice in the background. "Uh-oh. I'm in trouble for staying up so late. We'll talk more during our regular call. Love you, Court."

"Love you, Mom."

Jittery with anticipation, once Courtney had finished watering, she went for a run to the beach, eager to shed some of the excess energy that made it so hard to concentrate. Even in the forest's shade, it was hot, and Courtney paused on the beach, peeling away her sweat-soaked shirt to invite the ocean breeze to cool her skin. The water, calm as the tide receded, glittered in Little Bear Bay, and Courtney imagined Josh with shoulders and toned back rippling as he paddled. Then she remembered the feel of those same muscles beneath her searching fingers. Ooh, boy. She was in trouble.

Flushed and hot, inside and out, Courtney set the shower temperature to lukewarm, letting out a strangled squeak as the cool water hit her molten skin. She hadn't felt like this, lusty and preoccupied, in a very long time. It felt good to be back. Normal. As she rinsed the conditioner out of her hair, she paused, fingers tangled. What if it was simply a physical need that was pushing her toward Josh? It had been a long time for her, after all. Josh said he wanted more. A relationship. He was the one that was eager to go on dates. What if she was just horny? She would never forgive herself if she broke his heart. He was Josh; he deserved happiness.

As she toweled herself off, her more rational side spoke up. He'd been her best friend. Her first love. She felt safe and supported whenever she was with him. She cared deeply for Josh. She'd imagined herself with him at her grandparents' anniversary party. Surely, that wasn't just lust? As she combed out her wet hair, Courtney's heart hammered in her chest, and her mind churned. Did she love him now?

Afraid of what she'd see in her own eyes, Courtney let the comb drop into the basin and hustled out of the bathroom. As she pulled on clean underwear, her phone dinged.

Change of plans. Can I come over in about an hour?

Electricity shot up her spine.

Yes, you can, Constable Cameron. Want me to make some lunch, to fuel up?

Three dots appeared, then disappeared on her screen. Courtney scowled. Her heart thumped hard in her chest. Why was it taking him so long to respond?

Can't stay for lunch. See you in an hour.

What the hell? Courtney slumped onto her couch, her shoulders growing tense. She'd come on too strong and scared him off. Nonsense! her rational side yelled. You're being an idiot. Courtney shot off the couch, the jitters returning. Time to find something to do.

She settled on cleaning, getting lost tidying, dusting, and scrubbing. As the hour drew to a close, she decided to dash to the manor house to wash her sheets, and as she marched across the driveway, a tangled bundle of bedding tucked beneath her arm, a police cruiser trundled down the drive. See, he had a perfectly good reason to change your plans, her rational side gloated. He had to work. The tension in her shoulders eased, and Courtney raised a hand to wave. Josh pulled up beside her and rolled down the window.

Scowling, Courtney leaned into the window, surprised to see Russell riding shotgun.

"Uh-oh, was someone a bad boy?" Courtney reached in to pet Russell.

Russell's ears quirked up, and Courtney noticed Josh wasn't smiling. His shoulders were stiff, and his jaw set.

"Can Russell hang out with you?"

Nice to see you too, Constable Cameron. "Um, sure. Something up?"

"I can't get into it." Josh sighed and glanced at his watch. "Not sure when I'll be back to get him."

Was he serious? Courtney took a deep breath and reminded herself that he was a police officer, and there was a lot he couldn't share with her. She really shouldn't add to his stress. "We'll manage."

"Door's open," Josh said.

Courtney opened the passenger side door, and Russell paused to look at Josh.

"Out," Josh commanded, pointing, and Russell jumped down onto the drive to sit next to Courtney as she closed the car door.

"Thanks," Josh said, waving, then shifting the cruiser into drive and taking off, the tires crunching on the gravel drive.

Russell whimpered and nosed Courtney's hand.

"I know exactly how you feel, boy," she said as they watched the cruiser disappear.

Russell followed Courtney into the big house, looking as dejected as Courtney felt as she threw her laundry into the washer.

"I'm sure he's just busy, buddy," she said as she added detergent to the machine. "We'll have fun—you'll hardly know he's gone."

At that, Russell slumped onto the rag rug with a huff. He didn't believe her either. Her phone binged, and Courtney almost cheered. Saved by the bell.

It was Danielle.

Hey, you! How's the break going?

Great. How about yours?

I'm bored. I'd almost go back to work. Rethinking retirement. I'm terrible at doing nothing.

Courtney laughed because it was true. Then she had a great idea.

I can help with the boredom. Want to come over for drinks? My grandparents are away, and I have access to the manor deck. We can see who else is around.

OMG, yes! You're the best. I'll see who I can find. What time?

Is 5:30 too soon? If everyone brings an appy, we won't get too sauced.

Sounds like a plan. See you then!

In the end, Danielle; Kim Murphy; the librarian, Sheila; and their principal, Sandy, were all delighted to drink on a weeknight.

"This is the best part about summer breaks," Kim declared, accepting a glass of cider from Courtney. "Thanks for the invite."

The women raised their glasses to toast Courtney's last-minute invitation.

"I didn't know you had a dog," Sandy said, ruffling Russell's ears. Russell had perked up as soon as Courtney started getting ready for the party, and he'd greeted each lady enthusiastically. He leaned into Sandy, a dopey smile on his face.

"He's not mine. I'm looking after him for a friend. Josh Cameron?" Courtney sipped her wine, avoiding Danielle's eye.

"Oh, your *friend*, Constable Cameron. A little birdy told me you were more than friends," Danielle said, waggling her eyebrows.

Courtney's face flushed as pink as her wine. Marilyn! Nothing stayed private for long in Port Russell.

"Ooh, do tell, Courtney," Kim said.

"There's nothing to tell. We've been friends since high school. He's back in town because of the protests."

"So, he's not your boyfriend?" Sheila asked.

"No! We're just friends." The wine on her tongue turned sour with the lie.

"Me thinks the lady doth protest too much," Sandy said, and they burst into laughter.

Courtney wished the ground would open up and swallow her. I mean, her principal was teasing her about her love life!

"Hey, we don't mean to make you uncomfortable, kiddo," Danielle said. "We just want you to be happy. You deserve to have someone in your life, and Josh Cameron was a good kid. I'm sure he's a great guy. He'd be a catch if you wanted him."

Courtney flashed a grateful look at Danielle. "Thanks." Part of her wanted to tell them all, see the look on their faces, and engage in a bit of girl talk, but it felt too delicate. If she forced it, the spark would get blown out, and the fire would die.

"Ooh, did you hear, Court?" Kim deftly changed the subject. "The teacher they had in Jen's maternity leave took a position on Salt Spring."

"Oh no! Really?" Courtney gasped.

"The school board is getting really concerned. We're facing a substitute teacher shortage next year. It should make flu season a treat," Sandy said. "Know anyone who's willing to TTOC?"

"Maybe? I'll keep an ear open, for sure."

"It's too bad your parents are so far away. They'd be perfect," Sheila said, leaning over to help herself to some Brie and crackers.

Courtney laughed, imagining her parents' reaction to being called back in to teach elementary school. Her mother would be game, her father grumpy but secretly thrilled. Courtney rubbed at her chest, suddenly hollow. Man, she missed them.

"Hey, have you guys seen this?" Kim said, pulling up an ad calling for investors in a luxury development at Gnome Lake. "My friend from university is teaching in Thailand and sent this to me to ask if she should invest."

"May I see?" Courtney asked, and Kim passed her phone over. Cold dread washed over Courtney when she realized this ad was telling investors the development would break ground in September. They didn't even own most of the land they claimed they would develop. At the bottom, Eris Resources and CFI were listed as the partnered companies. Josh was right; his father and brother were involved in real estate fraud. And because he was a shareholder, he might be implicated too. "I'd tell your friend to steer clear." Courtney passed the phone to Sandy.

"Definitely fishy. The protests are growing, and I hear that progress is being made at the talks in Victoria. They think they may force an early sitting of the legislature to push through a bill."

Courtney fervently hoped that would happen while dreading the fallout for Josh once the public, and his bosses, realized what Josh's family was up to.

The conversation ebbed and flowed as the ladies shared their summer adventures. Inevitably, they started talking shop, regaling each other about funny classroom antics and lesson misfires. Courtney couldn't remember the last time she'd had a fun night out with the girls, though she was the youngest by at least fifteen years. She glanced around at her colleagues with new eyes and found herself looking forward to the new school year. It wouldn't be as lonely as the last.

The sun sank behind the looming cedars, and the temperature dropped. Courtney turned on the gas fire table and noticed Sandy was shivering.

"Anyone want a blanket? Gram has a stack in the laundry room,"

"Yes, please!" Sandy said, and Kim and Danielle nodded their requests.

Courtney hustled inside and pulled the stack of blankets from their home in the laundry room cupboard, pausing on her way back out to retrieve another bottle of wine from the fridge. She wasn't driving home, after all. Russell began barking, his oh-my-gosh-I'm-excited bark reserved for squirrels and other enticing situations. Chuckling, Courtney slid open the screen door with her toe to find the source of the duck toller's excitement. Josh. Anger over his behaviour when he'd dropped Russell off flared in her chest, and she realized she'd been hurt by coldness. She didn't deserve to be treated like that.

"Look who dropped by, Courtney," Danielle said, flashing a conspiratorial smile from behind Josh, standing on the deck in his duty pants and a form-fitting white undershirt.

"Sorry to drop by, but my shift finally ended, and I thought I'd better take Russell off your hands," Josh said, moving over to take the bundle of blankets from Courtney. She yanked them away.

"I've got them, thanks."

Josh's mouth quirked down, and he had the decency to look chagrined, as he should, given his stinky attitude earlier.

"We had a great day, didn't we, Russell?" Courtney said and the dog, bless him, looked up at her with love in his eyes. Her heart squeezed; he was just so sweet. "I'll be sorry to see him go."

Courtney distributed the blankets to the ladies, her back to Josh, and set her bottle of wine on the table. Please let him take a hint and leave before she had to offer him a drink.

"Want to have a nightcap with us, Constable?" Kim asked, reaching for a glass.

"Thanks, but I'm beat, and I've got a big day tomorrow. I'll leave you ladies to it. Thanks, Court."

She turned as he leaned toward her, and she sidestepped toward her empty seat to dodge his kiss. This time, there was genuine hurt in his eyes, and inwardly she kicked herself. Now who was being a jerk? She should use her words, not the cold shoulder, to get her point across. Was she avoiding him because she was angry or because she was afraid the ladies would find out they were dating?

"Come on, Russ. Good night ladies," Josh said, his words clipped.

Courtney watched as he strode across the deck, finally disappearing around the corner of the house, fighting the urge to run after him.

Once the mosquitoes made an appearance, the party wound to a close, and the ladies made plans to meet for drinks at Sheila's house in a couple of weeks. Returning to the deck to tidy up, Courtney was suddenly aware of how alone she was. Slightly creeped out, she gathered up the glasses onto a tray and straightened the deck, eager to head back to her cottage. As she carried the tray into Gram's kitchen, her phone dinged.

Sorry if I made your party awkward.

Courtney winced. She'd really hurt his feelings.

You didn't. I managed that all on my own.

I deserved it, considering what an ass I was when I dropped Russell off.

Courtney considered how gruff he'd been and had to agree.

You were a bit of an ass, it's true.

Don't hold back...

You know me. I tell the truth.

Courtney winced. Her behaviour toward him on the deck had been anything but honest. She leaned a hip against the counter as three dots appeared, then disappeared. She was just about to message him to see if he'd fallen asleep when he replied.

Why didn't you tell your friends we're dating then?

Her stomach dropped, and she was suddenly parched. Hands shaking, she got a glass out of the cupboard and filled it with water. What could she say to that? She'd had the perfect opportunity to acknowledge she was in a relationship, and instead, she'd denied it. Twice. She gulped the tepid water, wiping her lips on the back of her hand.

I'm so sorry, Josh. I can't explain why I didn't...

Look, Court, I want the whole world to know we're seeing each other. If you don't, maybe we shouldn't be.

Courtney's knees began to shake, and her vision blurred as her eyes filled. She felt stuck, this feeling so much like giving too much away, like she had with Nathan, but she was also terrified that she would lose Josh and be alone again. After dashing away the tears with her fingers, she typed.

Please. No. I don't want to lose you. I just need to wrap my head around things.

Time felt like it stopped as she waited for his response.

I don't want to lose you either, Court. I've got to head out of town for a few days. How about we talk, in person, when I get back?

The tension drained out of her body, and Courtney was suddenly exhausted.

Okay, it's a date.

Goodnight, Court.

Courtney's heart soared when she saw the red heart punctuating his message.

Goodnight, Josh.

She wanted to tell him she loved him but settled for the kissing face emoji. She wished they could talk right away, settle what was happening between them. It was going to be a long couple of days of waiting and overthinking. But she knew what she wanted now. A relationship with Josh. He would listen to her fears and be willing to work with her.

And she could finally tell him how she felt face-to-face when he got back into town.

CHAPTER 26

Saturday morning, Courtney threw on her light rain jacket and hustled to tend to the hanging pots before she drove up to the blockade. The light drizzle got her off the hook for watering the flower beds but wouldn't reach the pots tucked beneath the eaves. Gram had called and left a message saying they would be home tomorrow, and Courtney didn't want to drop the ball now.

As she watered, her brain seesawed between excitement and anxiety. She loved Josh but worried more with each passing day he was away. Would they be able to sort out all the issues between them? They'd been texting, but it was light and friendly banter only, no serious talk. She was headed out to the protest and worried about what might happen on-site and with Dissidence. Marilyn had called the night before to warn her Alex expected ERT on-site today, and Josh said they didn't play around. Would she be arrested again?

She was soggy by the time she finished, both on the outside of her jacket and the inside. She'd forgotten how hard it was to dress for summer rain, the warm temperatures making her sweat beneath her jacket. After peeling it off, she hung it back up in her cabin and grabbed a light hoodie, her backpack, and a to-go mug full of coffee. She'd rather be wet from rain than sweat.

Tense, she drove herself to the Gnome Lake blockade, the thwap and squeal of her wipers clearing the light rain off her windshield the only sound. She parked at the crossroads well off the road, remembering what Alex had said. There had to be at least forty cars already. She glanced at her watch and gauged the hike in. She was going to be later than she told Dissidence. The forest seemed to sigh beneath the welcome rain, the deep green cedar boughs brightening as they soaked in the needed moisture. Shoulders knotted, Courtney raised her face, closing her eyes, enjoying the patter of the rain on the salal and ferns, breathing in the damp richness of the forest, and trying to relax. A honk behind her startled her out of her reverie.

"Need a ride?" Alex asked, leaning an arm out of his open truck window. "Got supplies for the front line."

Front line. That sounded ominous, turning the protest into a war, which Courtney realized was the truth, especially for Dissidence and the others entrenched at the blockade. She really shouldn't sit back and let others fight for her home anymore. "Thanks. That'd be great."

Courtney circled around the back of the truck to the passenger side, noting the tarp-covered mound in the bed of the truck. "What do you have back there?"

"Cement. Good thing I had that tarp, else the rain would have turned the bags into bricks on the way up."

Cement? Courtney was afraid to ask what they were planning to do with it. The truck bumped and rocked over a series of potholes and speed bumps, and she grabbed the roof handle to keep her head from smacking the window as she was jostled.

"I see the boys were able to get the work done on the road," Alex said with pride. "I mobilized some of the Pacheedaaht youth to do a bit of guerilla road work overnight. Can't make it easy for the cops to get up here." He grinned wolfishly before turning his attention to maneuvering around the hollows and peaks decorating the forestry road.

Duane was minding the gate again and waved heartily as Alex drove into the protest camp. Several new banners were painted on sheets, and plywood was mounted in the trees on either side of the gate. One read "Worth More Standing" in bright pink block letters, while the other was beautifully painted with the "Respect Existence or Expect Resistance" motto Dissidence had used the last time she'd come up. Courtney spotted Dissidence speaking to a cluster of gray-haired women near the tent that served as the mobile command centre.

"Raging Grannies came out today—some from as far away as the Okanagan. Crowd is going to be massive today," Alex explained as he parked his truck next to the command tent, one of those large white marquees used for weddings and outdoor events. The Raging Grannies were a fixture at protests around the province, many attending the marches in support of BC education that Courtney had been involved with as she finished her education degree a few years ago. Too bad Gram wasn't here. She'd sign up in an instant, Courtney mused as she grabbed her bag from the truck floor. "Thanks for the lift. Need a hand with unloading?"

"Nah, my boys are here. Think Dissidence is eager to see you. She seems glad she's got a protest sister. Lots of dudes around here most of the time." Alex chuckled and opened his door with a creak.

Slinging her pack over her shoulder, Courtney joined the back of the crowd of grannies, raising a hand in greeting. Dissidence stood before the knot of old ladies, holding up a whiteboard that looked like it had instructions for a football play on it, and nodded her pink head in Courtney's direction.

"Right, so to recap, you lovely ladies will form lines the width of the road here using your coat loop lock-ons. When they come to arrest you, lie on the road, making it more difficult for them to remove you from the line. Our aim is to slow the arrests down and tie up as many officers as possible. We'll have a bunch of individual protesters chained to the large logs we've hauled over there past the second barricade."

Courtney turned her head in the direction Dissidence was looking and was shocked to see how much it had changed since the beginning of the week. Gram had called to tell her the bill had stalled in Victoria, largely thanks to interference from Marc Welton, the MLA likely in the Camerons' pocket. The energy of the protesters on-site was different. It had an edge of desperation and fear that was missing the last time she was up here. Victory seemed less certain. A small excavator was parked behind a dozen large logs arranged in rows across the narrow logging road just past a trench, six feet in width and who knows how deep, reminding Courtney of the old black-and-white photos she'd seen of WWI battlegrounds. She shivered.

"Questions?"

After answering a handful of questions, the grannies began organizing themselves into groups of ten, pulling old coats from their packs, while one of Dissidence's group made the rounds with lengths of chain and locks. Courtney joined Dissidence as she walked toward the large white pavilion.

"The coats are called coat loop lock-ons. They're modified with handles to grab. We make it even more difficult by winding a chain through and locking the line together. They'll have to be released from the chain and have their coats removed before they can be arrested and put in the police vehicles."

"Clever," Courtney said. "You have been busy." Courtney pointed to the new features past the tent.

"Not me personally, but yeah, crews have been sneaking on at night and making the modifications, thanks to Alex and help from the elders. They came in the back way from the reserve. The RCMP were busy guarding the roads in from town." Dissidence walked into the command tent, a generator humming behind, powering several laptops and even a coffee maker. Topographical maps of the area were taped to the tarp walls of the marquee. "Want a cup?"

"No thanks. Had one on the way up." Courtney waved at Martin, one of the Old Growth Guardians she'd met the other day. He was on the phone with someone in the corner. She perched in a chair across from Dissidence at the rectangular plastic table set up like a boardroom table on the other side of the tent. "So, what fun do you have planned for me today?"

Dissidence laughed, stirring her coffee with a piece of dried pasta set out to use as compostable stir sticks. "I think you'd like it. More comfortable than the arm lock and not as wobbly as the sit."

Courtney raised her eyebrow, curious.

"The large logs our friends from the reserve dragged back behind the trench there will have one prone person chained to each of them, the locks buried beneath the log."

"Those look like pretty heavy logs. How do you get the locks buried?"

"That's what the excavator is for. It will lift each log in the air as we wind a chain around the protester and log, setting them down once the lock is in place."

"Wow," Courtney said.

"Game to be chained to one?" Dissidence said, sipping her coffee. "I'll make sure we're next to each other so we can chat."

Courtney laughed, reminded of her students saving seats next to them for their besties during carpet time. "Well, as long as we can chat, why not?"

The clock was ticking. With the talks stalling in Victoria, if there were solid evidence of collusion between CFI and the protest group, the court could cancel the injunction they'd granted CFI, and the government could force the company to cease any timber harvesting while they investigated. It was faint hope, but it was all she had at this point. Once they started investigating CFI, Courtney was sure all the dirty dealings Mr. Cameron and Justin were involved in would come to light. Hopefully, it wouldn't touch Josh.

Martin finished on the phone and headed over to the table. "My contact says the police will be here at ten this morning."

"Sleeping in today. Nice." Dissidence glanced at her watch. "Just past eight now. That gives us lots of time. Can you track down the volunteers for the log sits? And let Duane know his driving skills are required. Maybe some of the new kids up from UVic can man the gate? That big one, Grady, and his girl would probably do a good job."

Martin nodded and hustled out of the tent.

"You'd make an excellent general," Courtney mused.

"So would you. Teachers are naturals when it comes to organizing people, and it is way easier to organize a bunch of adults committed to a cause than a bunch of kids. Ever taught kindergarten?" Dissidence shivered dramatically. "Now those kids are a challenge."

Courtney laughed. "Like herding cats, for sure."

Dissidence finished her coffee, and Courtney's worked its way to her bladder. "Where are the latrines? I am not getting chained to anything with a full bladder ever again."

By 9:30, Courtney was lying face down on a wide log, comfortable because of the foam cushion beneath her and the tarp blanket that shielded her from the persistent drizzle. They wrapped the chain around the length of her body, and she felt a little like a bacon-wrapped asparagus, she mused as she watched Duane and his crew set up Dissidence on her log. How quickly things had changed. How quickly she had changed. She marveled at her progression in just a few short weeks, from living in fear to fearlessly standing up for what she believed in.

"Comfy, hey?" Dissidence called once her log was back on the ground. Duane had turned the heavy machine away from them and was rumbling down the road toward the cultural centre. "He's got a hiding spot down there. Don't want to make the machine available to the cops."

"Ah. How long will it take them to bring their own machine up?" Courtney wondered if they could even find one in town, though she supposed they could subpoena one if they had to.

"Probably not as long as I'd like. Martin got word from his source that they know about the changes to the road. They might arrive late today because they've been waiting for its arrival."

Would Josh be back today? He'd been so guarded about why he was going out of town. Maybe he'd been doing special training to deal with these more extreme protest tactics?

Across the trench, the grannies began singing, and Courtney smiled. They took popular songs and changed the lyrics into their protest—so clever and often biting. They were singing a catchy song called "Radical Environmentalists," set to the tune of "She'll be Coming Round the Mountain," as their fancy hats drooped because of the drizzle. She'd always admired them and their stick-it-to-the-man attitude. Funny to now be allied with them.

"Show time," Dissidence said, a huge smile on her face.

Courtney lifted her head and turned it to look toward the gate, realizing she was excited rather than fearful. She knew what to expect this time, so she settled in to wait.

It took just two hours to clear the Raging Grannies, not because the coats didn't work, but because there were double the number of officers this time, some in the all-black uniforms of the ERT, and they seemed to have an endless supply of tools to work with. Courtney had to push aside disappointment when she realized Josh wasn't among the officers on site. She was sure he said he was working today when he texted last night.

There was some excitement when one of the older women collapsed after they freed her from her coat.

Dissidence started screaming, "She needs medical care. Stop! Paramedic! Paramedic!"

Courtney took up the chant. Soon, everyone was chanting, and the police paused to allow the paramedics they had on standby to attend to the lady. The crowd cheered when she waved from the gurney as they wheeled her to the waiting ambulance.

"Pigs," Dissidence spat. "Weren't going to stop to aid a helpless old lady."

Courtney turned to look at her new friend, noting her eyes glistening with tears. She was invested in her people and seemed to truly care. If she was faking it, she was a great actress. Courtney was conflicted, wondering how Josh would act if he were the arresting officer.

"She'll be okay now," Courtney said. Did Dissidence know what Justin was up to, or was she in the dark? Honesty wasn't Justin's strong suit; maybe he lied to the pretty protester to get her to help. It was time to get to the bottom of things.

Dissidence nodded, squeezing the tears from her eyes. "I just worry, you know. So much can go wrong. Emotions run high on both sides. I feel responsible."

"Hey, you promised me a chat. How is your man?"

Dissidence's face cleared, and she smiled. "He's good. We managed to meet up in Victoria, and I even snuck into his cabin at the beach earlier this week."

Had Dissidence been there the night she'd gone to the beach fire with Josh? Had she seen them together? Did she know Justin and Josh were brothers?

"He's a local?" Courtney played dumb, hoping Dissidence would finally admit she was seeing Justin.

"Not full-time," Dissidence glanced around. "Can you keep a secret?"

"Definitely."

"I'm seeing Justin Cameron. The CEO of CFI?" Dissidence looked pointedly at Courtney.

How should she play this? Would Dissidence know she and Justin knew each other? Sticking as closely to the truth as possible made for more believable lies.

"Justin, really? Did you know we went to elementary and high school together?"

"Really? I thought he went to some fancy prep school in Mulligan Lake?" Dissidence scowled, her furrowed brows creating a sharp crease.

"Um, he was here until Grade 11, I think?" Courtney felt the ground growing shaky beneath her. "Is Justin staying at Cedar Sands? Are they nice? I've always wondered." Courtney crossed her fingers beneath the tarp, praying that Justin had kept more than what high school he attended from Dissidence.

"Yeah. The ones on Cedar Bay? They are cute—can't beat being right on the beach. The stars were amazing the last time I was there."

Courtney did the math. She had been there the night of the campfire. Courtney wondered how she'd managed to get into Justin's cabin without her noticing. Beside her, Dissidence spoke quietly.

"Hey, please don't say anything about Justin. It's still hush-hush. Although I'm beginning to worry I'm more of a late-night booty call for him. We don't spend a lot of time talking."

Ew, gross. Revulsion was replaced by indignation on her new friend's behalf. "You deserve better than that, you know. Is he worth it?"

Dissidence grew dreamy. "I think he is. Circumstances are standing in the way now, obviously, but I really like him. We have a lot in common. What we have feels different. Important. Adult."

Courtney wondered what they had in common because they were as different as chalk and cheese on the surface. "How did you meet, anyway?"

"At a pub. I was there with some friends and ran into him."

Courtney raised her eyebrows.

"So cliché, right?" Dissidence chuckled.

A random meeting at a pub? How had Justin pulled that off? Had he had Dissidence followed? Creepy. Courtney suspected Dissidence knew nothing about Justin's true intentions for dating her.

Courtney's mouth grew dry, and she licked the rain off her lips to rehydrate. It tasted faintly of moss and cedar. She didn't have any right to tell Dissidence who to date. What was she supposed to say? It was a shame Dissidence was falling for a dirtbag like Justin, but Courtney had no way to prove that to Dissidence. If she said anything, it might stop this new friendship in its tracks. "I'm happy for you. Just do me a favour and make sure he treats you right. You deserve to have someone love and cherish you, not hide you away."

Dissidence's eyes widened at that. "That sounds like the voice of experience. Not your new guy, I hope?"

So Justin hadn't said anything about Josh to Dissidence? Interesting. A vision of Josh laughing the last night she'd seen him, face lit by the campfire, popped into her head, and Courtney smiled. "No. Not my new guy. An ex who stole years of my life from me."

Dissidence furrowed her brow. "That sucks. I hope it's better with this guy."

"It is." Courtney smiled, the crunch of boots on gravel behind her causing her to rotate her head away from Dissidence.

It was Constable Huong. She gave Courtney a sympathetic smile before glancing down at her phone. "Folks, I am here to remind you that you are in contravention of a court-ordered injunction," Emmy read from the document on her phone in a clear voice. "If you remain, you will be arrested. Do you understand?"

Chained to a log a couple over from her, Alex answered. "We're a little tied up, Emmy. Can you give us a minute?"

The other protesters laughed, and Emmy Huong signaled for the other officers to approach to start the long task of removing a half dozen people chained to logs. Frustration bubbled beneath Courtney's taut stomach. Even if Dissidence had any inside information, which Courtney was beginning to doubt, there would be no more questions today with police surrounding them.

Courtney sighed and settled in for the wait.

CHAPTER 27

"This is strike two," Emmy said, signing the paperwork to release Courtney. "I'm doing this as a favour to you and your grandparents. The next time you're arrested, there will be charges. Understood?"

Courtney took the pen from the stocky constable. "Understood. Thanks, Emmy." She signed where the Constable pointed. Courtney looked over at Josh's empty desk. "Did Josh call in sick? I thought he said he'd be working today."

Emmy smirked. "When was that?" Chuckling, the constable reached across the desk to staple the forms together for filing while Courtney flushed scarlet. "He's not sick. Took a personal day and headed to Victoria. He was in a rush when he dropped Russell off this morning, so I didn't get too many details."

"Oh. Glad he's okay," Courtney said weakly. Disappointment over his silence, not to mention not even asking her to look after Russell, stung.

"If he's not careful, my kids are going to kidnap that dog of his. They are in love."

"Russell is pretty lovable. Hey, I don't suppose I could get a ride home from you? Gram and Gramps are still out of town, and when I called Danielle earlier, there was no answer."

"They're in the Shuswap right now," Emmy said, and Courtney winced, remembering Danielle telling her about the houseboat they'd rented the other night. "I can give you a lift, but I'll be at least another forty-five minutes dealing with the rest of the paperwork." She quirked a thin black brow in question, and Courtney nodded.

"Sure. Thanks. Is it okay if I hang out here?"

"Actually, no. Just sit over at Josh's desk. He has a stash of candy in his bottom right-hand drawer," Emmy whispered conspiratorially before hustling back to holding to process another protester.

Courtney wandered over to Josh's desk, feeling a little like she was snooping in his room when she sat in his chair. She noted the framed photo of Russell on the prow of Josh's kayak, a huge smile on his dopey face, and she smiled. His two loves: the ocean and his dog. What would it be like if she were in a frame, smiling at him while he was a work?

She pulled open the bottom drawer and found a box of mini chocolate bars—KitKats, Smarties, Coffee Crisps, and Aeros. Most of the Coffee Crisps were already gone, being Josh's favourite, but there were plenty of KitKats. Courtney snagged one and laughed, remembering how they'd always swap one for the other from their Halloween stashes. She reached for a second dip into the box, shifting it slightly, revealing a framed photo beneath the box at the bottom of the drawer.

Heart thrumming, she tipped the box onto its narrow edge, revealing a framed photo of a smiling blonde, her arm wrapped around Russell. All the blood drained from Courtney's face as her brain madly connected dots that had been niggling her all week after Justin's cryptic warning and Josh's mysterious phone call the other night.

"Fancy meeting you here," Gram said, standing next to Josh's desk, causing Courtney to jump. The box thumped back over the photo, and Courtney slammed the drawer. When she looked up at her grandmother's familiar creased face and crown of white-sprinkled chestnut curls, relief washed over Courtney immediately, and she took a deep shuddering breath to stop the tsunami of tears that threatened to wash over her. "Hey love, what's wrong?"

Courtney wiped at her eyes. "Nothing, Gram, just surprise and a very long day. How did you know I was here?"

"How else?" Gram said, mouth quirked. "The Port Russell pipeline. We popped in to pick up the mail before we headed to the manor and ran into Stan. He told us you and Alex had been arrested."

Courtney stood, legs shaky beneath her. "I haven't been charged, though Emmy said next time I would be."

Gram pulled her in for a hug, running her hands up and down Courtney's back. "That's my girl! Are you done here?"

"Yeah, I'm free to go. Emmy was going to drive me home. Just give me a sec. I'll let her know I'll go home with you."

Constable Huong was processing one of the UVic students at her desk. Courtney waited until she looked up to wave and point at her grandmother. The constable called over.

"Hey, Court, I forgot to tell you, all the vehicles parked by the intersection were towed over to the impound in Jordan River. They're open until six today but closed tomorrow."

Courtney glanced at her watch. It was four; she'd have to hustle, or she'd be without her wheels until Monday. She sighed. "Thanks, Emmy."

Gramps was leaning against his truck in the parking lot. "Here comes my eco-warrior." He pulled her into a hug. "I'm proud of you, kiddo."

Courtney laughed. "Usually getting arrested is something families frown on, you know."

"We Merricks fight for what we believe in, remember? The arrests at the blockade are making people in Victoria mighty uncomfortable. It's helping. You're helping."

Gramps opened the door, and Courtney slid into the rear seat while her grandparents buckled themselves into their seats. She was ready for a nap. The adrenaline that had kept her going since her early morning start washed out of her body, but sleep would have to wait.

"Hey, Gramps, do you mind driving me to the impound lot in Jordan River? My car got towed there by the RCMP."

"Buggers. That's a bit mean-spirited. No problem, but I think we need to pick you up some food. You look a little pale, kiddo."

The taste of the KitKat on her tongue reminded Courtney of the photo hidden in Josh's desk, and though starving before, her hunger vanished. Who was she? Why had he buried her photo? Jealousy, hot and metallic, pierced her sternum when she pictured her arms wrapped around Russell and around Josh. Catching her grandfather's gaze in the rearview, she managed a feeble nod. "Sure, sounds good."

The burger they stopped to pick up tasted like sand in her mouth but did make her feel better once she'd eaten it. Gram caught her up while she munched in the back seat. They'd made great strides at the meetings until Marc Welton had mucked things up, causing a recess for fact-finding just when they'd been so close to getting the legislature to sit early. The delay could mean that the trees would be cut down before they could be protected. Frustrated, they'd accepted the invitation to visit their friend's interior acreage.

"You should have seen your Gramps. He was a force at those meetings," her grandmother said, raising her husband's hand to kiss the back of it as he gazed over and winked. "He's a large part of the reason the government almost agreed to an emergency session of the legislature to examine the protections of old growth forests in the province."

The love enveloping her grandparents was nearly palpable, and Courtney swallowed around the lump in her throat. Married almost fifty years, and they still looked into each other's eyes as if no one else in the world existed. She wanted that, desperately, despite how badly she'd been hurt. She had begun to hope that maybe Josh would be the one.

The road got twisty, and Gramps needed both hands on the wheel to navigate the bends and curves. Gram twisted, putting her arm on the back of her seat.

"You're awfully quiet back there, love. You okay? I know better than anyone what an ordeal you've had today. It's normal to be emotional once the adrenaline wears off. When we were arrested, I threw up after I got home."

"It's not that. Well, a little that, but more something else." Courtney looked down at her hands, worrying a hangnail with her thumb.

"Is it Josh?"

Courtney looked up sharply. "Why would it be Josh?"

Her grandmother batted her words away with her hand. "Oh please, Court. I've known since you came back from Victoria. We think it's wonderful."

"I have no doubt," Courtney said, sarcasm thick. "How ever did you find out?"

"I have eyes everywhere in this town," Gram said smoothly, straightening in her seat to look out the front once again.

Courtney didn't know if she was horrified or impressed at her grandmother's admission.

Gramps slowed the truck and turned into Jordan River, heading for the industrial area tucked up against the flank of the wooded mountain. They pulled up to the impound, a chain-linked lot attached to a mechanic's shop.

Courtney grabbed her bag, slid out of the truck, and trudged across the gravel parking lot to pull the door to the office open. The small space was full of people. Courtney recognized a couple of the Raging Grannies and gave a small wave before heading back out to her grandparents.

"You'd better just go. I'm going to be a while. There are a bunch of other people in line before me. They said as long as we're in line before six, we'll get our cars today." Courtney glanced at her watch. It was 5:30.

"As long as you're sure. I know I'm eager to get home to enjoy the patio tonight, and your gram wants to inspect the garden before the sun goes down."

Gram gave her husband a playful slap on the arm. "Hush, Charlie. I know you've done a good job, love. I just missed my plants."

"I know, Gram. Enjoy, both of you. Thanks again for driving me out here. I'm going to run an errand before I head home, so don't wait up for me."

"Whatever the issue is between you two, I know you and Josh are meant for each other. Enjoy making up," Gram teased, waggling her fingers as Courtney's face grew hot.

Gramps rolled his eyes and then put the truck in reverse.

In the end, it cost her 200 dollars to free her car from jail, and Courtney sighed. So much for her trip to the mainland for back-to-school supplies. Courtney glanced at her watch: 6:00 p.m. Pulling her rain-frizzed hair into a messy bun, she rolled her window down to enjoy the coastal drive back to Port Russell. The rain had stopped mid-afternoon, the clouds moving east over the mountains, and the evening promised a spectacular sunset. The air was clean after the rain, and Courtney reveled in the feel of the wind causing the tendrils of hair escaping her bun to dance around her face. Her bank account was slowly being drained, she could face charges the next time she was arrested, and they were no closer to stopping CFI. Now with the talks stalled, it was looking more and more like Justin and his scheming father were going to be the only winners. To top it all off, Josh had lied to her. She rehearsed what she wanted to say as she drove, half hoping he'd still be out of town.

She pulled into the parking lot of Cedar Sands, tensing when she saw Josh's truck in the lot. He was back. Rubbing her face with both hands, she pulled down the visor and inspected her face in the mirror. She was a disaster, bags under her eyes and a layer of grime coating her entire body, but she needed to know. Now. Having a shower wouldn't make the conversation any better.

Hands shaking slightly, Courtney slid them into her pockets, crossed the lot, and crunched down the path to Josh's cabin, pausing before his cottage for a deep breath. She mounted the wooden steps onto the porch and knocked, bracing herself for the door to open.

Nothing happened. She knocked again.

"He's out for a paddle," Justin said from behind her, causing her to jump.

Courtney closed her eyes. The guy was like a bad penny. She turned, schooling her face into stern teacher mode. "Thanks for the information," she said coolly.

"He'll be back soon. You could wait," Justin said, gesturing to the Adirondack chairs on the porch.

Courtney narrowed her eyes. Why was he being helpful? "Why do you care, suddenly?"

"I just want my brother to be happy."

Courtney barked out a laugh. "That'd be a first."

Justin splayed a hand across his chest in mock hurt. "You wound me, Merrick."

"Uh-huh. Why don't you concentrate on your own love life, instead of mine, for a change."

Justin narrowed his eyes, caught off guard. "What do you mean by that?"

Courtney watched his eyes and did an inward fist bump. She'd rattled him. "Oh, you know exactly what I mean. Say hi for me, by the way."

Justin's smile turned vicious, his armor back in place. "Enjoy your evening, Merrick."

He strutted across the beach to his cottage, wearing his ridiculous leather loafers, and Courtney flipped him the bird while she slumped into the nearest chair. Weary, she put her head back and closed her eyes, letting the setting sun warm her skin, taking slow, mindful breaths as she processed the events of the long, emotional day.

The sound of a kayak being dragged on shore pulled her from her meditation. She shielded her eyes with a hand over her brow as her stomach fell to her knees when she spied Josh on the shore talking to a woman. The blonde woman from the photo in his desk.

With a gasp, her brain made the connections it had been struggling with: Josh's comments about knowing what teachers go through. The truncated phone call. His weirdness with his brother the night of their fireside date. Justin's ribbing. His broken promise to talk about things.

She was his girlfriend.

Courtney stood, the chair scraping against the porch and clattering into the cottage wall. She needed to move. He was just as bad as Nathan. Saying he wanted to be with her while involved with another woman. Her legs carried her off the porch and toward the parking lot while her eyes burned with tears. She was such an idiot. She was vaguely aware of someone shouting her name over the roar in her ears but kept running. Dashing the tears out of her eyes, she yanked her car door open, threw herself into the driver's seat, and turned the key in the ignition, pulling out of the parking lot faster than she should have. She was such an idiot; she should have listened to her inner voice yelling at her not to get involved.

She peeked in the rearview to see Josh running to the edge of the parking lot, waving his arms. Her chest ached as the fragile heart she'd spent all year mending cracked within her chest.

CHAPTER 28

Courtney lurched to a stop and jogged into her cottage, peeling out of her protest clothes and pulling on a pair of running shorts and a singlet. Exhaustion was replaced by adrenaline after seeing Josh with the blonde woman on the beach. After lacing on her runners, she grabbed her headlamp out of the basket by the door and loped toward the forest path in the growing dusk. As she hit her stride on the soft forest path, the tension in her shoulders eased somewhat while her chest still ached. She was the other woman. Josh had lied to her.

Fury flashed like lightning, and Courtney curled her hands into fists.

How could he do this to her? She'd told him all about Nathan, how hard it had been to come back from how small he had made her, and Josh sat there, silent, while he did the same thing to her. While she knew Josh, the boy, she realized she did not really know who Josh the man was.

God, she'd been so stupid!

She should have known better. She'd come home to learn how to stand on her own two feet, and at the first hint of interest from a man, she'd rolled over and let him in—in more ways than one. Courtney ground her teeth.

No more. She'd rather be alone than be with someone who treated her like dirt.

Chest heaving, she ran into the tree house clearing. If she'd had a sledgehammer, she'd destroy the whole thing. Hanging onto the romantic notion of first love had been a fatal mistake on her part. When she got the chance, she would tear it down. Make a fresh start. A sob escaped as grief stabbed her hard and fast. She'd wanted Josh to be her home, to build something with him that would last fifty years, just like her grandparents. But he wasn't the one. Tears mingled with the sweat on Courtney's cheeks as she placed her head against the mossy trunk next to the ladder. Footsteps in the silent forest caused her to straighten in a panic.

"Court, thank God," Josh gasped as he jogged into the clearing. He leaned over, putting a hand on each knee as he sucked in a deep breath. "I was worried when you sped off."

Courtney narrowed her eyes and rolled her shoulders back, her heart hammering in her chest. She wiped the tears away with her fingertips. A vision of Josh, arms wrapped around the laughing blonde on the beach popped into her head, and she pushed it away angrily. It didn't matter. She could have him.

Josh stood, and Courtney noted the sweat staining the collar and underarms of his shirt. Good. Let him sweat. He was in the hot seat, after all.

"Court, I need to explain,"

"No," she said, cutting him off. Where had that come from? Conviction kicked in, and her legs stopped trembling. "No. I don't think you do. I've made a terrible mistake, and it's better that I find out now rather than later." She laughed, the sound humourless. "I should have listened to my instincts not to get involved. Your brother did me a favour."

Josh's face contorted in anger. "Justin did this?"

"No, Josh. You did. Justin only tipped me off."

Josh took a step back, the words hitting him like a slap. "I don't know what he told you, but I think you're misunderstanding the situation."

"I'm misunderstanding? You said you wanted a relationship, but you were in one with another woman at the same time? Did she know, or did you blindside her too? Maybe it's my fault for sending you mixed signals. I didn't claim you, so you went back to her."

Raising his hands, Josh took a step toward Courtney, and she sidestepped away from the tree. "It's not like that, Court."

"You know, I don't really care. I trusted you. I opened up to you about the hell Nathan put me through while you were doing the same thing to me." Courtney paused as her voice broke. "I trusted you," she said.

Anguish washed over Josh's face. "Please. Please let me explain."

Courtney wrapped her hands around her torso but nodded her head once, sharply.

Relief eased the furrow in his brow. "I've always wondered about what would have happened if I'd been brave enough to talk to you that day instead of letting that prick Nathan scare me away. I heard you'd moved back to Port

Russell, so when the temporary posting came up, I decided it was time to finally answer the question for myself."

"Did she know you were coming here to pursue a relationship with someone?"

"It wasn't like that. Ashley was my girlfriend, but we had decided to call it quits long before I came here because we wanted different things. I swear."

Courtney quirked a brow. "Quits or on a break? She just drove all the way here to go paddling with her ex-boyfriend? Justin said you were a couple."

"What the hell would he know about it?" Josh growled. "He met her once at a Christmas party a few years ago. He emailed her some bullshit story hoping to stir up trouble. She was traveling in the area because she's on school break, so she contacted me because she was worried. Ashley and I managed to stay friends after the breakup. You know Justin. Making other people miserable gets him off. Especially you and me. He's always been jealous of our relationship. Back in high school, he was furious when you picked me over him."

Courtney snorted. "Yeah, right—he had a thing for me."

"He did, even though he had a funny way of showing it, I know."

Courtney looked back over her memories and realized with a start that Josh was right. Justin had asked her to go to the Christmas formal in Grade 10, and thinking he was taking the mickey with a tenth grader, she'd refused him and gone with Josh instead. The bullying had escalated right after that. Courtney's heart squeezed. They were losing sight of the real issue here.

"I've never felt like I fit in anywhere but here in Port Russell. It's my home. You're my home, Court."

Courtney looked over at Josh, and every fibre of her being urged her to cross the distance and wrap her arms around him. Mold herself to fit against him. And that was the problem. She'd spent the better part of her adult years changing herself to fit into someone else's life. She had to stop and stand on her own. Work on building her own life so she could return to the girl she had been—was meant to be. Only when she found her again, owned who she was meant to be, would she trust she wouldn't lose herself completely again. It was clear she hadn't healed enough.

"I can't be your home, Josh. I'm broken, and in the space of a few weeks, I let you undo the progress I've made in coming back to the woman I'm supposed to be." With a stricken look on his face, Josh stepped forward again, and Courtney raised both hands to ward him off, taking a deep breath to bolster herself. "No. I'm sorry. As much as I want to be, I can't be with you right now. I think I need to be alone to find myself. I deserve that. And you deserve to be with someone who is whole and can be an equal in the relationship. I need to work on me, Josh, not an us."

"I'll wait," he said, voice cracking.

Courtney shook her head. "Please don't. You deserve to be happy, Josh. This could literally take years. I can't ask you to wait. That isn't fair." Courtney's swirling thoughts stilled as a kind of peace settled over her, even as her chest ached. She stepped forward and took Josh's hand, ice cold despite the warm summer night and his run through the forest, and she squeezed. "I am sorry. I'm making this decision because it's what's best for me. It doesn't have anything to do with you."

In the gloom of the darkening forest, anger flickered like a candle flame in his eyes. "I call bullshit on that, Court."

Surprised, Courtney dropped Josh's hand and took a step back.

"You're afraid. I get it. That asshole twisted and manipulated you, and you think I want to do the same thing, but I don't. I love you, Courtney. I want you to love yourself again the way I do. We can work on this together. You don't have to be alone."

Courtney had wrapped her arms around her middle again, fighting the urge to go back on her decision. No. She had to make a stand. "I won't change my mind."

Frustration erupted, and Josh threw his hands up. "Ashley warned me this might happen." He rubbed his hands over his face, stubble rasping against his callused palms. "I should just take the job in Victoria once my whitewater competition next month is over."

An icy curtain descended over Courtney at the mention of Ashley. He'd talked to her about their relationship? It was none of her business. He was still going to leave Port Russell? Even though she didn't want to be in a relationship with him? She didn't want him to leave his home. He loved it here. He shouldn't leave on her account. "What job?"

Josh shot her a look over his shoulder, filled with cold anger. "I applied for a position in the white-collar crimes division in Victoria before I took the temporary posting here. I've been short-listed."

Courtney staggered under the weight of his admission. He'd had an out the entire time? Of course he had. He couldn't count on her, broken as she was. Her heart pounded in her chest. This really was it. Her palms itched, and she ran her free hand over the side of her shorts. "That sounds like a great opportunity for you. I agree with Ashley."

He sneered. "Oh, you do, do you? Thanks for your opinion."

Courtney swallowed hard around the lump that had formed in her throat. "I want you to be happy, Josh."

"You make me happy, Court," he growled.

Courtney shook her head. "Take the job, Josh." Courtney lifted the headlamp and pulled it over her sweat-damp hair.

Hands trembling, she flicked the light on and ran out of the clearing, leaving Josh in the dark.

Courtney showered, allowing herself a good cry. As she dried off, her phone binged. Josh, please just go, she thought.

She lifted it off the counter, surprised to see it was from Dissidence. She pushed away the disappointment that there were no messages from Josh.

Up for a little adventure tomorrow?

Courtney wrapped herself in a towel and considered the offer. She was up for an adventure, especially if it forwarded the cause. She may have joined the protest under false pretenses, but she realized she felt strongly about seeing it through to its conclusion, although she faced possible criminal charges. It would get her mind off Josh.

Sure, what do you have in mind?

Don't want to get into it here, but can you be at the blockade for 6 a.m.?

Sure. See you then.

Courtney set down the phone and dried herself off, pulling on the soft cotton boxers and tank she'd brought into the bathroom. She was close to getting concrete evidence of Justin's conflict of interest to take to the authorities. With the talks stalled, time was of the essence. She would not let him cut those trees down. Toweling off her hair, she padded across the hardwood floor to close her blinds, just as Josh jogged across the driveway to his truck, parked next to Courtney's car. He looked at her cottage with longing, and Courtney wished he'd cross the distance and knock on the door. He jerked open the door of his truck and climbed into the cab, disappearing into the darkness. Courtney was glad she'd left the lamps off in the living room so he couldn't see her, and as he drove off, his aggressive start sending gravel flying, Courtney twisted the Venetians shut, her heart squeezing in her chest and her eyes swimming in tears. He didn't realize it now, but he was better off without her.

Wiping the tears from her eyes, Courtney focused on packing her bag for the morning, ignoring the voice in the back of her head, suspiciously similar to her grandmother's, telling her she was making a huge mistake.

CHAPTER 29

Eventually, she'd fallen asleep. When the alarm went at five, she groaned, wishing she could back out on her promise to Dissidence. But with no cell reception at the blockade, there was no way to call and cancel. And the clock was ticking without any solid legislative protection. Blurrily, Courtney pulled on the heavy Carhartt overalls Dissidence had advised her to wear, packing her rain suit as well. She usually wore them to help Gramps shovel the driveway when it snowed. Courtney prayed the temperatures were lower than they'd been yesterday or her clothes would fill with sweat long before she got to the protest site. She made coffee, its scent making her mouth water as she filled a thermos and a travel mug. Courtney grabbed a banana and stepped out into the mid-July morning, the chittering of birds and roll of the waves in Little Bear Bay drifting in the calm, clear air. She understood why the Pacheedaaht considered this forest sacred on mornings like today. She wanted to help them protect it for future generations to venerate and enjoy.

With her mind threatening to flood her with a replay of the terrible scenes from the night before, Courtney pulled up her favourite 2000s playlist. Soon the sounds of Taylor Swift's "Love Story" kept the thoughts at bay. She sang along off-key, then kept on when "Hey There Delilah" came on.

She parked her car at the crossroad, resigned to the fact she'd have to bail it out of car jail again, emptying her meagre trip fund completely. Never mind. She'd be busy up here for the rest of the summer. She didn't need to leave Port Russell. She just needed evidence that Justin was interfering with the protests, nullifying the injunction. Shouldering her backpack, Courtney waved at a carload of grannies arriving and waited for them to park so they could walk up to the blockade site together, using the path through the forest rather than the road to get past the RCMP posted at the site.

It was a bit of a slog over logs and through thick scrub. Courtney was always relieved to see the next route marker, stones painted in shimmery fluorescent green, as she and the grannies bushwhacked up to the site. They were spat out on the road behind the command tent, sweaty and shaking, thirty minutes later.

"You made it!" Dissidence crowed, getting up from her seat around the firepit set up in the middle of the road in front of the structure. "Sorry about the off-roading. Didn't want you hauled off before the fun started."

"Thanks." Courtney plucked the overalls off her sodden chest, sighing as cooler air wafted in while the grannies waved at Dissidence and made their way to the fire pit. "Tell me why I'm dressed for January instead of July?"

"You brought the jacket too?"

Courtney used her thumb to point to the pack on her back. "In here. What have I signed up for?"

Dissidence pointed toward Duane, using the excavator to scrape depressions into the hard-packed gravel of the forestry road.

Courtney winced. When this was over, this road would need major repairs if it was going to be useable. "Duane has been preparing some trenches, and Alex"—Dissidence pointed over to the side of the road where Alex was directing some young guys to empty buckets of water into the wheelbarrow he was stirring something in—"and his crew are preparing the cement. We'll cement protesters into the trenches. It's a riff on the sleeping dragon protest technique."

"Hence the heavy clothes."

Dissidence nodded. "Sorry I couldn't explain it before. Look, I don't want to force you into anything you aren't comfortable with, but I'd be honoured if you'd join me. "

Courtney looked over at the other protesters gathered around the fire. There were many gray heads and lots of young kids. She didn't feel comfortable letting them do something risky. That voice in her head sounded again, telling her she was being reckless and reacting to what had happened the night before, but she shushed it. She was an adult and could make her own choices. She wanted to do this.

"I'll do it. Where do you want me?"

By 8:00 a.m., two more six-foot-deep trenches had been dug into the road alongside the one from the previous day. Courtney prepared herself to lie down in the half foot of cement being poured into the bottom by pulling on her rain jacket and taping on some gloves to keep the cement from touching her skin. Just then, her grandparents stepped off the forest path near the firepit.

"Courtney!" Gram called.

Separated by the other two trenches, Courtney called back. "What are you doing here?"

"I could ask you the same. What's going on with all this?" Gramps asked, pointing to the trenches.

"Standard civil disobedience," Dissidence answered for Courtney. "Courtney, Alex, and I are going to be cemented into these trenches to slow down our arrests."

Gramps scowled. "Have you made sure the sides are angled properly? Six-foot trenches are deep—you don't want them to collapse on you."

"It's all good, Mr. Merrick. No need to worry. We had qualified people dig them. Thanks so much for joining us again today. If you see Martin in the command tent, he'll get you organized."

Gramps stood his ground, despite Dissidence's obvious dismissal. Courtney eyed the trenches. The sides looked like they were angled properly to her. Duane had dug them, and he had a lot of construction experience. "It's all good, Gramps, don't worry. Duane and Alex are supervising."

At the mention of the locals involved, Gramps's shoulders edged downward a notch. Gram laid a hand on her husband's arm.

"Courtney knows what she's doing, Charlie. Stay safe, love," Gram said, blowing Courtney a kiss.

"You too," Courtney returned the kiss.

"Ready for you, Courtney," Duane said, setting the wheelbarrow back down after dumping a load of cement into the trench Courtney was to lie in.

"Won't it take a while for the cement to dry?"

"Some," Duane said. "But it's quick-crete, so we can't dally too much. Maybe thirty or forty minutes?"

He held out a hand and helped Courtney lower herself down into the trench, the top a few inches taller than her as she stood in the puddle of concrete. The handcuff she'd locked onto her left hand cut into her wrist. She put her hand against the side of the trench, sending a shower of loose gravel spilling down and plopping into the wet mess puddled along the bottom of the trench. Dissidence appeared over the edge as Courtney contemplated the best way to lay herself down.

"Best thing to do is put your hood on and lower the length of your body into the cement, nestling in, making sure it comes at least halfway up your arms and legs, and the other end of the handcuff is submerged. Once you're comfy, Duane will shovel more cement around your perimeter if need be. Then, just lie still and let it set. I'll be doing the same thing right next door." Dissidence smiled down at Courtney.

"Got it," Courtney said, her heart pounding. This was madness.

Dissidence had suggested she put on a waterproof layer over the Carhartts she wore to keep the wet cement from soaking through her jacket and pants, so she'd put on a pair of yellow rain pants and a jacket. She'd duck-taped her gloves over her sleeves and around the cuffs of her pants. They'd likely cut her out when they came to remove her, another hit to her bank account. The handcuff would then slow them down as they chipped it out.

Courtney flipped both her hoods up and sat in the puddle of cement, shoulder checking she had enough room for her head before settling into a prone position. The cement oozed up the sides of her torso and limbs, from her shoulders to her ankles. The cool chill of the wet cement was welcome, given she felt like she was in a steam room underneath her extra layers. She could see a patch of sky above her, the early morning marine cloud whispy against the summer blue, the tops of the trees jutting upward like a palisade around her fortress for one. She tried not to think about cemeteries.

Duane appeared at the foot end of her trench, cheeks ruddy above his bushy red beard. "Ready?"

Courtney rotated her head to check that the other end of the handcuff was submerged and there was nothing poking along the length of her body too badly. "Ready as I'll ever be, I guess." Her voice echoed in her hood.

Duane gave the thumbs up and grabbed a shovel, gently emptying several loads of cement around the perimeter of her body.

"Not too squishy?" he asked.

"Nope. All good. Snug as a bug," Courtney said, and Duane guffawed. The wet mix came two-thirds of the way up her body as she lay at the bottom of the trench. Courtney felt like she was floating in the shallow end of a cement-filled pool.

"Good luck," he said, lifting the handles of the barrow and moving over to Dissidence's trench.

Courtney wished she'd thought to bring an audiobook or something. It was going to be a long day down here, alone with her thoughts. The sounds of the barricade camp drifted over the top of the trench, and even though they were metres away, they sounded much more distant. The cement was already viscous. It would take a lot of effort to free herself even now.

Courtney wiggled her legs a bit to give them a bit more space. Panic fluttered beneath her sternum, and she took a slow, deep breath in and out to calm herself, the wet mineral scent of the drying cement overpowering her. Josh's face, crumpling in pain the night before when she'd effectively cut him out of her life, popped into her head, and the panic deepened. Courtney whimpered.

"Courtney, you all right?" Dissidence's voice, muffled by the wall of dirt separating them, broke her out of her thoughts.

"Yeah. Just a lot of time to think in here. I'm okay," Courtney said, unsure whether she was trying to convince Dissidence or herself of that fact.

"What are you thinking about? Want to talk it through? I've got nowhere pressing to be," Dissidence joked.

"I broke up with my boyfriend last night." Courtney realized with a pang that Josh had been her boyfriend.

"Aw. Sorry to hear that. It sounded like you guys were going strong. What changed?"

"I went to his place last night, and his girlfriend was there."

"What! No!"

"He told me later she's his ex-girlfriend, and I want to believe him, but it's dredging up so much for me." Courtney paused to take a breath. "I realized that what I want right now is to learn to stand on my own. Before him, I was involved with a guy who abused me emotionally for most of my twenties. I need to find myself, the person I was, before I get involved with anyone. It's not Josh's fault."

"Your guy's name is Josh?"

Courtney winced at her mistake. "Um, yeah."

"My guy has a brother Josh. Weird coincidence."

Given that Josh was very unlikely to want to talk to her again, Courtney decided it was best to come clean.

"Dissidence, I have a confession to make."

"Oh? What terrible crime have you committed?" Dissidence laughed nervously.

"I not only know who you're dating. I've been dating his brother, Constable Josh Cameron."

Dissidence was silent.

"I've known Justin since we were kids. But, like I told you, we have a complicated history." Courtney recalled Josh's bombshell regarding her long-time tormentor. "His brother Josh was my best friend in high school, and over the last few weeks, my boyfriend." Courtney closed her eyes and said a little prayer before she spoke again. "Josh and I saw you and Justin in Victoria on Canada Day weekend. Did you know he was the CEO of CFI Industries before you started dating?"

Dissident was silent for a few moments, and Courtney's stomach roiled.

"Yes, but it's not what you think?"

Courtney's body felt like it was made of cement, not just lying in it. As Courtney had gotten to know Dissidence, she'd hoped her cohort was completely in the dark regarding Justin—a pawn in his scheme instead of a co-conspirator.

"He's a dirtbag, Dissidence, and he's got you ensnared in something really nasty. Justin Cameron is only ever looking out for Justin Cameron, despite what he may have told you. He tricked my grandfather out of his company and is tearing this community apart with his plans to log. He was the one who asked Josh's ex-girlfriend to come to Port Russell and then set me up to see her with Josh. Did you know about the Gnome Lake development? Did they promise you shares? Or maybe they're just paying you to provide a diversion."

"What! No! I believe in this cause. Look, I know it's a conflict of interest to be involved with him, but I swear I don't know anything about the development. I do know he's being manipulated by his father. You don't know the Justin I do."

"Apparently," Courtney said. She felt for Dissidence. She had no idea he'd played her. "I really like you, Dissidence. I meant what I said about you deserving someone who will treat you with respect. Someone who is honest and above board. Justin has told you what you want to hear to get what he wants. It's all he knows."

"You're wrong," Dissidence said, this time with heat in her voice. "I like you too, Courtney, but with all due respect, you don't know enough about me to tell me who I should or shouldn't be dating."

"Fair enough," Courtney said, feelings stinging. "Your involvement with him might negate CFI's injunction. Would you be willing to tell your group's lawyer? We have a chance to stop all of it, the logging and the development."

The ground beneath them began to rumble, and the lines of protesters nearer the blockade gate began shouting.

"They're here," Dissidence said.

It was hard to hear the shouts without being able to see what was going on. Fear gnawed at Courtney, the cement now stiff around her. She prayed her grandparents weren't being hurt, especially when the protesters began shouting about police brutality.

"Assholes!" Dissidence screamed at one point, maybe a half hour after the police arrived. "Pepper spray and roughing up senior citizens. Looks good on you pigs!"

A pair of combat boots appeared at the foot end of Courtney's trench, sending a shower of soil down the wall and onto her feet with a hiss. She looked up into the goggle-obscured face of an ERT officer in a black kevlar vest, a gun held across his body. He looked like someone deployed to war rather than a peaceful protest, and Courtney's heart thrummed, making her ears ring beneath her hoods.

"Three trespassers have cemented themselves into the trenches dug into the road, sir. We'll need heavy equipment to extricate them," the man, voice rough and clinical, spoke into his radio. He left without acknowledging Courtney or reading the injunction, like the officers in the past had.

"This is bad," Dissidence said.

"What's going on?" Courtney asked, her limbs trembling against her cement cocoon. "Why didn't he read the injunction? Isn't he supposed to do that?"

"They've sent the ERT," Dissidence explained. "I thought we'd have at least a few more days before they took over from the locals. They're called in when they want to clear out protests. Things are going to get rough."

"Rough! Dissidence, my grandparents are out there!" Courtney wiggled but was held fast in the now-set concrete at the bottom of her trench. God, if they got hurt. Courtney screwed her eyes shut against that thought. Gramps was tough, and he'd never let anything happen to Gram. Helpless, Courtney prayed. *Please let Josh be out there, looking out for them.*

The trembling beneath her increased, and a shower of dirt landed in her face. Turning her head, Courtney spat out a mouthful, teeth crunching as she clenched them.

"What's going on?" she yelled.

"They've commandeered the excavator. Don't worry. They will proceed with maximum caution. They have to offer you assistance if you ask for it. If you're uncomfortable, demand they stop."

Panic was raging in Courtney's body, the desire to run making her legs burn. Was she just supposed to ask them nicely to stop? They had an excavator, and she was lying here, totally helpless. What had she been thinking? The air filled with the screeching of the machine as it began scraping away at the sides of her trench, the shovel obscuring the sky above her head. The showers of soil became torrents, burying her legs and landing in her eyes.

"Stop!" Courtney screamed. "The walls are falling in."

When the scoop lifted with a metallic shriek, the hissing turned into a roar as the sides of Courtney's trench collapsed. The weight of the dirt pushed her down, knocking the air from her lungs, and white lights detonated behind her eyes. As she struggled to breathe, Courtney realized she was going to die and started crying. Scenes from her life flipped through her mind in flashes: Her parents' proud faces on her graduation day. Running in the forest, her feet bouncing on the soft ground. Gram laughing as they gardened together. Building the tree house with Gramps. The light in her student's faces when they grasped what she was teaching them. Russell's soft ears and constant smile. Josh's arms around her as his beard tickled her ear. He was the one. She loved Josh. She wanted a life with him. She couldn't die now.

The world grew silent, and then, darkness.

She awoke in a panic at the sound of her name.

"Courtney, open your eyes," an unfamiliar male voice said.

How had she slept through her alarm? She flailed her arms toward her bedside table but couldn't find her alarm clock. Why wouldn't her eyes open? Her eyelids were like thousand-pound sandbags. Someone grasped her hand, and the chaos in the trench hurtled back into her mind, forcing the air out of her chest with a whoosh.

"Breathe, love, breathe," Gram crooned, rubbing the back of Courtney's hand, brushing back her hair with the other hand. "You're safe. You're safe."

Courtney fluttered her eyes open, taking in an unfamiliar ceiling of fibre-glass panels and fluorescent light fixtures. She located the sound of the beeping: the row of machines lined up beside her hospital bed as a smiling nurse, the source of the voice, checked the settings on one of the machines.

"Welcome back," he said. "I'll be right back with the doctor."

With a start, she realized her left arm was resting on a slab of plaster, wrapped in a tan-coloured tensor bandage that reached from her armpit to the base of her fingers. A deep ache radiated from the arm beneath the fabric. An IV line was taped to her right forearm. She tried to speak but found she couldn't and began to panic again.

"Shh, love. It's okay. You're still on the respirator. The anesthetist said it would have to stay in until you're stable and show the strength to breathe on your own." Gram smoothed the hair from her forehead again, and Courtney closed her eyes and reveled in her calming touch.

The tail end of a horrific nightmare slithered away as she blinked her eyes open again.

"You're in Victoria General," Gram said, once again reading Courtney's mind. Gram flashed a smile meant to be comforting, but her eyes were awash with worry. "They airlifted you here after the accident at the blockade. You've been in an induced coma for the last five days." Gram reached over and pressed the call button. "Everyone's going to be so relieved."

Everyone? Courtney tried to remember, but her head was fuzzy. The light was giving her a headache, so she closed her eyes again. The squeaking of shoes on the linoleum had her opening one eye to see a lab-coated woman, a spring-green hijab covering her hair, stride into the room.

"Ms. Merrick, so nice to meet you," the woman said, her voice melodic and slightly accented. "I'm Dr. Zaina Hassan. I'm the doctor in charge of your care." She retrieved Courtney's chart, reading the last entry before approaching the side of the bed to grasp Courtney's wrist. The faint scent of laundry detergent drifted off the doctor.

"Let's see how that head of yours is faring," Dr. Hassan said, setting the chart on the bed and pulling out a small light from her coat pocket. Peeling Courtney's eyelid open, she swung the small light before the right eye, then repeated the motion for the left. "Your pupils are responding as they should. I imagine you have quite a headache. I'm afraid these may be with you for some time. Did your grandmother fill you in at all with what has happened since your dramatic arrival?"

Courtney shook her head slightly, pain stabbing her across the top of her head.

"You lost consciousness for several minutes after you were buried in the trench. The weight of the soil broke your humerus and caused some bruising to your internal organs. I understand it took some time to cut you out of your clothing as it was stuck in the cement at the bottom of the trench. This delayed your treatment. I was most concerned with the concussion you sustained and the damage that may have been caused by your lack of oxygen, so I induced coma to give your brain the opportunity to heal itself. The human body is an amazing thing."

Courtney snuck a glance at her grandmother, noticing the strain around her eyes as she stood off to the side, speaking to someone on the phone. The past few days must have been a nightmare for her grandparents, and guilt twisted Courtney's belly.

"You required pins in your humerus, above the elbow, and there are hairline fractures in the radius and ulna, as well. I will have the surgeon, Dr. Kim, come in to speak to you about that. If you are in pain, you can use the pump to administer pain meds, but no more than once every four hours, and we will closely monitor you due to the head injury. If you are stable for the next twenty-four hours, we will extubate. While I'm happy to see you awake, you have a lot of healing to do. Especially your brain. I will order some tests so we can determine the extent of the damage, and a nurse will come in and go over concussion protocol with you."

Courtney tried to get her mind to work, but it was stuck, and she couldn't get it to kick into gear. Dr. Hassan placed a slim, cool hand over Courtney's. "It is very normal to struggle with thinking and speaking following a traumatic brain injury. We are in no rush here, and you must be patient with yourself. You are out of the woods, so to speak, but there are still many miles to go in your journey."

Gram finished on the phone and stepped to the foot of the bed. "Thank you again, Dr. Hassan." Courtney shot her grandmother a grateful look for helping her communicate.

"Would you like me to help you sit up?"

Courtney nodded, careful this time not to jostle her head too much following the pain the last nod unleashed. Dr. Hassan angled the bed to a thirty-degree slope. "Is that all right? It is important to sit you up slowly, as the pressure can sometimes cause discomfort."

Courtney blinked, the pressure slightly elevated but manageable. Gram squeezed Courtney's hand, smiling in encouragement. Oddly exhausted, Courtney fought to keep her eyes open.

"Now rest, Ms. Merrick. I will check on you later."

Courtney was in hospital for another week as Dr. Hassan monitored her for complications. She was beyond grateful when she could get off the respirator, but her brain chugged like an out-of-tune engine, and Courtney was frustrated by the blank spots in her memory and how easily she was exhausted. Dr. Hassan assured her she was healing well, but Courtney just wanted to get out of the hospital and back to Port Russell.

The surgeon, Dr. Kim, came in and explained the surgery he'd performed, uncovering the half cast to check the three pins protruding just above her elbow. She'd have to stay in the soft-topped cast because of them and would have to keep her arm in a sling for at least four weeks and be careful not to bump it. They would remove the pins in six-to-eight weeks, depending on how quickly the bones knitted. The concussion protocol was the hardest to deal with, as Courtney wasn't allowed to use computers or to read or watch television for at least two weeks once she was discharged. It might take longer, according to the nurse.

After Dr. Hassan had left the day she'd woken up, Courtney remembered the last thought she'd had before she'd lost consciousness. As she'd laid there with nothing to do but think, she'd realized she had to talk to Josh. One thing had been clear since she'd woken up. She'd made a huge mistake in breaking up with him. She was grateful that Gram and Gramps were by her side, but she longed to see Josh. He was her person. She had to see if there was any way she could repair the damage she'd done. How was she going to contact Josh without access to her phone? It's not as if she could ask her grandmother to relay the message. It was too personal. Her grandmother had heard her thoughts once again.

"I forgot to tell you. I let Josh know you're out of the coma. Poor boy was beside himself. Didn't leave your side from the moment that trench collapsed till they wheeled you into surgery."

"Josh was there?"

"He was. He made sure they didn't manhandle us like they did with some of the other protesters. When the trench collapsed, he dove in and started digging with his hands." Gram let out a sob, covering her mouth for a moment. "Sorry. I don't think I'll forget that scene as long as I live."

Courtney reached for her grandmother's hand and squeezed. "He was livid they'd messed up getting you out of the trench and injured you, and he got into the air ambulance with you."

Courtney's mind chugged slowly, and her brow furrowed in concentration. "Where is he now?"

"He had to go back to Port Russell a few days before you woke up, and now, because of the investigation into the real estate fraud and his brother's interference with the protest, they've pulled him back to his post in Port Hardy, I've heard."

"They found out about the fraud? How?"

"Dissidence. She was horrified when she discovered what had happened to you and told the authorities about her relationship with Justin Cameron and what you had told her about the real estate shenanigans Wayne Cameron had been up to. Did you know he paid off Marc Welton? And it turns out he was playing his business partner, Eris Resources, as well," Gram tutted. "The accident shone a spotlight on the situation at Gnome Lake, and the government will be convening the fall session early to discuss the bill. Your sacrifice was not in vain."

"Oh," Courtney said, voice heavy with disappointment about Josh's absence, her bruised brain struggling to make sense of everything that had happened while she'd been in the coma and how she felt about it.

"Love, what happened between you? When I called him, he was relieved but said to pass on his best wishes to you. When I asked why he didn't want to give them to you himself, he said I should ask you."

Courtney winced at the memory. "I broke up with him the night before the accident. Told him I needed to find myself before I committed to being anyone's girlfriend. I told him he shouldn't wait for me."

"Courtney Norma Marie, why on earth would you do that? You were never more yourself than when you were with that boy, when you were kids, and lately."

Courtney's eyes filled with tears, and she blinked, sending them flowing down her temple and into her hairline. "Gram, I never told you the reason Nathan and I broke up."

"You said he cheated on you. That's reason enough." Gram pursed her lips as if she'd just sipped sour lemonade.

"That was what finally pushed me to walk away, but I should have left him years earlier. He was emotionally abusive, Gram. Controlling. He isolated me from my friends and my family. Made me doubt everything I said and did. He turned me into a version of myself that I hated."

"Oh, love, I had no idea. We thought you were just busy getting settled in your new career. When you came home, I thought you were just dealing with some misguided embarrassment over him cheating." Gram smoothed Courtney's hair, the sweet floral scent of her perfume replacing the harsh hospital disinfectant smell and the lingering scent of the lacklustre chicken soup they'd served her for lunch. "I never liked Nathan. I knew you deserved better."

"I know, Gram. I should have listened to you. The worst part is, Josh came to a meet not long after I started dating Nathan, and he prevented Josh from coming to see me."

"Forgive me, love, but I'm not sure why any of this is preventing you from being with Josh now."

"I'm broken, Gram. I don't know if I'll ever be whole. Josh deserves so much more than being saddled with my baggage."

"Does he know about what you've overcome?"

"Yes, he does." Courtney's head pounded in concert with her heart, boom-boom-boom, and she pushed the button on her pain med pump.

"And knowing this, he wants freely to be with you?"

"Yes, but..."

"Yes, but what? You can't make that decision for him, Courtney. We don't find ourselves all alone. We find ourselves in community, with the love and trust of our friends and family. This past month, following Josh's return to your life, you've been luminous. The strong, principled, passionate girl I knew came back. You claimed your power and put it to good use serving your community at the protest. I was in awe of you. You aren't a lone wolf, you have a pack, and Josh is part of your pack. I've watched and worried about you this past year as you isolated yourself. I should have done more to push you."

Courtney, eyes brimming with tears after Gram's compliments, barked out a laugh, then regretted it immediately. It rang like a gong in her head and lit her arm on fire. "You did plenty of pushing, Gram. I don't think you could have done more other than locking us in a room together."

"I've seen the way that boy looks at you, Courtney. How he's always looked at you. Please don't shut him out because you don't think you're worthy of his love."

Courtney's eyes widened. How did Gram always manage to see the depths of her soul? "I don't think that."

"Then you're lying to yourself and to me." Gram squeezed Courtney's hand and pushed her chair back from the edge of the bed. "I've said my piece. Now you need some time to chew on it. I'm going for a walk."

CHAPTER 30

Courtney received the all-clear to leave the hospital and return to Port Russell the next day, the Friday before the August long weekend. She'd spent the last two weeks of July in the hospital. Not exactly what she'd envisioned doing on her summer holiday. Despite realizing she'd messed things up with Josh, Dr. Hassan's strict post-concussion protocol meant that even writing a note was off the table.

"You may dictate a text or a letter, but only a short one," she had said. "Your brain is on vacation."

What she needed to say to Josh was too personal to dictate to her grandmother, or her mother, who was arriving from Australia to spend a month at home and help with the surprise anniversary party at the end of the week. Courtney resigned herself to waiting impatiently to ask one of her visitors to help once she arrived back in Port Russell. Anyone but Marilyn, that was.

Gramps arrived with a pair of truly hideous sunglasses for the ride home, the kind old ladies wore over their eyeglasses.

"I feel ridiculous," Courtney huffed.

"Think you'll feel different about that once we get you out into the midday sun, kiddo," Gramps said, chuckling. "Your chariot," he said, positioning a wheelchair next to her bed. A young nurse hustled over to the bed to help Courtney maneuver herself into her new ride.

Sighing, Courtney lowered herself down into the wheelchair carefully, body sore, still getting used to her left arm immobilized in the sling. She faced a long few weeks of recovery.

Gramps was right, Courtney conceded as soon as the double glass doors opened and the midsummer sun hit her square on. Without the old-lady sunglasses, her head would be on its way to exploding. Gramps helped her step up into the truck and carefully buckled her seatbelt while Gram returned the borrowed wheelchair.

"I'm sorry to be such a burden, Gramps," Courtney said, tearing up. "I'm the one that's supposed to be helping you."

"Hush. Families help each other out when there is a need. Right now, your need is greatest. We're just so relieved to be bringing you home, kiddo." With his hazel eyes glistening, Gramps leaned over and kissed Courtney's forehead before closing the truck door.

Courtney received her first visitor the next afternoon. She was set up in the shade on the patio, feeling guilty watching Gram toil in the vegetable patch, when she bolted, stunned by Dissidence rounding the corner, a travel mug in each hand.

"Dissidence, you're still in town," Courtney said, surprised when her chest loosened a notch. It was good to see her friend again.

"Yeah. The RCMP has asked me to stay close by, and as my home is wherever I park my van, I found myself a pretty spot at the Pacheedaaht campground. I brought you a London Fog from The White Raven, though it is a little warm for a hot beverage. They didn't have any cinnamon buns. Sorry." Dissidence waved at Gram weeding.

"Thanks. It smells heavenly."

Dissidence set the cup on the table in front of Courtney and then perched on the chair across from her, face belying her distress.

"Courtney, I can't tell you how sorry I am that this has happened."

"It was an accident, Dissidence. You had no way of knowing that the trench would collapse. Gramps told me that despite being asked to wait for a qualified heavy equipment operator, one of the special unit officers insisted and is now being investigated."

"Yeah, the tone really shifted with them on site. The local cops were way more respectful. But I should have done a better job of inspecting the trenches. They weren't angled properly for their depth."

Courtney looked at the misery clear on her friend's face. "I appreciate you taking responsibility, but it's no one's fault. I agreed to do it. Please know

I'm not angry with you. I should thank you—you told the police about the real estate fraud and Justin. Are you in any trouble? What about you and Justin?"

Dissidence frowned, her dark eyes swimming with tears. "Don't worry about me. OGG has a good lawyer, and I'm only sorry I didn't let the authorities know about Justin earlier. You were right about him."

"I am sorry. I know you felt things were serious between you." Courtney reached out her good arm and squeezed Dissidence's hand. "I'm here if you need to talk."

Dissidence swiped the tears off her cheek with her other hand and squeezed back before letting go of Courtney's hand.

"Hey, we need to count our blessings. We were successful in convincing the government to put the old growth protection bill before the legislature. Gnome Lake, and other magical places like it, will be safe," Courtney said. "You were instrumental in making that happen."

"Thanks," Dissidence said with a sad smile. "I still feel so awful. Look at you." Dissidence swept her hand in the air over Courtney's arm. "They told me you had to get pins, and you had internal injuries. I wish there were something, anything, I could do to make it better."

Courtney shifted in her chair, and her body complained loudly. "I'm on the mend, but there is one thing I could use your help with."

Dissidence leaned forward, broad face eager. "Name it."

"I can't use any devices at the moment or even write an old-fashioned letter. Would you help me send a text to Josh? I-I left things badly, and I want to let him know I'm okay."

Dissidence's thin black brows lifted. "You want to say you're okay? Couldn't your grandmother help with that message?"

Courtney pinked. "There's a bit more I want to say, not grandmother friendly."

"Gotcha! Do you have your phone?"

Courtney glanced over at her grandmother, making sure she wouldn't see her bring the forbidden device out of her back pocket. "I feel like a rebellious teenager, sneaking around."

Dissidence laughed and, making sure the coast was clear, took the phone. "Close your eyes, and I'll unlock it." She held the phone out briefly to scan

Courtney's face. "We're in. By the way, I thought I should let you know I've been using my real name since the blockade ended."

"Dissidence isn't your given name?" Courtney said, smirking.

"Oddly no. It's Song. Liu Song, in Mandarin."

"Nice to meet you, Song,"

"So, what are we texting to Mr. Hot Cop?" Song asked, fingers poised over the keyboard.

CHAPTER 31

The hot cop didn't text back. Not to any of the half dozen texts she sent. Song checked daily for Courtney. Three days passed, and Courtney found herself in familiar territory. It hurt as much as the first time Josh had left, and she longed to hit the trails to release the storm of emotion raging inside. But she was stuck on the patio, allowed only sedate, supervised walks, and she was going mad. Song encouraged her to confide in her grandmother, but Courtney found she couldn't. Gram had pinned so much hope into the idea of Josh and Courtney. She didn't want her grandmother to be disappointed or angry with Josh, especially when this whole stupid mess was her fault alone.

Courtney spent hours staring at the deep green of the forest behind the manor, dissecting every conversation she'd had with Josh. Analyzing every misstep. When she wasn't overthinking, she was napping off the headaches and the pain of her arm knitting itself. Who knew bones could hurt so much? Gram hovered and fussed, and Courtney was ashamed to admit how many times she'd snapped at her grandmother. She measured the days in weeks rather than hours.

Her parents, Carolyn and David, arrived, offering some distraction. Her mother, in particular, seemed determined to pull Courtney out of her funk, pushing her to get active again.

"Let's walk down to the beach, Court. Dr. Hassan said you can start more strenuous exercise, and it'll be a change of scenery for you. Plus, I need to discuss my thoughts about your grandparents' anniversary party without fear of having either of them walk in. What do you say?" Nearly Courtney's twin, except for her silver hair, styled into a smart, wavy bob, Carolyn fixed clear hazel eyes on her daughter in what Courtney and Josh had referred to as "mom eye" when they'd been kids. There was no escaping mom eye.

The day was beautiful, another spell of warm, dry weather having descended on Port Russell, delighting anyone involved with the tourist trade. Port Russell gleamed at the height of summer.

"Sure," Courtney said. "I'll get my sunglasses." The bright sun still made her head sear.

"Got them already. I had a feeling you'd say yes. Up you get," Carolyn said, holding out the glasses, Courtney's own, rather than the horrible ones she'd had to wear home from the hospital. "I think the activity will shake loose the case of the mopes you've settled into."

They stepped off the patio, Courtney wincing despite her sunglasses when unsheltered sunshine hit her, rambling across the lawn to the beach path. "I'm not moping," Courtney said, sighing inwardly once they entered the deep shade of the forest.

Carolyn laughed. "It's almost at teenage proportions, Court. What's going on?"

Courtney gently lifted her arm, still in its cast but no longer requiring the sling unless it was in danger of being jostled. "Hello, traumatic injury over here."

Carolyn's brow wrinkled. "Do you need to talk to someone about it? Dr. Hassan recommended a few therapists if that's the case. I can call and make you an appointment."

Remembering the dreams that had woken her the past few days, Courtney considered. "Probably wouldn't hurt to talk to someone. I've been having dreams."

Carolyn stiffened.

"It's manageable, Mom, more prevention than anything else."

"So what else has you struggling?"

The path crunched beneath their feet as they walked, an unfamiliar sound due to the lack of rain. "The headaches are awful, and I had no idea how miserable recovering from a broken arm would be. I will be way more sympathetic to people in casts going forward. But mainly, I'm mad at myself. I made a choice I regret deeply."

"And if I know you, you're beating yourself up over it."

"And I deserve it. I've ruined the best chance I've had at true happiness. I'm an idiot."

"I take it this has something to do with Josh rather than the decision that led you into that trench." Carolyn ran a hand over the waist-high sword ferns lining the path. Courtney realized with a pang they'd be passing the tree house soon.

"I'm sure Gram has told you all about it," Courtney snorted.

"Marilyn is the gossip, not Gram. She only told me that he was back in town and that you seemed to be yourself for the first time since you'd come home. That you were happy."

Courtney's eyes prickled with tears. They rounded the bend, and the tree house appeared, a shaft of sunlight illuminating it like a spotlight. Courtney could feel Josh's hand in hers, a phantom, and her heart squeezed like a fist. A lump in her throat made it impossible to speak, and her mother rubbed a hand lightly on her back, giving Courtney space to deal with the emotion. They walked on, and the forest opened up above the beach, the ocean breeze and salt-scented air welcoming after the closeness of the trees.

"I was happy," Courtney said. "And I ruined it, Mom."

Carolyn cupped Courtney's cheek."Who says it's ruined? This is Josh. He'll forgive you. That boy has always been yours."

"I texted him."

Carolyn's brows shot up toward her auburn curls.

"Not me directly. I had my friend Song deal with the electronics, and I dictated. He hasn't responded."

"It might have nothing to do with you. Dad heard he's been getting some heat over what he knew and when because of his brother and father's involvement in the whole mess surrounding the protests and the real estate fraud. Justin is facing a criminal investigation, and his father is in the wind, apparently."

"Really? Song didn't mention that."

They made their way down the path and onto the stone-strewn beach, the sound of the waves breaking on the rocks a familiar refrain. Courtney looked out at the endless blue Pacific, stretching to the horizon, feeling suddenly insignificant.

"Song asked around, but no one at the detachment knows exactly where he is right now. Emmy Huong told her Josh swung by with Russell to say goodbye to her kids, but she wasn't sure where he was headed," Courtney continued.

Carolyn picked up a smooth stone, running her fingers over it before skipping it into the waves. "Be patient, Court. Give him space. He'll answer you."

Courtney sat on a rocky outcrop, shuffling her feet in the sand. "Even if he does answer, what if he decides he just wants to be friends? I'm not sure I can go back to that."

Carolyn joined her daughter, leaning back on her arms and basking in the sunshine. "You're stronger than you give yourself credit for. I know Nathan spent the whole time you were together eroding that, but he never reached your core. You'll cross that bridge when you get there. But either way, you have a family who loves you, a community that values you. A home. He'd be an idiot if he passed on you, but you will survive if he does."

Courtney felt the band around her heart loosen just a bit. "Thanks, Mom." She squeezed her mother's hand. "So, what are your grand plans for the anniversary party? Please, please, give me something to do. I'm desperate for a project."

CHAPTER 32

Four weeks later, on the Thursday before Labour Day weekend, both parents insisted on taking Courtney to have her pins removed, which is why she was now sitting in the back seat of her own car at this ungodly hour.

"Honestly, I can do this on my own," Courtney complained, awkwardly buckling herself into the backseat of her car. It felt very wrong but nice, and Courtney was irritable. She'd been counting the days to pin and cast removal day. Dr. Hassan had given her the okay to start back on work half time once school started, and as long as she limited how much screen time she had and worked in short bursts no longer than three or four hours, she kept the headaches at bay. Courtney hoped that the teacher hired to work the other half of her week was competent. Sometimes teachers on call were scarce in Port Russell. She'd much rather be back full-time, but a full day of school, with its noise and constant action, would knock her on her butt. The most annoying impediment at the moment was her damaged arm. She would be grateful when she could finally get back to doing things for herself, though sad too. It had been nice to be babied over the last few weeks. It had been a long time since she hadn't been the one doing the caring.

"You need a hand, sweetie?" her mother asked from the front seat, twisting to pass back a travel mug.

"No, Mom, I'm fine," Courtney huffed, taking the mug. The coffee smelled heavenly. "Thanks for this."

Courtney ignored her father's smirk, clearly visible in the rearview mirror. "Ready, grumpy pants?"

Courtney harrumphed and took a long drink of the perfectly prepared coffee. Although she wouldn't miss Dad's terrible nicknames, spending so much time with her parents and grandparents was nice. She hadn't spent this much uninterrupted time with all of them since she'd been in high school. They did little, especially since she was still resting her noggin, as

Gram reminded her, but they went for rambles on the beach, hung out in the garden, and lingered over dinner on the patio. Last night they'd played card games until the wee hours. Not the best decision, given the early morning start on the docket for today.

"Yes. Let's get this show on the road!" Her parents laughed, that line usually her father's.

It was rainy again. Great for the garden but not the best weather for a surprise anniversary party. It would be a miracle if they could pull it off, given how hard it was to find a moment when her grandmother or grandfather weren't within earshot. They'd capitalized on Courtney's need for rest and quiet—Courtney retreating to her cabin to "rest" when she was actually making phone calls or sending out invitations. Gram had been so concerned about Courtney's backward slide that she'd threatened to call Dr. Hassan, and her dad had been forced to step in and intercede on Courtney's behalf. The party was set for Sunday when most of Port Russell would descend upon Merrick Manor, rain or shine. Hopefully, shine.

As they drove the coastal highway, the sky low over the steel gray waves pounding the shore, Courtney drank her coffee and schooled her mind to stay here in the moment rather than race ahead or rehash the past, practicing what the therapist she'd started seeing had counselled her to. She needed to prevent herself from getting carried away with the unhelpful narratives that normally consumed her. She'd balked at first, mostly going to therapy to appease her mother, but remembering she always told her students it was important to try, she did so and was pleasantly surprised to find it was beginning to work.

In the absence of her normal runs, which her therapist had pointed out were a form of mindfulness and a necessary coping tool for her, the work she was doing with the therapist had brought Courtney peace and clarity. Clarity about her past relationships, what she wanted out of life, and the situation with Josh. His rejection was still painful, but her therapist had encouraged her to sit with the emotion rather than run away from it. It was hard, like running after a long time away, but her stamina increased every day.

Just outside of Jordan River, they passed an RCMP cruiser, and Courtney searched the driver's side window as it passed, waving limply at

Constable Huong as disappointment crashed like a wave on the shore of her heart.

"Hey Court, that reminds me, I forgot to tell you I ran into Emmy at the grocery store when I ran out for ice cream last night. She told me she'd finally located Josh," David said. Courtney's stomach soared and then hit the ground hard. "He's returned to his post up island in Port Hardy and will be going to Oregon for some big kayak event at the beginning of September."

"Oh," Courtney managed, ignoring her mother's not-so-furtive glance into the back seat to see how her daughter took the news. Courtney focused on the waves crashing against the stony beach just outside her car window, willing the tears welling not to fall. What did she expect? That he'd change his life for her, especially when she'd told him not to?

"It's nice to know he's not in too much trouble," Carolyn said. "I worried he'd have to face disciplinary action because of the investigation into his brother and his father. Charles mentioned Josh's name was still on the board of directors for CFI, unbeknownst to him."

Courtney allowed herself to be diverted from dealing with the news Josh was not coming back to Port Russell. "Has there been any more news about Cameron senior's role in this whole thing?"

David sighed. "No. Justin is still maintaining he acted alone, and Wayne Cameron is nowhere to be found."

Courtney ground her teeth. Song had mentioned that Justin took direction from his father regarding the protests, but no links could be found, and apparently, Justin refused to implicate his father. Courtney almost felt sorry for Justin, remembering how domineering and cruel Mr. Cameron had been to both his sons when they were growing up. Josh had freed himself, but Justin was tied to Wayne through the family business and was now poised to take the fall for his snake of a father. What a waste.

Courtney dozed off in the back seat, despite the coffee, waking as her father bumped over the grate at the entrance to the hospital parking garage.

"Sorry, I dozed off," Courtney yawned, stretching her neck.

"It's okay, sweetie. You need to rest up for the start of school. You didn't miss much other than the audiobook," Carolyn said.

"Let me guess. It was a thrilling non-fiction account of some key battle from two hundred years ago. The author must be glad that at least one person bought their book."

"Hey, I'll have you know that the Battle of Lode turned the tide for the Swedes," David protested as Carolyn laughed.

"How do you manage to listen to that stuff without falling asleep?" Courtney asked her mother as her father pulled the Subaru into a parking stall.

"I get my revenge when I make him listen to podcasts about female empowerment," Carolyn said, caressing David's cheek. A blaze of warmth washed over Courtney. If only she had what her parents and her grandparents did. When would it be her turn? Dismissing the tidal wave of regret that washed over her, Courtney busied herself unbuckling and extricating her cast from the seatbelt. Her father opened the door for her.

"Need a hand, invalid?" He extended his hand, and Courtney grasped it gratefully.

They made their way to the cast clinic and checked in. The clerk asked if Courtney wanted someone to go in with her.

"I should be good," Courtney said, sliding her care card back into her wallet.

The clerk, her name tag read Soleta, was a petite woman with jet-black hair gathered into a neat bun at the nape of her neck. "It says your pins come out today. You may want to have someone to support you."

Icy dread spread out from behind Courtney's navel. "Is it really that bad?"

"It doesn't hurt," the clerk said, her accent lilting. "Though it can be uncomfortable."

Her dad came up behind her. "You look a bit pale, Court. Everything okay?"

"Um, would you mind coming in with me?"

"No problem, bean," David said, squeezing her shoulder.

Dr. Kim hurried in from a door Courtney hadn't noticed before, giving a perfunctory hello before examining Courtney's arm, his bedside manner as brusque as she'd remembered. He bent her at the elbow, pulling it gently to straighten it. She winced when he twisted it, even though it didn't hurt. She was just so used to not using the arm that the muscles were stiff from lack of use.

"Good. Good. X-rays show complete knitting of the bone. You may need some physio to work on the lateral movement of your arm. The muscles in your bicep"—Dr. Kim ran a thumb over the muscle—"have shortened and will require stretching in order to achieve full extension. I will give you the names of some good physio clinics."

Dr. Kim grabbed the pliers, and Courtney's eyes grew round. "I will hold your elbow and pull on the pins with this. Try to relax your arm." He placed a hand behind her elbow, jiggling it. "I said relax."

"I'm trying," Courtney said, taking a deep breath. Her dad squeezed her hand.

"It's easy," Dr. Kim said, bending to grasp the head of the first pin.

Easy for him to say, he didn't have metal sticking out of his arm.

Courtney felt a tug on the skin at the base of the first pin and bit her bottom lip as it let go, and the pin began to slide. There was a perfectly round hole in her arm, and as she marveled at it, burgundy-coloured blood spurted out of the hole. Courtney gasped, blanching as the pin hit the kidney-shaped pan with a clatter.

"Don't worry," the nurse said, blotting the blood away with a square of gauze. "It's just bone blood."

"Bone blood?" her dad said, echoing her thoughts exactly in the tone of his voice. "What the hell is that?"

"It's a good sign. Means the bone is healthy," Dr. Kim said, bending to grasp the second pin.

"Thanks for the heads up," Courtney said.

The nurse and Dr. Kim shared a look that screamed "wuss" and Courtney turned her head to focus on the waffle knit pattern of the pale blue blanket on the bed, breathing in through her nose and out through her mouth to control the nausea washing over her.

Dr. Kim removed the next two pins, then lowered the pliers to the table.

"All done. Keep the area covered until the holes scab over. I'd recommend waiting a few days before starting physio so the scabs don't tear open."

"Sure," Courtney said as the nurse cleaned the holes and covered them with a bandage. "Thank you, Dr. Kim."

He nodded once and then hurried off to his next victim. The nurse flashed the blood-covered pins in Courtney's direction.

"Want to keep these?"

"No. I'm good." Courtney swallowed, her stomach burning. What a weird experience.

"All right then. You're free to go. "

Her dad nodded his thanks as the nurse bundled up the blood-soaked gauze and the kidney-shaped container with the metal that had been in her arm just minutes before, then made his way around to help Courtney slide off the edge of the bed.

"Whoa there, kiddo," he said as Courtney wobbled. "That was intense. Let's get you something to eat."

Courtney squeezed her dad's hand, grateful Soleta, the clerk, had given her the heads up about bringing someone in with her.

CHAPTER 33

"Girls, it looks spectacular," David said, carrying more chairs out of the borrowed truck, setting them around the tables scattered around the lawn.

The weather had cooperated, thank goodness, and with a small pavilion set up for the cake, photo display, and electronics, just in case, they could safely hold the anniversary party in the manor garden as planned. Bouquets of sunflowers and asters, set in mason jars and assorted vases, graced the tables—a hodgepodge of furniture borrowed from friends and neighbours. It shouldn't have worked, but it did. Perfectly laid back and welcoming, just like her grandparents.

"Do you think we left enough room for people to mingle, maybe dance?" Courtney asked, biting her lip, while Song adjusted the tablecloth and centrepiece on a nearby table.

"I'm sure it will be fine, Court," her Dad said. "If people need more room, we'll just move the tables."

Carolyn rounded the corner with a box full of more flower centrepieces. "If you girls want to shower, head in now. Marilyn just texted to say they'll be heading our way for 6:30-ish."

Courtney glanced at her watch. Quarter to five. They had asked the guests to be at the manor for six, so they could be in place for the surprise.

"What has she had them doing all day, anyway?" Song asked, rubbing her newly shorn hair absently. The pink dreads outed her as Dissidence, she said, so she'd convinced Courtney to help her hack it off. She wanted a fresh start, to put the mistakes, aka Justin, behind her and go forward as Song.

"A bit of volunteer work this morning up at the cultural centre followed by mysterious errands and a long lunch," Carolyn said, setting out more centrepieces. "Go, now, while you can. I'm just going to meet the caterer out on the driveway in a minute, and get her set up in the kitchen. Your dad just has one more load of chairs, I think."

Courtney and Song headed to her cottage to shower and get ready.

"You go first. Your hair will take longer than mine," Song said. "You can manage on your own?"

Courtney nodded. It felt strange to be able to get her arm wet; she'd spent weeks putting it in a bag to keep it dry. She still had to use just her right hand to shampoo her hair because she couldn't straighten her left arm all the way. Courtney wasn't sure just how much physio would allow her to have a normal range of motion. She towel-dried her hair, wrapped herself up in another towel, and swapped places with Song. When her grandparents found out how much Song was paying to stay in the campground, they'd insisted she park her van on the driveway. It had been nice to have someone her own age around the last couple of weeks, and it looked like Song might decide to stick around into the fall, teaching on call. Courtney had encouraged her to apply, hoping she may benefit during her own gradual start back at work. If Song was offered the position to help with Courtney's gradual return to work, it would be fun to partner with her. If Song started at Port Russell Elementary, it might even open the door to a longer-term contract if a maternity leave or long-term illness created an opening. There was also zero chance of Justin returning to Port Russell, an added benefit.

Courtney combed out her hair to let it air dry a bit, then slid into her soft yellow sundress, the memory of the last time she wore it threatening to overwhelm her. She looked at herself in the mirror; the sight of the large bandaid covering the three holes on her left were adding to her funk. She sighed. She'd have to wear a sweater, or she'd spend all night answering questions. She pulled on a white cotton cardigan, pushing the sleeves toward each elbow. Once the sun went down, she'd probably be glad for it. She eyed the hair dryer lying on her bureau, contemplating the best way to make her hair look half decent, given her uncooperative arm.

Song poked her head in, her pink-ended crop somehow making her elf-like.

Courtney sighed. "It's so unfair. If I had your haircut, I'd look like a seven-year-old boy, whereas you look like a creature out of a fantasy novel."

Song laughed. "Need a hand? Best part about this situation is the lack of fuss it requires." She was wearing a cropped jersey jumpsuit in a gorgeous rust colour.

"You don't mind?" Courtney could count on one hand the number of times someone else had blow-dried her hair.

"Not a problem. My auntie runs a salon, so I've even got professional experience."

Song had said very little about her family, and Courtney figured she had a good reason, so she hadn't pushed. "You have a lot of aunts on the mainland?"

"Yes and no. Blood aunts, no. Village aunts, lots." Song pointed to the chair, and once Courtney was seated, she picked up a round brush and the hair dryer.

"Village aunts?" Courtney asked as the dryer roared to life.

"They're not related to me by blood but come from the same village as my parents. Important support network for immigrants," Song explained, expertly moving the brush down the length of Courtney's dark brown strands, following with the dryer.

"Your parents are immigrants?"

"Yeah, me too. I was born in China. We came to Canada when I was a toddler."

"Wow. I didn't know that."

Song shrugged. "As my mother likes to remind me, I'm only Chinese in appearance."

Courtney caught the look of pain that flashed over her friend's face and decided to let it go. Song concentrated on drying, then, using the round brush, created soft curls and waves.

Courtney took in her glorious waves, running her fingers through the soft curls as she turned her head one way, then the other. "Oh my god, you undersold your skills, girl. Thanks!"

"My pleasure," Song said, setting the tools down and pulling her phone from her pocket. "Mind if I take a photo?"

Courtney laughed. "Sure." They posed in mirror, and Song took the pic, flashing it toward Courtney. They looked nothing like the women who'd been chained to trees just weeks before. "What filter did you use? We look awesome."

"Just our amazing selves, I assure you," Song said, pocketing her phone. "It's almost six. We better head over."

David and Carolyn had worked out a deal with Duane to pick people up at the elementary school and bus them over, so the extra cars wouldn't tip off the surprise. The yellow bus arrived as Song and Courtney stepped off the cottage's porch. When the doors opened, Courtney could hear the party had already started, and pushing aside a sudden rush of sadness, she made her way over to greet the party-goers. She'd been busy for the last few days with last-minute plans, then the decorations, so she'd been able to compartmentalize the loss. Song squeezed her elbow.

"We can do this. We'll be each other's dates, okay?"

"Yes. We can," Courtney smiled at Song. "Thank you."

People streamed off the bus: former employees, neighbours, and family friends. Constable Huong stepped off, a can of cider in her hand, face flushed.

"Ladies! Look at you, all cleaned up and not chained to anything."

"Haha, very funny. Aren't you on duty?" Courtney asked, waving at Emmy's husband, Mike.

"Nope. New guy's turn," Emmy said, waggling her eyebrows. "We're kid-free, and I've got the next three days off! I plan on enjoying myself tonight!" The off-duty constable grabbed her husband's hand and shimmied off toward the lawn.

Courtney directed the attendees to follow Emmy to the backyard, and Duane called down from the driver's seat, "Just one more load to go. I'll be back by 6:15."

"Thanks, Duane. When you come back, pull into the garage bay. Once the door is closed, you can use the side door to join us in the backyard."

Duane gave Courtney a thumbs-up and then pulled the bus doors closed.

Courtney heard music drifting in the night air. They'd have to turn that off, or Gram would be tipped off for sure. When she rounded the corner of the house and took in the manor yard, Courtney smiled as she saw everyone oohing and aahing over the decorations, clustered together, chatting and laughing, bright pops of summer colour in the dusky garden.

It had been a lot of work, but her grandparents were going to love this. Their family and community celebrating—they lived for stuff like this. David waved Courtney over, pressing a glass of rosé into her good hand.

"You earned this, kiddo. Smile! The hard work is done, and the party starts now!" The group of people nearby sent up a cheer.

"Thanks, Dad. Duane said he'd be here at 6:15 with the next load. Then we'd better turn off the music and get everyone into their hiding spots."

David saluted. "Yes, ma'am."

Carolyn wandered over and laced her arm through her husband's, rolling her eyes at her husband's high spirits.

"How much have you had to drink, Dad?" Courtney asked, sipping her chilled wine. She waved at Song, chatting with Sandy Munro near the deck.

"I'm just happy. All my family is here, and we're celebrating." David pulled Courtney into a side hug and kissed her head, then his wife's. "Life is good."

Courtney smiled, though it didn't quite make it all the way to her chest, where a wedge of loneliness, like a block of ice, sat just behind her sternum. She took another sip, the wine sour in her mouth. It was going to be a long night of pretending. The person she most associated with home wouldn't be in attendance tonight or ever.

At 6:15, as promised, the second bus load of partiers streamed into the backyard, among them Danielle O'Halloran, decked out in a sparkly silver top, who waved as she joined a group of people admiring the photo display Courtney and her mother had set up. This was the event of the summer for Port Russell, it appeared. David made his way over to the tent and, turning off the music, lifted the mic to address the crowd.

"Carolyn just received a text from Marilyn. The guests of honour are about ten minutes out. So, if everyone could please take a seat, we'll keep the music off and the chatting to a minimum, and maybe we'll actually pull off this crazy surprise!"

The crowd laughed, and people moved to sit at the scattered tables perched on the lawn and patio, the noise lowering to a soft hum. Courtney joined her parents at the marquee tent, a romantic table for two arranged in front of it. David checked the champagne chilling in the bucket next to the silver tablecloth-clad table while Carolyn leaned over to turn on the battery-operated fairy lights wound through the flowers on the table.

Across the yard, the guests did the same thing, the lights shimmering in the dusky blue garden. Song plugged in the fairy lights wound through the trees and shrubs, and the crowd gasped. The manor was a fairy garden, glimmering and gorgeous. Courtney's stomach danced, jittery, and she smiled as she imagined her grandparents' faces when they rounded the corner. Duane, bushy red beard neatly combed and sporting a collared shirt for the occasion, crossed the lawn from the garage, waving at Courtney and her parents.

Carolyn's phone dinged. "They're at the manor gates, everyone. Shh."

The crowd grew silent, the sound of the waves in the bay drifting over the deep-green cedars surrounding the manor garden. They heard a car door slam and someone in the crowd giggling softly before stifling the sound. Courtney gripped her mother's hand, eyes glued to the path that wound around the side of the yard. Her grandmother's voice echoed in the quiet.

"Honestly, Marilyn, you are so bossy. It's so much easier to use the front door."

Her grandparents rounded the corner, and the crowd yelled, "Surprise!"

For as long as she lived, Courtney would remember her grandmother's eyes round with surprise, her hand splayed across her chest, and the smile that lit up her face.

"Happy anniversary, Mom and Dad!" David said into the microphone Carolyn held, as his hands were busy with the cork on the champagne bottle. A loud pop, followed by a fizz, filled the air, and the crowd cheered. Courtney made her way over to her grandparents, hand extended, and her grandmother took it and squeezed while Marilyn laughed.

"You sneaky so and sos," Gram said, shaking her finger at Marilyn and then Courtney.

Courtney laughed.

Gramps, beaming, put a hand under his wife's elbow. "I believe we get the seat of honour, my dear."

David handed each of his parents a glass of champagne, then Carolyn handed one to him and Courtney. "Please join me in a toast to celebrate fifty years of wedded bliss for the cutest couple in town. Your dedication to each other and to this community is inspiring. I am so proud to be your son." David's voice cracked, and he paused before lifting his glass. "To Charlie and Norma Merrick!"

The crowd lifted their glasses and toasted as the couple of the hour kissed.

After the toast, the DJ, one of Marilyn and Stan's many nephews, began playing the happy couple's favourite song. As the John Denver classic "Annie's Song" drifted on the night air, Charlie led Norma onto the dance floor, and Courtney teared up, watching how in love her grandparents were still. The song continued, and Courtney stifled a sob. She would never have a moment like this with Josh for certain, perhaps never with anyone, given her terrible track record with men. Stepping into a pool of darkness, she palmed away the tears flowing over her cheeks. She needed to get it together, or she would spoil her grandparents' special day.

The song shifted into Van Morrison's "Brown-Eyed Girl," and others joined Charlie and Norma on the dance floor. Throat aching from her stifled tears, Courtney headed to the drinks table and helped herself to a glass of wine, the tart chill of the rosé easing her throat. She sensed someone at her shoulder and fixed a smile on her face before turning to chat, the false face melting away when she saw it was Song.

"You okay, hun?" Her brown eyes were understanding. "They're playing my song. Want to dance with me?"

Courtney smiled, though it didn't reach her eyes. "That's quite an offer, but I'm having a moment."

Song squeezed her elbow. "Offer stands all night."

Something wet brushed the back of Courtney's leg, and she startled. "Ach!" She turned to see what was tickling her, and her stomach fell. "Russell? What are you doing here?"

Russell was wiggling his rear end so much Courtney feared for the drinks table, so she crouched down to give him pets. He rewarded her with a wet kiss right on the lips. "Yuck! I missed you too, buddy. Where's your person?"

Song touched her shoulder. "Over there, talking to your grandparents."

Dressed in his uniform, Josh shook her grandfather's hand, then leaned in to give her grandmother a hug. The sounds of the party disappeared, drowned out by the roaring in Courtney's ears. Her heart thrummed in her chest, and her hand shook so much that she set her wine glass down. Her grandmother gestured toward the drinks table, and Courtney froze to her spot as Josh's eyes landed on her.

"He's coming over," Song said. "I'll leave you to it."

The mistakes of the summer, her rejection of Josh, hurt over his missing-in-action routine, and the overwhelming fear he was going to break her heart washed over her like a tsunami.

"I can't," Courtney spluttered, struggling to take a breath before pivoting and running for the path to the beach.

Head pounding and arm aching, Courtney ran the path through the dusky woods, muscle memory, and Russell, who'd caught up to her guiding her through the deep gloom. By the time she entered the tree house clearing, she was sucking in air, a stitch in her side, sobbing. Her shins ached along with everything else. The sandals she'd put on were definitely not cut out for a run in the forest. Or her tender head. Courtney rubbed her temples with a thumb and index finger. Russell bumped her other hand, whimpering.

"Can't go any farther, buddy, sorry. I'm out of shape." With her head pounding, she smoothed the fur between his ears, trying to sort through the tangle of emotions she was experiencing: chiefly embarrassment, quickly followed by bewilderment and anger. How dare he just show up here after ghosting her texts? She'd poured her heart out, and he'd completely ignored them. Courtney's heart stopped for a moment as she pictured the way he looked at her across the manor lawn. Josh was a stand-up guy. He probably wanted to let her down in person.

"Oh, God," Courtney moaned. "I'm such an ass."

"If anyone's an ass, it's me," Josh said quietly, his voice arriving before he did in the deepening forest shadows.

Courtney whirled, flashing a look of irritation at Russell. "Thanks for the heads up," she muttered before finding Josh standing at the entrance to the clearing. He stepped closer into a puddle of light created by the setting sun as it found a path through the maze of trees. His blue eyes fixed Courtney with a look she couldn't quite decipher. Courtney's legs quivered.

"Look, Josh—"

"Court, let me go first. It's my turn," Josh said at the same time.

"What?" Courtney's brow furrowed in confusion.

"Diss—I mean, Song told me about your texts."

"Oh." Courtney's chest swelled as she thought of Song. It felt good to have someone in her corner.

"I want you to know I'd never ghost you. I honestly didn't get them. I didn't turn my personal phone on while I was in Port Hardy because I was busy doing overtime shifts and spending every spare moment I had training for my competition. To be honest, I was hiding out from the world a bit, embarrassed, once again, by my family. I headed straight for my shift when I got back into town today. It was selfish of me, and I am so sorry. For everything."

A flash of anger tightened the tangle of emotions knotted in Courtney's chest.

"You're sorry? You left me unconscious in the hospital and never checked in with me. No one had any idea where you were. I was worried, Josh. Especially once we learned the extent of your dad's real estate scheme and how you might get in trouble because your name was associated with CFI." The knot gave and loosened as Courtney realized what was at the centre. She'd been genuinely worried about what would happen to Josh.

Josh's face crumpled, his eyes filling with tears, reflecting the scant light. He moved toward Courtney. "God, Court, when I saw that trench collapse"—Josh's voice broke, and he took a deep breath—"I thought I'd lost you forever. I've never been so scared in my life." Russell whimpered and nosed Josh's hand. Absently, Josh began to stroke the dog's velvety ears.

Heart blooming in her chest, Courtney stepped forward and laid a hand on Josh's arm. She breathed in the subtle cedar notes in his aftershave and licked her lips."Gram told me you dug me out and stayed with me the whole way to the hospital. Thank you."

Gingerly, holding her gaze, Josh ran a finger down Courtney's mending arm, then lightly down the side of her head. "I wanted to be there when you woke up, but I got a text from Justin."

"Justin?" The irritation returned. Of course he was at the centre of this Romeo-and-Juliet-level misunderstanding.

Josh raised a hand. "I'm not making excuses for him. He still has to face the consequences of his actions, but I've been in contact with him a lot more over the last few weeks—a reconciliation of sorts. It's my father who's at fault here. Justin is taking the fall for him. Unwillingly, I might add. I'm trying to convince him to cooperate with the crown attorney and give evidence against Dad, so when he turns up again, he'll be arrested and finally face the consequences of his actions. Justin and I have also been trying to support Mom. We've all been victims of Dad's abuse for too long."

"Oh, Josh. I'm sorry." Courtney thought about Song for a moment—maybe her taste in men wasn't quite as bad as Courtney had concluded. "So you and Justin have buried the hatchet?"

"We're on our way there. I mean, you know, there are years to unpack. But, in the end, we've both been victims of my father's greed. His narcissism. It took me years of therapy to get to this point in my life, and I'll likely be working on my issues for the rest of my life. Justin really needs someone on his side right now."

Courtney rubbed her hand lightly down his arm, her fingers tingling as they passed over his solid warmth. "Well, that's something, I guess. Are you in any trouble because of this?"

Josh looked confused. "What do you mean?"

"We heard you were facing disciplinary action."

"I was investigated, yes, but I've been estranged from my family for years, so I was cleared pretty quickly, despite Dad leaving my name on the board of directors."

"So, why didn't I hear from you?" The edge in Courtney's voice caused Josh's eyes to widen.

"I had to finish some business up island before I started my new posting. I worked twelve-hour shifts to clear my caseload."

Courtney pursed her lips and considered what this meant. "Your new posting? So, you decided to take the position in Victoria?" Courtney's stomach clenched painfully. Victoria was closer than Port Hardy, but realistically, she'd still only be able to see him occasionally. Could she manage a long-distance relationship? "Congratulations."

Josh shook his head, his face cracking into a wide grin. "No. I didn't take the post in Victoria. It's too far away from home."

"Home?" Courtney's stomach wiggled and fluttered beneath the yellow linen sundress.

Josh took both Courtney's hands, being extra gentle with her left. "Port Russell is my home. I want to be here. You, Court. You're also my home. I want to be with you, in Port Russell, always. I want to build a life and a family here with you."

There was a pop in Courtney's chest, like a cork leaving a champagne bottle, and she burst into tears.

Josh looked stricken.

"You're moving to Port Russell?" Courtney said between sobs. "For real? Despite my baggage and drama?"

"Yes. For real. I want to be with you and face everything life throws at us with you, my best friend and the love of my life." Josh put a hand to Courtney's face, wiping the tears away with his thumb. "Is that okay?"

The sight of her grandparents dancing beneath the twinkling lights popped into her head. It was now or never. Courtney grasped Josh's duty vest, her stiff left arm complaining loudly, and pulled him into a deep, passionate kiss. Russell jumped up, barking, then twined himself around his people as they wound their fingers into each other's hair, consumed with exploring every inch of the other's lips. The setting sun filled the clearing, gilding everything with gold.

They were home.

Acknowledgements

Five years ago, a writer friend of mine a little further along the road than me told me she felt it took her a decade before she felt like she knew what she was doing as a writer. It made me want to cry because it seemed like I'd already struggled for so long, but because time is so fleeting for adults, the next five years passed by in the blink of an eye, and I find myself here, with a shiny new book in my hand. I'm so glad I persevered. That I kept learning and growing so I could bring share this story with the world.

I had a lot of help along the way. I'm blessed to have many people who picked me up when I fell down, celebrated my wins and commiserated my losses. If it weren't for my people, I would have thrown in the towel a *long* time ago. On my writer journey I've had the privilege of meeting some truly amazing human beings who are generous with their time and expertise. I've learned so much from them, and I hope I can pay it forward as I continue along my way.

So, in no particular order of importance, here's the list of some of those I'm so, so grateful for.

- My editor, Melanie Cossey. I wish I'd chosen to work with you years ago; it might not have taken me a decade to publish if I had, lol. I've learned so much from you, and become a much more confident writer.
- Bailey McGinn of Bailey Designs Books. My first book has a stunning cover- thank you.
- The staff and students of Kanaka Creek Elementary school for inspiring my classroom scenes and lending their names for my student and teacher characters. I so wish I could figure out how to write and teach at the same time because I miss you guys.
- My RCMP expert Commander Gander and his awesome wife

Shannon- thanks for the insight and good times. Our chats are always illuminating!

- The Creative Academy, particularly Eileen Cook, Donna Barker, Crystal Hunt, and Stephanie Candiago. Thank you for your expert advice and steadfast support of new writers. A special call out to my fellow academy writers, Bonnie, Leslie, Jenny, Tracy and Erryn and all the other inspiring, creative individuals around the world I've hung out with and learned from. Thanks for cheering me on and sharing your knowledge with me.
- My local, in person writing group, Golden Ears Writers, for helping me be brave enough to tell other people I'm a writer (always a scary step). Special thanks to Katherine Wagner, a wise friend further down the road, for inspiring by example and stepping up to organize events for us introverts so I can get out of the house occasionally and interact, in person, with other writers.
- My literary coven, the best critique group a person could hope for, Maureen Butler, Margot Spronk, Diane Walsh, Kristi Lewis and Allie Lahn. Thanks for your honest critiques and whole-hearted cheerleading. I love you all fiercely and the love, support and gentle guidance you've gifted me with these last ten years are an integral part of this book. I literally couldn't have done it without you. Nor would I have wanted to.
- My fantastic kids Jin, Vivian, and Jocelyn; your support and patience allowed me to make this dream of publishing a novel come true. Thanks for putting up with me when I'm lost in my work. I hope that I've shown you that with perseverance and hard work, you can make your dreams come true.
- Twix and Hazel, my Schnauzer sidekicks. Thanks for getting me outside for a walk every day and always making sure I'm safe in the bathroom. I put a dog in every story just for you.
- And last, but certainly not least, my wonderful husband and best friend, Dale, who gave me the courage to see this dream come true by being 100% in my corner. Thanks for lifting me up when I'm down and for pushing me past my fear. I'm living my own HEA. I love you...more.

Don't miss out!

Visit the website below and you can sign up to receive emails whenever Keay Francis publishes a new book. There's no charge and no obligation.

https://books2read.com/r/B-A-LSGV-VWQEC

BOOKS 2 READ

Connecting independent readers to independent writers.

Also by Keay Francis

Port Russell Romance
Resistance

Watch for more at https://keayfrancis.com/.

About the Author

Keay Francis is a rehabilitated Canadian prairie girl who writes love stories set in the spectacular landscapes and warmer climes of her adopted province of British Columbia. When she's not writing, Keay can be found driving her kids to extra-curricular activities, walking her very demanding Schnauzers (even in the rain) or enjoying an Americano or glass of red wine with her husband.

Author Photo courtesy of Amy Williams Photography.

Read more at https://keayfrancis.com/.

Manufactured by Amazon.ca
Bolton, ON

35536034R00139